Approaching voices shattered the moment and they pulled apart. When the people passed, Carmen kissed her temple gently. "Will you come back to my room?"

Judith never considered saying anything but yes.

Moments later, they were in a taxi speeding toward the hotel. As they pulled into the valet circle, Carmen tossed a twenty into the front seat and told the cabbie to keep the change. Together, they rushed inside and strode quickly toward the elevators, oblivious to the people who milled about. They grabbed the first elevator and Carmen pushed the button before anyone else could board. The instant the door closed, she pinned Judith to the wall with a crushing kiss. "I want you everywhere," she murmured. Her hands snaked inside Judith's parka to massage her breasts.

Judith gave herself up completely to the hungry assault. If Carmen's lovemaking was as fierce as her foreplay, she was about to go somewhere she had never been. She clung to Carmen's arm as they exited the elevator and hurried to the room. Carmen swiped her key card and the door opened into a suite, where cardboard boxes lined the entry.

"Hi, Carmen."

They froze in the entryway. "Raul."

Also by KG MacGregor (available from Bella Books):

Just This Once
Mulligan
The House on Sandstone
Sumter Point
Malicious Pursuit

OUT of LOVE

KG MacGregor

Bella
BOOKS
2007

Bella Books, Inc.
P.O. Box 10543
Tallahassee, FL 32302

Printed in the United States of America on acid-free paper
First Edition

Editor: Cindy Cresap
Cover designer: LA Callaghan

ISBN-10: 1-59493-105-4
ISBN-13: 978-1-59493-105-5

Thanks to Cindy Cresap for her usual lumberjack . . . I mean, crackerjack editing job. Thanks also to Jenny and Tami for their technical edits, and to Karen, who collects all the dropped words at the bottom of the page and pushes them back up to where they belong.

I'm dedicating this one to all of you who can't help falling in love across the miles. May your love be worth it.

About the Author

Growing up in the mountains of North Carolina, KG MacGregor dreaded the summer influx of snowbirds escaping the Florida heat. The lines were longer, the traffic snarled and the prices higher. Now that she's older, slightly more patient and not without means, she divides her time between Miami and Blowing Rock.

A former teacher, KG earned her PhD in mass communication and her writing stripes preparing market research reports for commercial clients in the publishing, television and travel industries. In 2002, she tried her hand at lesbian fiction and discovered her bliss. When she isn't writing, she is probably on a hiking trail. www.kgmacgregor.com

Chapter 1

" . . . so, next item of business. I need someone to take Bill Hinkle to dinner on Saturday night. Anyone?"

From her position at the head of the conference table, CEO Carmen Delallo tilted her head to catch the eye of a reluctant volunteer. Seeing none, she chuckled and honed in on Lenore Yates, one of her three senior research associates.

"Come on, people. He's one of our biggest clients. Which one of you wants to make a splash?"

Lenore sighed dramatically and tossed her pen on the table. "Fine, I'll do it."

"That's the spirit." Carmen was pleased at the sentiment, if not the lack of enthusiasm. Bill Hinkle was the CEO of Franklin Resorts, a Philadelphia-based time-share vacation company. He was also a sexist womanizer, but as a major client, he deserved personal attention from The Delallo Group.

"But he's not going to be happy about having to settle for an underling."

"I have an idea how we can head that off," Carmen said, reaching into a paper bag at her feet. Sliding a small box of business cards across the conference table to Lenore, she cleared her throat. "Ladies and gentlemen, boys and girls, children of all ages . . . please give a nice warm welcome to the new vice president of TDG, Lenore Yates."

The room went silent for several seconds as the shocked staffers, including Lenore, digested the news. Then the cued applause broke out as excited congratulations were shouted from around the room.

"Carmen!" Lenore dropped her jaw in amazement.

"I know, I know. I should have talked to you first, but Cathy told me I needed to share the workload and you seemed like just the sucker to take the job." She grinned back at Lenore, proud of her decision. Lenore was the only one on the senior staff she trusted to work with complete autonomy on the company's behalf.

Lenore fingered the new embossed business cards. "Am I getting a raise?"

"I haven't decided," Carmen answered smugly, her tone teasing. "Speaking of Cathy, who's in charge of the Rosen Track?"

Everyone laughed as one of the research assistants spoke up. "She called in from Harrisburg about an hour ago. She said you owe her big-time for this and that she charged a bottle of their best wine for dinner last night."

"Figures. With a whole bottle of wine, we probably could have gotten her on an airplane."

Cathy Rosen was Carmen's administrative assistant, and also her oldest and dearest friend. And she had a mortal fear of flying. She rarely attended travel conventions like the one this weekend in New York, but Carmen depended on her totally and had begged her to make the overnight trip from Chicago by train.

There was a lot on tap for The Delallo Group this weekend, including Carmen's keynote address on Saturday and a Sunday night reception for clients at Central Park's Tavern on the Green.

"She also says to tell you she's taking Tuesday off to recover from the return trip."

Carmen shook her head. "You know, sometimes I fantasize about being the one in charge."

Everyone laughed.

"Lunch is here," their receptionist announced from the doorway.

"Have them set it up in here," Carmen said, standing to stretch her legs. She hated these long meetings as much as anyone, but they had a lot of ground to cover before heading out en masse for the Association of Travel Professionals convention. As her crew bustled around the food cart, she walked to the window and peered out. Their twenty-first-floor offices in the Sears Tower afforded a marvelous view of the sparkling Chicago River.

"Here, Carmen." A research assistant handed her a plate with a half-sandwich and a scoop of pasta salad. "Cathy told me to make sure you ate."

"She doesn't even trust me to feed myself?"

"Apparently not."

Carmen took the plate and returned to her seat as the staff settled back in. "Okay, what else is there to talk about? Raul?"

The young Hispanic man sat up straight and shuffled his papers, pushing his lunch aside for the moment. "I'll have three terminals up and running in the exhibit hall by tomorrow afternoon. We should be able to demonstrate all the new software upgrades and give people a chance to train. Everything has to come down at four o'clock on Sunday."

"Need any help with that?"

"I can handle it, but I won't complain if somebody brings me coffee and cookies every now and then."

Carmen turned to Richard and Kristy, her other two senior staffers. "A lot of our clients will be coming through there. I'd like to have at least one of you in the hall with Raul at all times. Can you two work that out?"

They glanced at each other and nodded.

"Anything else we need to talk about?"

Kristy checked her notes. "Any advice on how to handle Art Conover?"

Carmen grimaced at the mention of their chief rival and shoved the last of the sandwich in her mouth. "Mace?"

Her answer was echoed by others offering similar suggestions. Conover Data Source analyzed credit card expenditures to compile profiles of travelers according to their zip code, and Art Conover coveted TDG's clients. His line of services was inferior to TDG's, but adequate for media buys. It was also considerably less expensive. Though Carmen refused to regard him as a serious threat, he had successfully skimmed off a few of TDG's budget-conscious clients.

"You all know what to expect from Art," she mumbled as she finished chewing her lunch. "He's going to come sniffing around to see what we're up to. Be nice. Laugh him off if you have to, but don't talk business with him. I'll get Cathy to set up a breakfast or something on Sunday and I can feed him everything he needs to know."

"I have a few ideas for what you can feed him," Richard said.

"Don't worry about Art. It never hurts to know what he's up to. We all need to get out there and meet people this weekend. Make a good impression, especially at the Tavern on Sunday."

She looked around the room at their confident faces.

"Okay, if that's it, let's call it a day. I know you've all got planes to catch this afternoon. We'll regroup at lunch tomorrow. See Cathy in the morning for where that will be. Safe travels." She stood and gathered her papers. "Oh, and Lenore . . . I guess we need to talk about how much more work you're willing to do for an extra ten dollars a week."

"I can tell you that right now."

Carmen laughed and led the way into her expansive corner office. Despite all the last-minute obsessions, she was excited about this year's convention, especially with the opportunity to present Lenore as her new vice president.

"What's all this going to mean?" Lenore asked.

"Obviously, the biggest thing is that you'll have the title to go along with all the duties you've been pulling for the past couple of years. My hope is that clients start to feel that doing business with you is like doing business with me."

"I can't imagine people will ever feel like that."

"Then we have to fix that. I want this company to be more than me."

"Cathy was right. You really have been spread pretty thin."

"Tell me about it. But it was my own fault for not delegating. And when I started handing things off to you, the first thing I noticed was how it helped our bottom line. Now I feel like I'm getting twice as much done."

"There's no way I can match you on a scale like that, Carmen. Unlike you, I go home sometimes."

"Now, now. No picking on my personal habits. I have Cathy for that."

Lenore studied the new business card again. "I really am honored by this."

"You deserve it," she said sincerely. "And just in case the honor alone isn't enough, I'm offering you twenty percent on both your salary and profit sharing."

"Wow."

"I know, I know. You're willing to do it for free because I'm the best boss in the world. And you'll always be grateful for this wonderful opportunity to work with me side by side. You don't have to say it. It just makes us both blush."

Lenore shook her head and smiled. "You really are the best boss in the world, Carmen."

"I appreciate what you bring to the company, Lenore. And I'm the one that's grateful." She handed over a copy of the press release that would go out on the business wire that afternoon. "Now go catch your plane."

Judith O'Shea paid the clerk and collected her generous slice of pizza. Her friend and coworker Celia was standing at a tall table, already eating her lunch. Judith shouldered past the crowd to the far side of the table, where she was out of the cold air from the open door. Their favorite West Village pizza stand was always packed at midday, but the pizza was worth putting up with the crowd.

Celia meticulously picked the black olives off her slice and dropped them onto her paper plate. "Did you see the new commission structure on Todd's desk?"

"I don't have to go looking for bad news," Judith answered with a groan. "It always finds me."

"The bottom line is it's going be another half a percent, effective next month."

"Shit."

"I know. They're all greedy bastards."

"True, but that's not the worst of it, Cee. There just isn't as much to go around anymore with so many people doing their own bookings on the Internet. And it's only going to get worse."

"I know. You remember that lady that had me put together the trip for all those women going down the Amazon?"

"The one that turned around and booked it herself on the Web?"

"Asshole. After I'd done all the work."

"Don't you miss the old days when we used to go on all the tours? I think I'd rather make less money and do that than grind out every single dollar on the phone."

"Me too." Celia finished her pizza and wiped her hands on a paper napkin. "Sometimes I just want to go into Todd's office and put both my hands on his scrawny neck and squeeze."

Judith had to admit the image of her hefty friend strangling their boss had appeal. Todd wasn't a bad manager. He just had a different formula for success than his Aunt Myrna, a flamboyant lesbian with an Auntie Mame streak. Myrna had built the company as a boutique agency servicing New York's gay and lesbian community. Todd, who wasn't gay, kept the niche market, but he wanted higher volume with a lower margin, a formula that relied on Internet marketing and national sales. It meant more customers, but with less of a personal touch.

"I don't blame Todd. He just has a different vision. The only thing that matters to him is if bookings are up."

"I know, but it's not fun anymore. We might as well be working at a factory."

Her appetite gone, Judith wrapped the rest of her pizza in paper and wiped her hands. "Think you'll talk to anyone this weekend?"

"Don't say anything, but I have a friend who works in corporate travel at one of the TV networks. They've got an opening, and she's going to try to get me an interview with them."

"I bet they have good benefits. I have something lined up too."

"At the conference?"

Judith nodded and took a sip of her drink. "There was an ad on the Web from Durbin Dreams, so I sent them a résumé. They called me back last week. I'm supposed to have lunch with Bob Durbin tomorrow to talk about it."

"Durbin's big!"

"Not all that big. But they probably have about thirty or forty agents."

"Compared to our six."

"Right, but they're no Zeigler-Marsh. Z-M's probably got a couple thousand all over the country."

"Where's Durbin's office?"

"Lexington. Upper East Side." It would be a schlep from her apartment in Chelsea, but Celia was right about the factory atmosphere at Rainbow Getaways. If she was going to work in a boring job like that, she wanted better benefits and higher commissions. A larger agency would do that.

"You'd make a lot more money there, that's for sure."

"That's what I'm thinking."

Celia gestured toward the remains of her pizza. "Is that for Agnes?"

"If she's out."

"Let's go see."

Judith zipped her parka and pulled on her gloves. The late winter cold front that came in last night had her chilled to the bone. "I don't know about you, but I'm looking forward to a few days out of the office."

"Me too. I can't believe Todd isn't even going to the convention. It's like he doesn't care at all about the travel business."

"That sums him up, though. At his core, he's not really interested in what we do at the agency. He likes the business part, all the figuring out how to squeeze margins from this and that, how to consolidate the media buys, and so on. He just doesn't care what we're selling. It might as well be curtain rods."

"Probably make more money," Celia groused.

Judith and Celia turned the corner toward their office, dodging the garbage cans that lined the sidewalk. Up ahead, an elderly woman held up a tattered towel salvaged from someone's trash. As they drew closer, she looped it around her neck as if it were an elegant scarf.

"Looks good, Agnes," Judith called.

The old woman's toothless face lit up as she recognized them.

"I have a little pizza left over. You hungry?"

She nodded and held out her hand eagerly.

"Did you sleep inside last night?"

"Yeah." That was the most conversation Agnes could manage.

"Good for you. It's supposed to be cold again tonight so you better find a place to stay warm, okay?" Judith knew Agnes was a regular at the shelter on Barrow Street because the priest had told her so when she dropped off a bag of old clothes.

"I'm surprised she doesn't follow you home," Celia said as they continued down the street.

"I worry about feeding her sometimes, you know? What if she starts depending on me and I end up working somewhere else where I don't see her every day?"

Celia shrugged. "You don't see her every day as it is. And it's not like she comes looking for you."

"I guess that's right. She probably gets lunch at the shelter and whatever I give her is extra." That thought made her feel better in case she got the job with Durbin.

"Hey, do you want me to ask my friend at the network to try to set up something for you too?"

"No, just toss me your bones when they want to do escorted tours."

"Ha! If I get any escorted tours, I'm not handing them off to you."

"You're breaking my heart, Cee." They reached the front door of Rainbow Getaways and Judith held it for them to enter.

She walked past Todd's office to her cubicle, rolling her eyes as she saw him check the clock and shake his head. Like five minutes extra at lunch was going to break the bank.

Two messages were lying on her chair, one from a client and the other from her mother. Knowing that Todd was straining to eavesdrop, she dutifully pulled the client's file and called her first.

"Hi. Judith O'Shea returning your call. Sorry we missed each other. I'll be in the office all afternoon if you have a chance to call back. Thank you."

One good thing about working at a bigger agency like Durbin's was the privacy that came from having lots of agents on the phone at the same time. In a small shop like Rainbow, there were no secrets at all.

"Hi, Mom. What's up?" Judith listened while her mother detailed the events of her day. As she swiveled in her chair, she studied the photo that was taped to her computer. It was the three of them, Judith, her mom, and her older brother Victor, taken last Christmas by a neighbor who had stopped by the house in Brooklyn. "No, I can't come this weekend. I have a convention at the Grand . . . It's for travel agents . . . just seminars and meetings, nothing that important." She checked her watch, knowing that Todd was doing the same. "I have to get back to work. I'll call when I get home . . . No, I'll go by and see Victor one night next week."

As she hung up the phone, she was tempted to yell out to Todd that she was finished with her personal call. But if things went well tomorrow in her interview with Bob Durbin, she would be out of here in a couple of weeks, and there was no point in leaving the job on a bad note.

Rainbow Getaways had been a fun place to work for most of the past seventeen years. Judith hadn't known the first thing about the needs of gay and lesbian travelers until that fateful cruise she had taken her first year with four dozen single lesbians. By the time she got back, she knew all about what lesbians wanted, and not just their travel needs.

From the corner of her eye, Carmen saw the blinking light again. The phone didn't ring through to her office, but the persistent flashing meant she was alone after hours, which wasn't unusual at all. She jabbed the button for the speaker phone.

"This is Carmen Delallo."

"Get the hell out of there or you're going to miss your

plane!"

Carmen whirled around in her chair and checked the clock. An hour and ten minutes before takeoff and she had to get to O'Hare in rush hour. "Shit, Cathy."

"I've been calling your cell phone for an hour."

"It's probably on vibrate at the bottom of my briefcase."

"That's what I thought. Now get out of there."

"Okay, bye." She punched the button to hang up and shoved her papers into her briefcase. A quick check out the window confirmed her limo was waiting at the curb. She grabbed her rollerbag and raincoat from the closet and headed out, latching the door behind her.

Five minutes later she was in the backseat on her way out of the city on the Kennedy Expressway. Indeed, her cell phone showed six missed calls from Cathy, and one from a number she recognized as belonging to Healey Vassal, her goddaughter.

"Hi, honey. It's Carmen . . . I'm on my way to the airport now . . . Don't tell me she called you too." Cathy tracked her practically everywhere.

As she talked, she sorted the papers she had crammed in her briefcase at the last minute. Everything was ready for the weekend, provided she made her plane on time.

"No, just the plain old dog food—cold, right out of the can. That's all she gets. The little princess can take it or leave it." Healey was dog-sitting her one-year-old dachshund, Prissy, who could be the most ornery animal on earth. "I bet it's because you fed her chicken the last time you stayed there. I tell you, she never forgets anything."

Carmen put her hand to her forehead as she listened to Healey's next request.

"I can't believe you're doing this to me." Healey was a twenty-one-year-old junior at DePaul, old enough to sleep with her boyfriend if she wanted to, but not in Carmen's apartment. "What would your mother say about that? Wait, I know. She'd tell you to ask your father and then she'd say just the opposite."

That was Brooke Nance in a nutshell, still doing battle with her ex-husband over everything having to do with her two girls.

"Okay, here's where I stand. I can't believe I'm actually saying this." She drew a deep breath. "Craig can stay the weekend, but he has to sleep in the guest room . . . I don't care where you sleep, but you know I don't like boys in my bed. Capiche?"

She looked up at the driver's rearview mirror, wondering what was going on in the poor man's head.

"I love you too. And if the shit hits the fan with your mom, you're on your own. I'm denying everything . . . Yeah, I'll be back on Monday, but I'm going straight to the office, so give the little princess an extra scoop of dry food before you leave, okay? And tell your mom I'll call her for dinner next week . . . bye."

The terminal signs for O'Hare came into view as they pulled onto I-190 and Carmen checked her watch. Thirty-five minutes to get through security and to her gate. Plenty of time.

Chapter 2

Carmen grappled for the chirping phone on the bedside table, momentarily disoriented by her unfamiliar surroundings. A cheerful voice told her it was six thirty a.m. and directed her to one of the restaurants downstairs for breakfast.

She collapsed back onto the bed with a groan. There wasn't a soul on earth besides her who cared if she made it to the treadmill this morning or not. It was grueling to work out on the road, but forty-seven was too young to throw in the towel on staying fit. Reluctantly, she dragged herself from bed and pulled on her spandex tights and trainers and walked out, sifting through the papers in front of her door until she found the *Wall Street Journal*.

The fitness center was already humming with a dozen people who seemed much happier than Carmen about being there. She claimed a treadmill in the corner farthest from the blaring television and put on her reading glasses to set the controls. When she reached her desired pace, she scanned the front page of the paper, where a small blurb directed her to an article inside on the association's meeting in New York. She skimmed it quickly, pleased to find her name as one of the plenary speakers. Her first instinct was to call her youngest brother Mark to brag. Of the six siblings, she and Mark were the only ones who hadn't followed their father into the medical field. Theirs was a friendly but intense competition for achievement in their business careers. Making the *Wall Street Journal* was a coup. Too bad her sister-in-law wouldn't appreciate a trumpeting call at this early hour.

Giving the keynote address this year was a shining moment for Carmen and her company, a sign their work in research and consulting was worthwhile and appreciated by industry professionals. Not that she ever doubted it, but it was nice to get recognition from the group that mattered most.

She went on to read the story, barely noticing the figure that suddenly occupied the adjacent treadmill.

"Carmen Delallo!"

"Art." Art Conover, the last person she wanted to see . . . with the possible exception of Bill Hinkle. "Good to see you."

"You too. You're looking fit."

"Thank you." Art was a handsome man in his early forties. Carmen considered him a gentleman, someone she might have enjoyed being friends with if he wasn't always trying to steal her clients. "We all have to work at it." She hoped their small talk might continue, but it was not to be.

"So . . . rumor has it The Delallo Group is rolling out something new . . . some kind of advertising tracker?"

In fact, TDG had put out a press release describing the features of the new software in detail. Art was just being Art, fishing for whatever extra tidbit he might learn.

"Not a rumor at all. We'll have the demo out this afternoon in the exhibit hall. You should check it out."

"Any secrets I can steal?"

Carmen laughed, appreciating his frankness. "Cathy Rosen handles all the patents and copyrights. You'd better check with her first."

"Maybe I'll ply her with a box of chocolates."

"Trust me. You'd be wasting your time. Her husband uses jewelry and expensive wine."

"I'll have to check my budget for that."

"Check your calendar too while you're at it. Maybe we can have breakfast on Sunday."

"Won't that get the tongues wagging?"

She hit the kill switch on her treadmill and grasped the rail as it slowed to a halt. "They've got to talk about something, Art. Might as well be us."

"Good point."

"I'll have Cathy set it up and give you a call."

"Have her call my office in Dallas. They'll plug all the info in and send it to my Blackberry."

"Of course. I'll tell her." That was Art's way of letting her know he too was important enough to have a staff of his own to manage his schedule. "See you soon."

On the way out, she checked her appearance in the mirror, congratulating herself for her efforts. Her friend Brooke was right when she said butts didn't just tighten themselves. But then Brooke had a lot more free time than she did, exercising for hours a day with her personal trainer or Pilates coach. She was a living commercial for a tight butt. Carmen had noticed.

Judith stepped onto the broad platform above her living room. She always thought she deserved an award for maximizing the space in her apartment, which was barely over two hundred square feet. The loft she had installed held her clothes racks, shoes and stackable drawers, allowing her to clear the clutter from her tiny living space below. If only she didn't have to climb the steep stairs several times a day. But cramped quarters were a staple of life in Manhattan for people of modest means. Most New Yorkers simply adapted.

She had her three nicest outfits cleaned and pressed for the weekend, including the tan gabardine suit she planned to wear today. With its plain styling and a hemline just above the knee, it was her most conservative, perfect for a job interview. She tossed her brown dress shoes onto the futon below and carefully descended the ladder, clutching the rail erected alongside.

In the small bathroom, she opened the clear glass shower door and turned on the spray. It was anyone's guess how long the hot water would last, but after six years in this apartment, she was an expert at getting through her routine in a very short window. The key was to take the initial plunge while the water was still warming. She preferred that to having it run tepid before she had finished rinsing.

The four-cup coffeemaker gurgled through its cycle in the kitchen, well on its way to being ready by the time she finished her shower. Coffee and a toasted bagel with jam would have to last till lunch. She was too nervous today to eat more than that.

Her anxiety about the interview with Bob Durbin had cost her a couple of hours of sleep last night. She didn't want to blow this chance, because there weren't many jobs out there for travel agents at her experience and pay level. Though she preferred to work primarily with the gay and lesbian segment, she was open to whatever Durbin needed, even if it involved switching her specialty. Whatever she did, she couldn't afford to take a pay cut at this stage in her career, nor could she manage without health insurance.

It wasn't as if Judith was barely scraping by. Her apartment was rent-stabilized at twelve hundred a month, and she was far from extravagant when it came to clothes or other expenditures. But like so many others her age, her main focus was saving for retirement. She didn't expect the small pension Myrna had set up ten years ago to amount to much with inflation, especially in one of the world's most expensive cities. That's why she put away extra every month in a mutual fund.

Fresh from the shower, she pushed a comb through her light brown hair and shook her head at her non-existent options. Some people had the luxury of wearing their hair in different styles according to their plans for the day. Not Judith, whose hair wouldn't hold a curl or wave, no matter what she did to it. Her friend Celia had just the opposite problem. Celia's hair curled to the point of wild abandon, despite dozens of treatments and styles. Both women had finally given up, Judith settling for a flattering cut just above her collar that showed off her hair's thickness and natural shine.

As she dried her hair, she thought again about Celia's decision to switch over to corporate travel. Maybe that was the right idea. It wasn't a glamorous job, but it paid better and had decent benefits. Judith figured if she got in with the right company, she might even be able to finish out her career in one place.

No matter what she decided, it had to be soon. She wouldn't put it past Todd to weed out the senior agents like her who were making more money.

She checked her makeup and buttoned her suit coat, satisfied there was no more she could do to look better or more professional. If she made a good impression on Bob Durbin, today could be a turning point in her life.

Carmen twisted the valve to stop the hot, pulsating spray, then stood on tiptoes to inspect the showerhead's configuration. One of these would be nice in the master bath at her apartment, she thought.

Since she traveled at least ten days a month for business, Cathy usually booked her in first-class accommodations. It wasn't that she was particular about things or self-important, but Cathy felt she deserved pampering because she worked so hard on the road. Carmen had learned to appreciate the extra touches, even to depend on them to help her relax so she could be at her best when she met with clients.

She grabbed a towel off the top rack and vigorously rubbed her head, squeezing as much water as she could from her thick black hair. Then she pulled it off her forehead and peered into the steamy mirror to examine the graying strands. She didn't mind a few gray hairs here and there, but that bit Cathy always gave her about it making her look distinguished was crap.

Carmen would never have been successful in business without Cathy's help because she would have burned out long ago. In the early years of her company, work-related stress landed her in the hospital with high blood pressure, chest pains and fatigue. That's when Cathy, who had been her college roommate, came on board to take control.

Fifteen years ago TDG was a simple consulting firm consisting of Carmen, her two assistants and a secretary. Back then, they shared office space above a restaurant with a personal injury attorney who advertised his services on cable TV late at night. Now they were the major supplier of sales and marketing information for the travel industry, with luxurious offices, a dozen full-time staff, hundreds of clients and millions in annual billings.

"I'm ordering breakfast. Have you eaten?" The subject of Carmen's ruminations made her presence in the adjacent parlor known.

"Not yet. I was going to," she shouted back through the open bathroom door. She waited until she heard Cathy hang up the phone. "Are you by yourself?"

"You mean is the whole staff here to watch you parade out of your bathroom naked? Afraid not. You'll have to settle for an audience of one."

Carmen laughed and wrapped herself in a long towel. "I have a robe around here somewhere, but I'll be damned if I'm going to put it on for you."

"You've got nothing I haven't seen a thousand times."

Still toweling her hair, Carmen walked into the parlor and slumped into one of the stuffed chairs. This room, with several couches and chairs, a conference table, a wet bar and refrigerator, and a half bath, would serve as the company's headquarters for the weekend. Boxes of bound reports and marketing materials were stacked against the wall, and a projector and laptop were set up on the table. "Is your room nice?"

"Not as nice as yours."

"Want to trade?"

"No, I'd rather complain."

"I knew you were going to say that."

"I got you this at the coffee kiosk in the lobby." Cathy held out a paper cup with a plastic lid. "I'm getting too old to travel with you."

"How can you say that? We're the same age."

"But you didn't raise three kids."

"The hell I didn't! You can't spit without hitting one of my godchildren—including one of yours."

"Speaking of godchildren, did Brooke find you?"

"No."

"That tells me you probably haven't turned your cell phone on since your plane landed. How are people supposed to get in touch with you?"

"That's what I have you for."

"Don't get used to it."

Carmen ignored her friend's surly mood. "I bet I know what Brooke's calling about. Healey's at my place this weekend with Prissy and I told her Craig could stay too, as long as they didn't . . . you know . . . in my bed."

Cathy let out a raucous laugh. "That's definitely one conversation I don't want to miss, but I don't think she was calling about that. I got the feeling there was some kind of trouble in paradise."

Carmen put her bare feet on the coffee table and leaned back, sipping her latte. "That hasn't been paradise for three or four years. She probably needs to vent some more about Geoffrey."

"She needs to find a good therapist and quit dumping on you."

"I don't mind."

"I know you don't, but that's not the point. If she really wants things to work with Geoffrey, they need professional help."

Carmen had always been protective of Brooke, taking her side automatically with no questions asked. She thought Cathy was hard on Brooke, not cutting her any slack for what she had been through as a child. Sometimes the best way to deal with Cathy on this was to change the subject.

"I ran into Art Conover down in the fitness room this morning. Can you set up a breakfast with him Sunday morning?"

"Here?"

"I'd rather do it in the restaurant."

"And give everyone a heart attack thinking you two are going to merge or something?"

Carmen laughed. "That's what he said. It doesn't hurt for us to play nice. Oh, and send Richard to check out his booth in the exhibit hall. I want to know what he's hawking this year."

"Richard will like that. He'll probably manage to break something."

"What's on our schedule today?"

Cathy flipped open her leather folder. "The Seattle people are coming here at nine to talk about the Asian project. I've ordered coffee and pastries, but you don't get any of either. And you wanted to sit in on Priscilla's panel at ten thirty. Then there's the staff meeting at lunch, the plenary at two, and you're meeting the Cayman group at four in the bar."

"Where are we going for lunch?"

"I haven't decided, but you'd better bring your raincoat when you come downstairs."

"Why can't we just eat in the hotel restaurant?"

"Because I haven't been to New York in eight years. I want to see more than just the airport and the hotel."

A knock at the door announced their breakfast delivery. Carmen hurried into the bedroom and shut the door while Cathy dealt with the waiter. Emerging moments later in a thick, white terrycloth robe, she took a place at the small table and spread her napkin on her lap.

"Get out and see things while you're here. I want you to have a good time, Cathy," she said hopefully.

"It isn't going to make me want to travel with you."

"But you can see how much I need you here. And there's the trade show in June. You can bring Hank. Maui . . . beaches . . . palm trees."

"Airplane over the ocean . . . nowhere to land."

Carmen sighed and removed the aluminum cover from her plate. Underneath was a bowl of yogurt and granola. "I was so hoping for bacon and eggs."

"I know. Aren't you lucky I was here to save your arteries from certain death?"

"Excuse me," Judith said, putting forth her best smile. "I was wondering if there was a way you might be able to print a new nametag for me. This one has my name spelled wrong." Her last name was spelled O-'-S-H-A-E.

The woman's retort was surprisingly rude, even to a New Yorker. "It's spelled exactly the way it was submitted."

Judith usually avoided confrontation, but she didn't appreciate the implication that she was an idiot who didn't know how to spell her own name, especially with so many people standing nearby. "Actually, not in this case. See, I have the printout from when I registered on the Internet." As she spoke, she unfolded her registration information alongside the errant nametag. "As you can see, the nametag is different."

"Well, I can't print another one. You'll have to hand-write it," she said curtly, handing over a label and black marker.

Judith forced another smile. "Thank you very much. May I borrow those scissors too?"

The woman pushed them across the table without making further eye contact. "Who's next?"

Judith slid sideways to the far end of the table, where she carefully printed an E and an A in block letters. Then she cut them out and plastered them over the last two letters on her nametag. She was trying to slide the label back into its plastic holder when a woman she didn't recognize approached her.

"Sorry, do you need this marker or the scissors? I'm finished."

The woman stared at her as if studying her face. Her nametag was hidden behind a leather folder she held to her chest.

"No, I just wanted to say hello and introduce myself. I'm Cathy Rosen, from The Delallo Group." She smiled broadly and held out her hand.

"Judith O'Shea. At least I will be when I fix this." She held up her doctored nametag with one hand and shook Cathy's with the other.

"Is this your first convention?"

"No, my second. I went to the one in Boston three years ago." She couldn't help but notice that Cathy seemed intensely interested in her reply.

"I missed that one. Was it a good one?"

"It was nice, but there's nothing quite like having one in your hometown."

"Oh, they'd never have one of these in Chicago. Not sexy enough."

"I hear Chicago's a wonderful city."

"I think so, but then I'm biased. Say, since you're from around here, maybe you can recommend someplace nearby that would be good for a working lunch."

"I know there's a great Irish pub around Park and Thirty-Ninth. But I've heard the hotel restaurant is nice too. I'm supposed to meet someone there to talk business. I guess he thought it was a good place for something like that."

"Well, thank you. We may check it out. It was very nice meeting you, Judith. Maybe we'll see each other again this weekend."

"I hope so, Cathy."

Judith watched with curiosity as the woman walked away. It wasn't unusual for convention-goers to be friendly as they networked with one another, but few seemed as genuine as Cathy Rosen.

Chapter 3

"I need a table for eight, please."

Judith smiled as she recognized Cathy at the hostess stand. So she had decided to eat here in the hotel after all.

The hostess studied the layout as she collected a handful of menus. "I can have something in about five minutes."

"That's all right. We're not all here yet," Cathy answered, glancing back again to the busy hotel lobby.

"What's the name?"

"The Delallo Group."

Judith wondered if Carmen Delallo would be part of Cathy's lunch group. Several people were clustered together with Cathy at the entry, but Judith didn't recognize any of them as the company head, at least not as she was pictured in the session guide.

Probably everyone at the ATP convention knew Carmen Delallo, if not personally, then by reputation. Each year, her company put out a syndicated study of lifestyles and travel behaviors that predicted all the hot new destinations and amenities. Agencies used it as a roadmap for marketing and advertising, and swore by its recommendations. Myrna used to say it was as if Carmen had a crystal ball.

When Myrna ran the agency, Rainbow Getaways subscribed to TDG's annual marketing guide, but Todd killed that budget item as soon as he came on board and discovered that Conover's report was less expensive. It was also useless as anything more than an ad-buying tool, Judith thought, but Todd rarely let facts come into play once his mind was made up.

"Carmen, over here!" Cathy waved through the crowd, and the rest of her party bustled forth. "I hope this is okay. I didn't think anyone would want to go out in the rain."

The impeccable Carmen Delallo stood out in the crowd. Judith had always been a sucker for Mediterranean women, but Carmen took the look to a whole new level. She had the characteristic olive skin and onyx eyes, and her wavy collar-length hair was so dark it seemed indigo. She also possessed elegance and grace that came only to women who were certain of their strength.

Standing just five feet away, Judith was instantly infatuated.

Bob Durbin suddenly pushed through the crowd and Judith straightened her stance, eager to get on with the next phase of her life, a new job with better benefits, bigger travel budgets and support staff.

"Hi, Mr. Durbin."

"Julia, sorry to keep you waiting."

"It's Judith. That's okay, I—"

"I'm afraid I'm not going to be able to keep our lunch date. I just ran into a colleague from Atlanta and he reminded me of something important we need to discuss."

Judith carefully masked her annoyance. If the asshole was going to cancel, he could have done so twenty minutes ago. But she couldn't let her irritation show. She needed to be polite and get this interview rescheduled. "That's all right. I understand. Maybe we can . . ." Just like that, Durbin was gone. And to her supreme embarrassment, Carmen Delallo was looking right at her and had probably overheard the whole brush-off.

Apparently, so had the hostess. "Table for one?"

"Fine," she grunted, following her to a row of narrow tables for two against the wall where one side was a padded bench facing the dining room and the other side a chair facing inward. She hated having her back to people when she was alone, so she chose the bench, instantly regretting that she would now have to look at all the other diners. There she sat, feeling ridiculously conspicuous. She should have canceled her table and grabbed something from one of the vendors in the train station tunnel below the hotel. All she wanted now was to eat something fast and get out of there.

A large table was positioned on a riser across from where she sat, and that's where they seated The Delallo Group. All sharply dressed and carrying business folders, they looked like the smartest people in the room. No wonder people in the industry seemed to hang on their every word.

Alone against the wall, Judith was apparently invisible to Jose the waiter, who stopped first at Carmen's table to get their orders before ever nodding in her direction. When he finally made it over, she ordered food and drink all at once, choosing the tomato bisque because she thought scooping up a bowl of soup would be quick. When a raucous laugh erupted at Carmen's table, she looked up to see Cathy talking animatedly. That was the kind of atmosphere Judith wanted at work. Too bad she wasn't trained in research. She would just walk over there and introduce herself.

She laughed softly and shook her head. As if she would ever have the nerve to do something like that.

Thinking she would look less stupid if she appeared busy, she opened her convention packet. It was full of freebies—pens, pads, calendar magnets—and marketing materials, such as the brochure from The Delallo Group. On the front was a picture of Carmen, her arms folded and her eyes boring into the camera. The photo definitely did her beautiful features justice, but more important, it conveyed certainty. That's why people followed her around waiting for whatever information nugget she might share.

Judith's stomach filled with hope every time the door from the kitchen opened, but the staff in the back didn't seem to care she had ordered something simple. The Delallo Group was served first, sandwiches and salads, it appeared. It all looked good, especially the forkful of spinach salad Carmen was holding up . . . as if she were offering Judith a bite.

Judith felt her face grow red as she realized Carmen had caught her staring and was grinning directly at her. Nervously, she smiled back, afraid to be too obvious in case her eyes were playing tricks on her. She'd had enough embarrassment for one day. When Carmen showed no signs of breaking off the gaze, Judith finally blinked and looked away, thrilled to see Jose headed her way with what looked like a simple bowl of soup.

Finally, she could eat and get out of there.

But just as Jose reached the table, the hostess called his name and he turned his head. Judith watched in horror as the tray tilted, the bowl slid across the plate, and rich, red soup poured down her jacket and into her lap. Immediately, she and the stunned waiter grabbed every linen napkin within reach to mop up the mess, but she was left with a red stain on her tan suit that looked like a map of North and South America. Every eye in the room was on her, no doubt waiting for her to tear Jose's head off. But even in her frenzied state, she collected herself, knowing an eruption would only make matters worse.

The manager rushed over to take charge. "I'm terribly sorry, madam."

She saw Jose cowering as if he feared being fired on the spot.

"It's all right. It was my fault. I stuck my foot out accidentally."

"We'll be happy to take care of the cleaning, and, of course, your lunch is on us."

Judith wanted to point out that her lunch was on her, but that was just too obvious. She wasn't even hungry anymore, but no way was she going to get up and walk out with everyone staring.

Miraculously, Jose brought the next bowl of soup immediately and she nursed it, waiting for all the people who had witnessed the disaster to leave. But The Delallo Group stuck around long after Jose cleared their dishes. Judith could hear Carmen giving each of her staff an assignment of some sort. Questions were asked and answered, and one by one the notebooks were folded and the staffers left the table. Only Carmen was left to sign the bill.

Judith plotted her strategy. When Carmen left, she would make a run for it, straight for the coatroom to get her rain jacket—which wouldn't begin to cover her ruined suit—and right out the front door. Attending the afternoon sessions like this was out of the question.

Carmen stood, but instead of heading for the exit, she walked over to stand in front of Judith's table.

"Hey, sorry about your accident."

Judith tried to smile, but failed miserably. "Just that kind of day, I guess."

"Yeah, I saw Bob Durbin break your lunch date. That was pretty rude of him if you ask me."

"I guess he couldn't help it if something came up."

"You're more forgiving than I would have been. Same thing with the waiter. That was pretty classy, what you told his boss."

Judith couldn't believe this was really happening. Carmen Delallo was calling her classy. "It was just an accident. I didn't want to see him get fired over it."

"Like I said, pretty classy." She stuck out her hand. "I'm Carmen Delallo."

"I recognize you." Judith indicated the picture on the brochure. She took Carmen's hand in her grip and held it long enough to marvel at both its softness and strength. "I'm Judith. Judith O'Shea."

"Pleased to meet you." Carmen smiled and looked down at their joined hands, which forced Judith to finally let go. "Look, I just happened to have my raincoat with me. I thought we were going out for lunch, but my assistant booked us in here instead." She held out the black overcoat. "Why don't you put this on so you can go up to your room and change?"

"Thanks. I appreciate the offer, but I'm not staying here at the hotel. I'm a local."

"Then keep it and wear it home. I won't be going out today. You can bring it back tomorrow."

She held it open and Judith gave in, standing up to push her arms through the sleeves and pull it closed in front. "I really appreciate this."

"It's no problem." Carmen straightened the collar and smoothed the fabric. "Looks great on you."

Actually, it was big through the shoulders, but the extra length was good since it went below her skirt hem. It felt expensive. "I'm afraid it's going to come back smelling like tomatoes."

"No big deal. It's washable."

In a nervous gesture, Judith stuck her hands into the pockets and pulled out a small stack of business cards. "Oops, these are yours." She took one for herself and smiled, tucking it back into the pocket. She would memorize it later, right down to the fax.

"Thanks. I'll need these to drum up business."

"That shouldn't be a problem. I've heard people talking this morning about your new service. They're excited about it." They walked out of the restaurant and entered the hotel lobby, where several people made it a point to greet Carmen as they went by.

"I hope so. I'm giving a presentation on it tomorrow morning at ten. Stop in if you're interested."

A presentation? Carmen Delallo was acting as though she was just an ordinary presenter. She was the plenary speaker for Saturday, the convention's busiest day. "I'm sure we'll all be there taking notes. And I'll bring your raincoat then."

"Or you could just bring better weather." Carmen smiled one last time and turned to greet a man Judith recognized as the president of the association. Carmen was one of the most sought-after people at the convention.

And Judith was wearing her raincoat.

"What did I tell you?" Cathy asked, her voice low enough that no one else could hear.

"Unbelievable," Carmen answered. She stared across the lobby as Judith collected her own jacket and departed through the revolving glass door.

"Rainbow Getaways. What else could that mean?"

"Hawaii."

"Come on. Didn't you get any sense at all?"

"Mine doesn't work as well as yours. Go figure."

"I do not have gaydar!" Cathy said, lightly stomping her heel on Carmen's toe.

"Well, I certainly don't. But it's fine with me if you're right."

"What are you two conspiring about?"

Carmen and Cathy turned toward the familiar voice and shouted in unison, both holding out their arms for a hug. "Sofia!"

The newcomer, stylishly dressed and wearing a Bluetooth earpiece, greeted her friends warmly.

"What's this?" Carmen gestured at the cell phone gadget. "Afraid you'll miss a call from your broker?"

Sofia jabbed her in the ribs. "I'm working for the Secret Service now. You've been identified as a threat."

"Of course I'm a threat. I plan to take over the world."

"Actually, I was checking my messages. In fact, I just got one for you."

"For me?"

"Brooke said to tell you to call her."

"She's calling you too?" Cathy's voice was tinged with concern. "Something big must be going on with her, Carmen. You'd better go call."

Carmen checked her watch. "I don't have time right now. The next session starts in three minutes, and I'm supposed to meet the Cayman people after that for a drink."

Sofia grabbed her sleeve as she took a step in the direction of the meeting room. "We're all still on for dinner tomorrow night, aren't we?"

"I saw Priscilla this morning at her panel and she said yes." Carmen tipped her head toward Cathy. "But I always have to clear everything with my handler."

Cathy didn't miss a beat. "That's right. I think I'm going to have Bill Hinkle bring her breakfast in bed."

Carmen made a face. "If that's what you're planning, I can think of someone else I'd rather have you line up." She nodded her head toward the revolving door.

Sofia glanced from one woman to the other with obvious interest. "Do you mean to tell me Carmen has her eye on somebody?"

"I'll let Cathy tell you all about it. I have to run."

Chapter 4

Judith closed her door and turned both locks. For a fleeting moment, she felt guilty for not going in to work after dropping off her soiled clothes at the cleaners. But then she reminded herself how Todd had insisted she and Celia take vacation time to attend the conference. So instead of feeling guilty, she would take advantage of the time off to get ready for the next two days.

It wasn't as if she had a lot to do to prepare. Mostly, she wanted to look over the panel descriptions to anticipate which sessions Bob Durbin might attend. Then she could intercept him and set up another interview. The worst possible outcome for the weekend was coming away without at least a prospect for a new job.

She spread the conference materials on her futon, which she folded each morning to the upright couch position. Page four of the detailed conference agenda gave a little background on the main speakers, and her eyes were drawn immediately to a stunning head shot of Carmen Delallo. She pulled out the brochure she had been reading at lunch and compared the photos, both of which were serious and businesslike. Carmen was definitely photogenic, but she was even more beautiful in person. Maybe that was because she had been smiling in the restaurant. Perfect teeth . . . perfect lips.

She shook her head in a futile attempt to clear her wandering thoughts. Carmen was *that* kind of beautiful. The blurb next to the picture didn't yield much that wasn't common knowledge. It was more about the work of The Delallo Group than Carmen herself. Basically, the company had two divisions, called TDG Syndicated and TDG Custom. The syndicated studies, like the annual reports they provided on national and regional trends, were available to anyone who paid the subscription fee. That's what Myrna used to get for Rainbow Getaways. The custom studies were specially designed for individual clients, tailored to give them a competitive advantage.

At the bottom of the blurb was a URL for the company's Web site.

Judith pushed the papers aside and went to her desk in the alcove beneath the loft. From the bottom cabinet, she drew out her laptop computer and settled into a swivel armchair by the window. In moments, she was surfing the Internet, paging through the staff bios they had penned themselves.

Carmen wrote that she had lived in Chicago all her life, attending DePaul for a bachelor's degree in social and behavioral sciences, and Northwestern for her MBA. She was the third of six children . . . a lifelong Bulls fan . . . and she loved her work. The rest of the piece she devoted to praising her staff and thanking her longtime customers for pushing TDG to be the best.

Judith clicked on the tab for Cathy Rosen and saw that she too had attended DePaul, which made her wonder if the two had been classmates. Cathy's heavier frame and graying hair made her look older than Carmen, but not by much. Husband Hank was a history professor at Loyola, and they had three children and two grandchildren . . .

Clicking through to the next staffer, Judith recognized Lenore Yates as the TDG associate who had presented on a panel that morning. The Web site said she was senior associate, but she had been introduced today as vice president. Unlike Carmen and Cathy, she had gone to Yale. She and her husband Troy were marathoners, sailboarders and eco-tourists . . .

Richard Henderson . . . University of Illinois . . . wife and two sons . . . little league baseball coach . . .

Kristy Burgess . . . Loyola . . . four Pekingese show dogs . . .

Raul Sanchez . . . first baby . . .

The list went on and on until something leapt out at Judith and she paged back to Carmen's bio. Surely she did more than work and watch Bulls basketball games. And where was the info on her family? No husband or children? No one important enough to mention?

It was hard to imagine the charming woman who had so kindly come to her rescue in the restaurant had nothing more in her life than her business. Sure, successful people dedicated long hours to their jobs, but someone as warm and personable as Carmen would need relationships with others.

Maybe she was single . . . or perhaps she didn't think her personal life was anyone's business. Carmen Delallo as an available lesbian made a nice fantasy.

Judith wondered what her life was like. Everyone at the conference seemed to know her, so she must travel a lot to meet with clients. Obviously, she made a lot of money through her business—her Burberry raincoat probably cost several hundred dollars—but Judith guessed she earned every penny, not only by working hard but by innovation. No one else anticipated the market curve the way she did, or knew what tools travel agents needed before even they did.

Myrna always swore by TDG's annual reports, and she had regular phone contact with someone at the company to talk about the peculiarities of the gay and lesbian market. She always said TDG's expertise helped her maximize Rainbow's limited advertising and marketing resources. Judith wished now she had fought harder with Todd to maintain their subscription.

She picked up the conference agenda again and scanned through the sessions for Saturday. She no longer cared about hooking up with Bob Durbin—she would follow up with him when the conference was over. He would have fewer distractions then anyway. But how many more chances would she have to see and talk to someone like Carmen Delallo?

Besides, she had a built-in excuse to seek her out tomorrow. She had her raincoat.

Carmen entered her suite and sent her shoes flying across the room into a stack of cardboard boxes.

"Whoa!"

"Hey, Richard. I didn't know you were here. Lucky for you I didn't lead with my bra."

One of the things Carmen cherished about her company was its family atmosphere. Through years of working together, TDG's staff had shared weddings, divorces, babies and funerals, and Carmen wasn't afraid to let her hair down and be herself with these people she had hired and come to love. She was more guarded when it came to clients, unless it was an old friend like Priscilla or Sofia.

"I'm working on the slides for tomorrow. There was a mistake in the third part where we show the magazine reach."

"A mistake?"

"Yeah, it looks like you transposed the numbers or something, and it affects about eight or ten slides in the next part."

Carmen sighed. "We've checked those numbers twenty

times. How'd you find it?"

"I didn't. I was going over the presentation down in the booth and Raul looked over my shoulder and said it was wrong. He remembered it from the printout."

"He remembered one number out of thousands from a printout?"

"The guy's got a photographic memory or something. I bet him he was wrong and we logged on and looked it up. The little shit was right."

Carmen laughed. "Remind me to give the little shit a bonus. That would have been a disaster because you know as well as I do the magazine people are going to be in the audience tomorrow."

Richard made a few more changes to the program and saved the document. "That should do it. I'll get out of your hair now."

"You're not bothering me. Take as long as you need."

"I'm done. We're meeting here in the morning to go over it one last time, right?"

"I think Cathy said eight o'clock. She'll order breakfast for everybody."

"I don't even want to think about food. Raul dragged me to Chevy's in the Village and I ate way too much Tex-Mex."

"Wish I'd gone with you guys. I went to the steak place on the top floor with the Texas group, but Cathy was there and made me get fish."

"I'm sure it was better for you."

Carmen snarled. "You're all in this together, aren't you?"

"Cathy says our mission at TDG is to deprive you of joy."

"It's working."

Richard closed the cover on the laptop. "Okay, I'm out of here."

"Thanks. I'll see you in the morning."

Carmen threw the safety latch on the door as he left. Because the suite was their staging area, practically everyone on the staff had a key card, but now that she was settling in for the night, she wanted her privacy.

She collected her shoes and carried them into her bedroom. As she got undressed, she thought of Brooke, who had left another message for her while she was at dinner. She dug for her cell phone and clicked two numbers on her speed dial. Her friend answered at once.

"It's me . . . Yeah, I'm sorry. It's really hectic here." With her free hand, she awkwardly tugged off her skirt and tossed it over a chair. The pantyhose proved even more of a one-handed challenge. "Hold on, I'm going to put you on speaker phone. I'm here by myself, but I'm trying to get ready for bed."

"I'm just glad you finally got a chance to call," Brooke said. "I've been dying to talk to you about something important."

Brooke sounded very unsure of herself, prompting Carmen to worry that Cathy had been right about things between Brooke and Geoffrey. She hated inserting herself in the middle of their home life, but she had never felt Geoffrey Nance was right for her friend. He was nice enough, and she appreciated how well he treated the girls, but Brooke needed someone who could boost her confidence and make her feel loved. Geoffrey was too wrapped up in himself and his engineering work to do that.

"I'm always here to listen. You know that. But what I say shouldn't matter as much as how you feel about things yourself."

"But it does matter, Carmen. Every time I make a decision by myself, I fuck it up."

"That's not true. I can think of two things you didn't fuck up, and I bet you're looking at their pictures right now." In her mind's eye, she could picture Brooke in the family room of her suburban Chicago home. That was her space, where she watched television, read or talked on the phone. Geoffrey's was his office in the attic.

"I got lucky with them. Besides, you had a pretty big hand in their lives too."

Carmen couldn't argue with that, having taken in Brooke and

her daughters for almost four years when Brooke left her first husband. Not only was she godmother to the oldest, Healey, she had been a surrogate parent to both girls while Brooke recovered from the emotional trauma of her divorce. Despite the circumstances, Carmen remembered it as one of the happiest times of her life, and she was as close to all of them as she was to her own family.

"So what's up, sweetie? What can I do for you?" She braced herself for bad news.

"You know how much time I've put into redecorating our house? I can't remember when you were over here last, but I'm finished with the living room and the kitchen, and I just have the girls' bedrooms left on the main floor."

Carmen wasn't sure she had heard right. "I . . . you . . . I think you told me about it." What was so urgent about redecorating her house?

"I've been spending a lot of time at Chicago Living, that interior design store on Monroe. I took you there to show you the fabric for the sofa."

Dragged would have been a better word. "I remember. The red."

"It was tomato."

Of course it was. How stupid could she be?

"Anyway, the woman that worked there . . . her name's Gisele Martin"—Brooke used the French pronunciation—"always said I had a very good eye for what looked good together."

"I've always thought that. You did a great job on my place." She had given Brooke free rein to decorate her apartment on Lincoln Park.

"Thank you. So Gisele asked me if I would be interested in working for them. They have a lot of clients who sell real estate and they decorate some of the models and upscale homes so they'll be attractive to potential buyers. It's called staging, and she says I can work part-time or full-time, whatever I want."

"Wow, that's fantastic!"

"You really think so?"

"It sounds like it's right up your alley." Except Brooke had never had a job in her life. "What do you think about it?"

"It's exciting. I can't get it out of my head."

Carmen carried her cell phone into the bathroom and began taking off her makeup. "What does Geoffrey have to say about it?"

"I haven't talked to him. I wanted to talk to you first."

Carmen knew she shouldn't feel good about that, but she liked being the first person on Brooke's list of people to call when she needed to talk something out. "Would you have fun with it?"

"Are you kidding? I can't believe they would pay me to do something like that. It's a dream job."

"Actually, I think dream job is an oxymoron."

"That's easy for you to say. You haven't sat at home watching your ass grow for thirty years."

"Neither have you, Brooke. You've always had plenty to do with the girls. And you volunteered all those years at the library and the March of Dimes." Carmen wet a washcloth and wiped her face. "Besides, if your ass has grown, what does that make mine?"

"You know what I mean."

"No, I really don't. Lots of women go back to work once their kids are grown."

"Well, that's one of the problems. Amie's just seventeen. I was there for Healey all through high school, and I'm worried how Amie will feel."

"Did you talk to her?"

"She said it didn't matter, but you know kids. They're all waiting till they hit thirty to tell you how you fucked up their lives."

Carmen laughed at the image, not caring that Brooke was

probably being serious. "If one of your kids ever says that, tell her it was the four years you lived with me. Who knows? You might even be right."

"My kids were never happier."

"I know, but all that happiness has to be bad for you, doesn't it?"

"You crack me up, Carmen."

"So go on. Tell them you'll take it. If Amie starts to feel cheated, maybe I can help out a little."

"I know she'd like that."

Carmen toweled her face. "Okay, I have to brush my teeth now so you do all the talking. Tell me what you'd have to do in your job. Oh, and did they say how much they'd pay?"

Brooke rattled off all the details. She was especially excited about the salary and potential for benefits. Right now, she was on Geoffrey's insurance, but it was nice to have an option in case something happened. That last bit got Carmen's attention, and she had to ask.

"How are things with Geoffrey?"

Brooke hesitated before answering, giving Carmen the chance to rinse her mouth. "Okay, I guess. We always get along better when he brings home a lot of work. He just goes upstairs and I don't see him till he comes to bed."

Carmen shook her head, holding back a discouraged sigh. She hated knowing Brooke was unhappy, but there wasn't anything she could do. "Have you guys thought about talking to somebody?"

"I don't think Geoffrey would go."

"You could always go without him."

"I guess . . . hold on." Brooke left the line to take another call. Moments later, she was back. "Police benevolent fund. I wasn't benevolent. Did you see Sofia today?"

"I did. She looks great, as usual."

"I'm so jealous. I wish I was there with all of you."

"Why don't you get on a plane tomorrow? We're having dinner in Little Italy tomorrow night."

"I can't. Amie's got a band concert tomorrow night. She's been practicing for months. Even Geoffrey's going."

"I forgot about that. She invited me too."

"It's probably a good thing you're out of town. I think Anthony's going to be there."

Carmen cringed at the idea of running into Brooke's ex-husband. Their last few exchanges—twelve years ago, right after the divorce—had been acrimonious, with Carmen refusing to pass on Anthony's messages or allow him to come to her house. She didn't know how Brooke could stand to be in the same room with him after the way he had behaved.

"I bet I'm keeping you up," Brooke said. "You're an hour ahead of me there, aren't you?"

"Yeah, I'm getting into bed. But we can talk as long as you want."

"Tell me what's going on at your conference."

"Not much. I've had meetings all day . . . dinner with clients . . . that kind of thing." For a fleeting moment, she considered telling Brooke about meeting Judith O'Shea, but something stopped her, an uncomfortable feeling she didn't want to share. "And I'm giving the keynote presentation tomorrow morning. I get to put on my blue silk suit and play big shot."

"I love you in that blue suit. God, you're going to have everybody there eating out of your hand."

"I hope so." Carmen couldn't stifle a yawn.

"Okay, I heard that. I'm hanging up now."

"You should take the job."

"I think so too. Thanks for calling me back."

"Anytime, sweetie. Love you."

"Love you too."

Chapter 5

Judith checked her watch for the tenth time as the morning's first panel of speakers wrapped up its comments. She had barely remembered a word from the session, she was so focused on Carmen's presentation, which began in twenty minutes. When the moderator stood and opened the floor to questions, she quietly slipped out from her seat in the back row, hoping for a chance to see Carmen before the plenary session began.

Carmen's freshly laundered raincoat was folded neatly inside a Saks Fifth Avenue shopping bag, one Judith had saved from two years ago when they had a massive after-Christmas sale. It was a silly gesture, she knew, but the bag seemed more fitting for the expensive coat than anything else she had. It didn't take a fashion mogul to see she bought her clothes off the rack at discount stores. But then Judith did very little that required her to dress in expensive suits or skirts. Besides, it wasn't as if she had unlimited space for an elaborate wardrobe. She had barely pulled together three nice outfits for the weekend.

From the deserted hallway, she peered through the crack in the door into the main ballroom, where hundreds of chairs were set up for the plenary session. The room seemed cavernous with only a handful of people inside making last-minute preparations. Carmen was at a table on a platform with the young man Judith recognized from the company's Web site as Richard Henderson. Cathy Rosen and Lenore Yates were there too, along with a woman Judith thought she recognized as the vice president of the Association of Travel Professionals.

She felt a little guilty for intruding at this critical time, but she had promised to return Carmen's coat before the session. The smart thing would be to give it to Cathy, but that meant she wouldn't get to talk to Carmen, which was all she had thought about for the last twenty-one hours. Once the presentation was finished, Carmen would probably be inundated with people congratulating her or asking questions. No, now was definitely a better time.

As she drew closer to the end of the platform, she saw them deep in concentration and changed her mind, deciding instead just to give the coat to Cathy. Carmen's time was too important for something—or someone—so trivial. But then Carmen looked up from her notes and saw her. Her face broke into a sudden smile followed by a look of confusion, which made Judith worry for a moment that Carmen didn't recognize her. After a moment's hesitation, Carmen jumped up from her chair and stepped down off the platform. "Good morning."

"Hi. I'm so sorry to bother you. I was afraid I wouldn't have another chance to see you." She handed Carmen the shopping bag. "I brought your coat."

"Thank you. There wasn't any hurry."

Judith noted with embarrassment that everyone on the platform had stopped talking and was looking in their direction. "I had it cleaned."

"You didn't have to do that."

"Yes, I did. It reeked of tomatoes by the time I got home. I couldn't bring it back like that."

"Still—"

Judith fumbled for the business card in her pocket. "Look, I don't want to keep you. Here's my card if there's a problem with anything. I really appreciate you coming to my rescue like that."

"You're welcome." Carmen looked over her shoulder at her staff. "I'm sorry. I have to get back to this."

"I know. I just wanted to say thanks."

"I'm glad I was there to help." Carmen smiled warmly before hurrying back to check her presentation.

Judith could feel her face burning with embarrassment as she walked toward the doors at the back of the room. The way they had all gaped at her from the platform, they must have thought she was an idiot for interrupting at a time like that. After all the hours she had spent imagining how nice it would be to talk to Carmen again, she had ended up blowing it by coming at a bad time.

A few early birds were coming in to claim the good seats. Judith figured she had just enough time to grab a cup of coffee from the beverage bar out in the hall. As she was going out, she was practically bowled over by Bob Durbin, who mumbled a token apology without even making eye contact. Carmen was right about him. He was rude.

When she returned with her coffee, Celia waved her over to a seat in the fifth row.

"Judith, I wanted you to meet my friend Denise. She's the one who got me the interview at the network. I go next Tuesday."

"That's great." Judith set her coffee cup on the chair and held out her hand to Denise, who seemed oddly anxious about her arrival. "I'm really glad to meet you. You're going to love working with Celia."

"Aw, you're sweet," Celia said.

"Is it okay if I sit here?"

"Sure." Celia indicated the open seat on her other side. "So how did your interview go yesterday?"

"It got canceled."

"That sucks."

Judith waved it off. "I'll deal with it later. I saw they have a job board out by the registration desk. Maybe something good will be on it."

Celia settled back in her seat and whispered something to Denise that made her smile. Then she looked toward the podium and leaned into Judith. "Do you remember back when Myrna used to call The Delallo Group?"

"Uh-huh."

"I always thought she sounded like she was flirting. I think I just figured out why."

Judith followed her friend's eyes to the platform, where Carmen sat smiling and relaxed. She looked absolutely fantastic in her dark blue suit. Judith had also noticed her understated, but obviously expensive, jewelry—a gold chain necklace and bracelet, with hoop earrings. On her right hand was a wide platinum band decorated with small diamonds, an heirloom perhaps. Her left hand was unadorned.

"Have you had a good look at that woman?"

Still embarrassed about interrupting Carmen earlier, Judith decided to let that be a rhetorical question. She didn't want to share anything about her unfortunate encounters with Carmen. "Very nice."

"Very nice?" Celia pulled off her glasses and handed them to Judith. "Here. Look again."

Judith chuckled. "Okay, she's very, very nice."

"I'll say. Ol' Myrna was up to something, all right."

The crowd grew quiet as one of the women rose and took the podium. She too was smartly dressed, and wearing a ribbon on her nametag that announced her official position. This was the one Judith thought was the vice president of the association, Sofia somebody. She was a slender, striking woman, her hair more silver than black.

"Good morning."

A few hundred attendees murmured a response.

"Oh, that didn't sound good at all. Let's try it again." Comically, the woman went back to her chair and sat, where she smoothed her skirt and primped her hair as the audience giggled. Then she stood and returned to the podium. "Good morning."

The crowd roared its enthusiastic response.

"For those of you who haven't had the pleasure of meeting me yet, I'm Sofia Santini, and you elected me vice president last year." She took a sip of water as the audience applauded. "Over the summer, those of us on the program committee met to talk about you behind your backs. While we were together, we read some of the evaluations of last year's conference and found that a number of you wanted to be tied to your chairs and have needles shot into your eyeballs with an air gun."

The audience chuckled nervously.

"We didn't have enough air guns to do that, so we asked Carmen Delallo to speak instead."

That brought a raucous round of laughter. Judith studied Carmen, who was pinching the bridge of her nose and shaking her head.

"If you don't happen to know Carmen, you can read her official bio in the program. But see me later if you want to know the real dirt." Sofia glanced back at Carmen and smiled. "Seriously, Carmen is one of my oldest friends. All the others are much, much younger."

By this time, Carmen was sneering.

"Folks, let me tell you a little about the presentation you're about to see. I had the chance to look through the slides this morning, and you're in for a real treat. The numbers are very encouraging for next year. I'm going to get out of the way and let her get started so we'll have time for questions. So without further ado"—she looked back at Carmen again—"and further shenanigans on my part, please welcome one of the smartest people I know, my friend, Carmen Delallo."

Judith joined in the applause, mentally adding kind and generous to Sofia's list of platitudes. Then she sat mesmerized for forty-five minutes as Carmen went on to present the highlights of TDG's annual study of travelers. She was funny and engaging, and as Sofia had promised, obviously smart. When the last slide faded and the lights went up, Judith was ready to rush back to her office and plan her next marketing campaign using all the information Carmen had just shared.

As the final applause rang out, Celia burst her bubble. "Can you imagine Todd letting us do a campaign like that?"

"Not really."

"I can't believe he thinks that Conover report is all we need to know."

"I don't even bother to look at it."

"Me neither." Celia stood and slung her purse over her shoulder. "You want to go with us for lunch?"

Judith had entertained a fantasy of having lunch today with Carmen, an invitation that would have come when she returned the coat. They would talk about work, their favorite travel destinations, what they did for fun, and maybe even a little about their personal lives. It would have been the beginning of a great friendship.

Except important people like Carmen Delallo didn't strike up friendships with people like Judith.

"Sure, thanks."

Carmen folded her arms and listened intently as Lenore described their plan for servicing Bill Hinkle's account. It was a good strategy for TDG Syndicated since it created an enormous revenue stream. But Hinkle wasn't going to like the fact that his competitors would be able to buy the information too.

"Bill, I think Lenore's on to something. She's been studying this for quite a while. Adding time-share data to the syndicated study would help your whole industry. It's a fact of life you guys are gobbling up a good-sized chunk of the travel business, especially in the south."

"But I don't see how going syndicated is going to help us at Franklin," Hinkle interjected.

"You said yourself you wanted to branch out and develop resorts in New England and out West. You don't want to put all that money into regional research by yourself. This way, you get to share the cost."

"But my competitors are going to know everything I know."

"These numbers are just going to give everybody the big picture. You can spend the money you save from this on testing your ad campaigns or finding ways to make your package better than the others. You'll not only have the edge, you'll have it in a national market."

"What's to stop them from spending more money too?"

"Nothing, but they aren't going to spend it with me," Carmen answered. "As long as Franklin Resorts is our client, The Delallo Group won't do any strategic work for your direct competitors."

That brought a smile to Hinkle's face. "You think you'll have it up and running by this time next year?"

Carmen glanced over at Lenore and gave her a quick wink out of Hinkle's line of sight. "Lenore says we'll have it off the ground by this summer."

"That's right," Lenore said, clearly trying not to show her panic. "We've already agreed on the major components. The rest is just a matter of writing the software and getting the vendors into place."

"So we're done?" Carmen stood and stretched. She was certainly done. Five straight hours of client meetings had rendered her numb. She followed Hinkle into the hall and let the door close. “I appreciate you being on board for this, Bill. Lenore really knows what she’s doing.”

“I enjoyed having dinner with her last night. You better watch that one, Carmen. She’s almost as pretty as you.”

“If you’d open your stubborn eyes, you might realize that women can be a lot more than pretty. Lenore’s probably smarter than both of us put together. That’s why I made her vice president.”

“She is smart. I’ll give her that.”

“I hope you’ll give her more than that because I think she can help Franklin a lot. But if you make her feel like she’s just a pretty face, she’s going to want to give her attention to someone who appreciates what she can do.”

Hinkle made a face, realizing he was getting called on the carpet. “I don’t mean anything by it, Carmen. You know that, don’t you?”

“What I know, Bill, is that I can’t send my people out to work in places where they feel like they’re not being respected. They’ll hold me accountable for that.” She could see that her message was getting through, and decided to end things on an up note. “I know she’s looking forward to working with Franklin on the syndicated study, but I’m afraid it’s because of the business potential for both of us, not your handsome mug.”

Both of them began to chuckle, breaking the mild tension.

“I guess I ought to behave myself before word gets back to Sheila that I’m checking out one of my vendors. I sure don’t need another ex-wife.”

“Your wife is a saint.”

“Don’t I know it!”

She punched him lightly on the shoulder. “Thanks for sticking with us so long, Bill.”

“My pleasure.”

Carmen turned and grabbed the door handle, only to find she had locked herself out of the suite. Her knock drew the expected response from Cathy.

"We don't want any."

"Good, because I don't have any."

Cathy opened the door and held out a small stack of messages. "You'd better get some because you're not finished."

"What do you mean I'm not finished? I didn't even get to eat lunch." She flipped through the messages, seeing only two that asked for a call back. "Did Durbin say what he wanted?"

Lenore was still at the conference table. "I saw him having lunch today with Art Conover."

Carmen sighed. "Great. He's going to try to squeeze me for a discount."

Cathy peered over her glasses. "Can you just throw in an extra consultation?"

"Bob Durbin's a jerk. If he wants to go with Conover, let him."

Lenore gave Cathy a quizzical look. "Why don't I give him a call? I bet we can work something out."

Carmen grabbed a seltzer from the refrigerator and twisted the top. As she took a hefty swig, she analyzed her reaction. The constant nuisance of Conover pitching her clients was like being nibbled to death by ducks. But it was Durbin who annoyed her more. She had long suspected he was sharing her reports with another agency and splitting the cost, a strict violation of their contract because it robbed her of a customer fee. On top of that, he had blown off Judith O'Shea. She spun around and spotted the Saks bag. She hadn't thought of Judith at all since the morning session.

"Carmen?"

"Yeah, go ahead and call him. Thanks." Carmen handed her the message and reached into the bag for Judith's card.

"Our dinner reservation's for seven thirty," Cathy said. "But you have to put in an appearance at the cocktail party downstairs. That started ten minutes ago."

Carmen blew out a raspberry. "I'm so tired of being nice." She slung her purse over her shoulder and started for the door.

"Just one more hour. Then you can take it out on us."

In the hallway, Carmen pushed the elevator button and checked her appearance in the mirror as she waited. The woman looking back at her was tired. She had a right to look tired, having worked twelve days in a row to get ready for this weekend.

"Screw the tight butt, Brooke. I'm sleeping in tomorrow."

The elevator opened and she climbed aboard. On the way down, she made small talk with fellow passengers, several of whom mentioned her earlier presentation. When they reached the lobby, she fell in step toward the cocktail party until her eye caught a familiar figure standing alone at the job board.

Judith O'Shea was checking the posts and making notes on a small pad. At a conference with more than a thousand attendees, it made no sense at all to Carmen that someone as nice as Judith wouldn't be surrounded by friends.

"TDG's got a couple of openings. Ever considered coming over to the dark side where the vendors are?" Carmen smiled as she peered over Judith's shoulder.

"God, you scared me."

"Sorry." She leaned a hip onto the table by the board. "And I'm sorry I didn't have more time to talk this morning. Things were kind of hectic."

"No, that was my fault. I should have had more sense than to bother you before your presentation . . . which was great, by the way."

"Thanks." Carmen nodded toward the board. "You're not happy where you are?"

Judith shook her head grimly. "I used to be, but the commission cuts are killing us. That's why I was hoping to talk to Bob Durbin yesterday."

"Yours is one of the boutique agencies, right?"

"Yeah, we specialize in . . . gay and lesbian tours . . . things like that."

Carmen picked up on Judith's hesitation. It didn't mean she was a lesbian herself, but the odds just went way up. "Have you talked to Zeigler-Marsh?"

"I'd love to work at a place like that, but they're not advertising any openings."

"That doesn't mean anything." The next words came out before Carmen could stop herself. "I'm having dinner with some friends tonight down in Little Italy. Sofia will be there, and she's a partner at Z-M. Why don't you join us?"

"Oh, I can't horn in on you and your friends like that."

"Sure you can." The idea of her friends meeting Judith was growing on her. She wanted them to see what a nice person she was. "None of us are working tonight, though. We're just going out to have a good time."

"Well, if you're sure . . ."

"I'm sure." She gestured with her thumb in the direction of the ballroom, where the cocktail party was well underway. "But I have to go show my face in there for a while. Are you coming?"

"Yeah, I was going to stop in."

"Good. My assistant, Cathy Rosen—well, she's also one of my best friends—is making the taxi arrangements. I'll tell her to find you when we're ready to leave."

"That'll be great."

"See you in a few, then." Carmen spun away, her mind already working on how she was going to explain her impulsive invitation to her friends.

As Carmen walked away, Judith replayed the conversation in her head. She couldn't believe she had just been invited to have dinner with not only the keynote speaker at the conference, but also a partner at Zeigler-Marsh, who just happened to be the vice president of the association. She wanted to pinch herself. Never in her life had she kept company with people like that. How ironic that all the good things happening to her right now were the result of disasters—Bob Durbin canceling their interview and Jose the waiter dumping soup in her lap.

She looked numbly back at the job board. Was Carmen really serious about her applying for an opening at TDG? There was a posting for an account rep . . . another for a software programmer. She was neither, so it didn't matter if Carmen had meant it or not. Besides, TDG was in Chicago.

Judith folded her notes and stuffed them into her coat pocket. From the job board, she had three new possibilities in the New York area, two in corporate travel departments and one at an airline club lounge at JFK. And now Carmen had suggested there may be a chance to get on at Zeigler-Marsh, one of the biggest agencies in the country. No question which was the best opportunity.

Inside the ballroom, Judith breathed a sigh of relief when she spotted Celia and Denise at a table near the center of the room. She would have hated standing around by herself waiting for Cathy's cue that it was time to go.

"Hey, you guys mind if I join you?"

"Of course not," Celia answered. "This is a great spot. All the waiters come by here with the hors d'oeuvres."

Denise stood and rested her hands on Celia's shoulders in what looked like a gesture of affection. "I was just going to the bar, Judith. Would you like a glass of wine?"

"Yes, thank you. Whatever you're having." She pulled out a few bills.

"It's an open bar. The airlines are sponsoring this."

Judith peeled off three ones. "Tip the bartender, then."

When she disappeared into the crowd, Celia whispered excitedly, "What do you think of Denise?"

"You mean Denise who's practically all over you?" Judith grinned, happy to see that her friend had hooked up with someone nice. "I think she's cute."

"She is, isn't she?" Celia checked over her shoulder to make sure Denise wasn't nearby. "I had no idea it was even happening till this afternoon when we were talking about me maybe getting that job at the network. She said she hoped I didn't have a problem with going out with somebody from work."

"That's really great, Cee. I thought I saw something between you two—"

"Excuse me, Judith?"

They looked up to see a smiling Cathy Rosen.

"Hi, Cathy."

"Sorry to interrupt. I just talked to Carmen and she said you were coming with us tonight. I wanted to let you know that we'll be taking two taxis. You can ride with me if that's all right."

"Of course."

"Great. I'll give you the signal in about fifteen minutes."

"I'll be watching."

As she walked away, Denise returned and placed a glass of wine in front of her. Judith became aware of Celia's fingers digging into her forearm.

"Did I just imagine all that, or are you actually going to dinner with Carmen Delallo?"

"It's not a big deal or anything. I was just talking to her and—" There was no point continuing in this vein. She wasn't kidding anyone. "I might as well tell you guys the whole sordid tale." She went on to relate the story of her humiliating experience in the restaurant and Carmen's rescue.

"I bet she thinks you're hot."

Celia and Denise giggled with mischief, causing Judith to cover her face with her hands. "Stop, you're embarrassing me."

"Well, it might be true. You never know." Celia grinned at her smugly. "You two would make a cute couple, don't you think?"

Denise nodded. "Maybe we can double date."

"You guys are killing me." Judith had enjoyed that fantasy too, but refused to give it serious credence. There was no legitimate reason to think Carmen was a lesbian, or if she were, that she was interested.

Chapter 6

"You invited her to dinner?" Priscilla stared across the ballroom as Cathy spoke to Judith. "What's going on inside that head of yours?"

"Nothing at all," Sofia answered instead, lightly rapping her knuckles against Carmen's head. "Because there's nothing in there."

"I felt bad for her. Bob Durbin blew her off."

"So you just offered her a job at my agency instead."

"It's not like I promised her a corner office or anything."

"Small wonder," Sofia said, her smirk a sign that her annoyance was all for show. "We actually could use somebody to help grow the gay segment. But I have to make sure I have an empty desk before you bring her in and give her my parking spot."

"Just meet her," Carmen snapped. She had expected a hard time from her friends so this was no surprise. At least Cathy wasn't busting her chops. She seemed to like Judith and was patting herself on the back for being right that she was a lesbian. "And be nice."

"We're always nice," Priscilla said. "But we don't get to tease you like this very often. When's the last time you got the hots for somebody?"

Carmen was about to take issue with the verbiage but knew it was a waste of time. "When was the last time I had the hots for somebody and didn't feel like shit about it?"

That quieted both of her friends for a moment.

"Speaking of which, did you ever get in touch with Brooke?"

"I called her last night."

"Is she all right?"

"She's fine. She's decided to take a job with a decorator, fixing up houses and apartments for sale."

"Brooke's going to work? That I have to see," Sofia said cynically.

Beneath her calm exterior, Carmen seethed with frustration. It was an age-old pattern for her friends to come down on Brooke this way. It wasn't fair they mocked her choice to be a mother and housewife, then did the same when she decided to get a job. "She's always had a job. It's just one you don't value."

"Now, now, girls," Priscilla said. "We're supposed to be having fun, remember?"

Carmen felt guilty, as she usually did when she lashed out at her friends in defense of Brooke. It was a firmly established dynamic in their complex relationship, but their friendship flourished despite the friction.

"There's Cathy waving at us. I have to go upstairs and get my coat. Hold the taxi, will you?" Priscilla hurried out, leaving Carmen and Sofia in awkward silence.

"Carmen, you know I love Brooke like a sister. And I'd tease her about getting a job to her face."

"Yeah," she conceded. "But she's not here to defend herself."

"You don't have to treat every little comment like it's an assault. But we shouldn't have to walk on eggshells with each other. We've been friends too long."

"I know." Carmen sighed. "She sounded really excited about it. I guess I wanted you guys to be excited too."

"Fair enough. I'll give her a call tomorrow and she can tell me all about it."

"She'll like that."

Each helped the other with her coat and they said good-bye to colleagues on their way out of the ballroom. When they reached the valet circle, Cathy was leaving in a taxi with Judith.

"So what exactly are you up to with this Judith person?"

Carmen shrugged. "A little diversion maybe. You know how conventions are."

Sofia wouldn't look directly at her, as if knowing she was treading on thin ice. But she wasn't the kind of friend to ignore questions that needed to be asked. "Carmen, I'm as happy as anybody to see you interested in somebody."

"I told you, it's not a big deal. I doubt I'll ever see her again after this weekend."

"You will if she comes to work for Z-M."

"Then I can deal with that."

"Fine. Just look me in the eye and promise me you don't have any weird shit going on in that head of yours."

Carmen laughed self-consciously at her old friend's choice of words, but she knew Sofia was being dead serious. "I don't. I met her at lunch. I've talked to her a couple of times. She's very nice."

Sofia gave her a skeptical look. "And she just happens to be a dead ringer for the woman you've been hung up on for almost thirty years."

"I'm so glad you could join us," Cathy said, leaning across the backseat to pat Judith's knee. "But I have to warn you, crazy things have been known to happen when this crew gets together."

Judith couldn't get over being invited along on this outing. "Who all is going to be there?"

"Just two others. There's Sofia, the woman who introduced Carmen today."

"God, she was so funny."

"She and Carmen both are like that. You never know what they're going to say, so watch out."

"You can tell they're great friends."

"Oh, they are. We all went to DePaul together. We've known each other for ages."

"And you've been working together ever since?"

"Mostly. Sofia was the first one to go into the travel business. She took a job with Zeigler-Marsh in Chicago right after she graduated. Carmen went on for her MBA, and I got married and started popping out kids." Cathy interrupted her story to remind the driver of the address. "Even though we were all doing our own thing, we were still close with each other. You know how girlfriends are."

Judith nodded absently. She had casual friends like Celia and the young couple next door, and even an ex-girlfriend she stayed in touch with. But there was no one with whom she shared a bond like the one Cathy was describing.

"Priscilla Magee is really the one who started it all. She worked in the tourism office for Cook County and needed a market research project done on short notice with almost no budget. Sofia put her in touch with Carmen, because Carmen had gotten interested in that sort of thing at Northwestern. So she did the project and they liked her work so much they asked her to do some more things. Before long, she hired a small staff and hung out a shingle."

"What a great story."

"It really is. Now Carmen has her own company, Sofia's a

partner at Zeigler-Marsh here in New York, and Priscilla is the director of travel and tourism for the city of Chicago. She's the other one who's going to be there tonight."

Judith still couldn't believe the clumsy chain of events that had led her to be on her way to dinner with such powerful women in the industry. This was going to be a night to remember.

The driver turned onto Mulberry Street, the heart of Little Italy, and pulled to a stop in front of Pellegrino's, which Judith considered one of the best restaurants in the neighborhood. The three twenties she had in her wallet would probably be enough unless her companions chose expensive wine. Then she would have to pay her part with a credit card, but it was more than worth it. For this one night, she could pretend to be just another successful, cosmopolitan professional.

"What part of the city do you live in?"

"On Fifteenth in Chelsea, not too far from here. I've walked down here with friends a few times, in fact."

"You've eaten here before?"

Judith nodded. "I love it."

"Carmen ate here a few months ago. It must have made an impression because she actually remembered the name long enough to tell me about it. I wrote it down so I could find it again."

"So you're Carmen's administrative assistant. Is that right?"

"I'm the person who keeps her on schedule and gets her where she needs to be."

"I bet that's a challenge."

"You have no idea. For a genius, she's a space cadet. Wait till you get to know her."

Judith liked the sound of that. She was looking forward to finding out more about Carmen, who was now pulling up in a taxi with her other friends.

All three were laughing as they poured out of the cab. Cathy made the brief introductions and led the way inside, where they were seated at a round table. Judith found herself between Cathy and Sofia.

Cathy opened her menu and scanned it, then closed it and slid her reading glasses across the table to Carmen.

"Get something I like, Carmen, so we can trade if mine isn't any good," Sofia said.

Carmen peered through the lenses and smiled. "I'm going to have the filet with wine sauce."

Cathy cleared her throat and stared at her, her head tilted to one side.

"I didn't eat lunch," Carmen whined.

"You told me not to let you eat a heavy meal at night anymore."

"I didn't mean tonight."

"Fine. It's your stomach."

Carmen gave her a satisfied smile. "Filet, then. What are you having, Judith?"

"Umm . . . maybe the shrimp scampi."

"Good choice," Sofia said. "Steak on one side, shrimp on the other. I'll have the calamari. You can get whatever you want, Priscilla. I can't reach yours."

"Why, thank you, Sofia. That's very generous of you. I'm going to have the quill pasta."

"And I'll do the veal scaloppine," Cathy decided, waving at the waiter.

The women ordered, with Carmen selecting two bottles of wine for the table. Then they launched into a catty discussion of an eccentric old-timer at the convention whose biggest complaint about the industry was that travelers didn't dress up anymore.

"So, Carmen, did you bring my little namesake in your suitcase?" Priscilla asked.

"I most certainly did not. She's probably tearing up my furniture as we speak."

Everyone at the table seemed to know Priscilla's namesake. Judith looked from one to another until Cathy noticed her confusion.

"Priscilla gave Carmen a dachshund puppy a few months ago. Carmen named her Prissy."

"She was a behavioral reject," Carmen explained evenly. "Someone brought her to the humane society because she destroyed their home every time they left her alone. Now, thanks to Priscilla, she's at my place eating the couch."

"Admit it, Carmen. You love that dog."

"She's a misfit."

"She sleeps on your bed."

"That's because she barks all night if I lock her in her crate. The neighbors probably think I'm beating her." She tasted the wine and nodded to the waiter, who filled all the glasses at the table.

"And you just left that poor baby alone this weekend?"

"Not this time. Healey's there with her."

"Along with Healey's boyfriend," Cathy added.

"Little Healey has a sleepover boyfriend?" Sofia expressed such dismay that Judith thought Healey must be a teenager.

"Little Healey's twenty-one years old," Carmen answered.

"What did Brooke say about the boyfriend staying over?"

"Who says I told Brooke?"

"I can't believe those girls are already grown up."

Cathy turned to Judith to explain. "We're talking about Brooke Healey—Brooke Nance, I should say. That's her married name."

"Her current married name," Sofia corrected.

Judith could have sworn she felt the table move, as though someone had just kicked Sofia underneath. Cathy ignored it and went on.

"Brooke was Sofia's roommate at DePaul, so we go way back

with her too."

"Is she also in the travel business?"

"No"—Cathy looked over at Carmen—"but didn't you tell me she was about to take a job somewhere?"

Judith listened as Carmen told the group about her phone conversation the night before. It was obvious from Carmen's tone she thought a lot of Brooke, and the two of them were quite close. "It's too bad Brooke couldn't be here tonight too," she offered.

"Oh, it really is a shame," Sofia said seriously, turning away so Judith couldn't see her face. From the way all four women seemed to be fighting the urge to laugh, Judith knew she was missing out on an inside joke. But the uncomfortable silence ended abruptly when the waiter appeared with their entrees.

"Have some more wine," Carmen said, filling all the glasses with the second bottle.

True to her word, Sofia helped herself to a bite of steak from Carmen's plate before swiping a shrimp from Judith's. "So, Judith, you work at an agency?"

Judith nodded, her mouth freshly full of linguine.

"Here in New York?"

Judith nodded again, trying not to laugh as everyone chuckled at her dilemma.

"Do you like it?"

"Mmm-hmm." Her eyes began to water as the questions persisted.

"So why were you looking at the job board today?"

Judith grabbed her water glass and washed down the mouthful. "Whew! Because the owner's nephew took over the shop where I work and we all think it's just a matter of time before he cuts our commissions to milk money."

"It's a small agency," Carmen explained to the others. "You specialize in gay and lesbian tours, right?"

Carmen said it so matter-of-factly Judith assumed no one at

the table would have a problem with it. She hadn't actually said she was a lesbian herself, but she didn't mind if they came to that conclusion on their own. She had always found most people in the travel industry to be accepting of gays. "We used to, but we don't do tours anymore. We just do straight bookings now for commissions . . . well, not that kind of straight. We still have our same clientele."

"You need a lot of volume for in-bound bookings," Sofia said.

"And heavy-duty marketing," Priscilla added.

"We're mostly on the Internet and niche magazines. The business has grown, but it's not as much fun as it used to be when we worked our own client base."

"You guys got caught behind the eight ball when the Internet took off, didn't you?" Sofia asked as she nicked another shrimp.

"Yes and no," Judith said, hesitating to voice her own business philosophy with these experts. The last thing she wanted was to appear uninformed. "I think it's tough for all the small shops, but it hit us at a time when our owner was getting ready to retire. She could have cashed out by selling the business to somebody who wanted the segment, but she decided instead to leave it to her nephew, who didn't really know the industry well enough to make the transition."

Cathy spoke up. "Who was your owner? Anyone we know?"

"You might know her because she used to get your annual reports. Her name was Myrna Greenbaum."

"There's a name my mother-in-law would have loved. Instead, she got a Righetti and three Catholic grandchildren."

"I remember Myrna!" Carmen said excitedly. "I used to talk to her all the time. She was such a character. I don't know why I didn't make the connection with Rainbow Getaways. Where is she now?"

"She moved to West Palm Beach about two years ago."

"That's about when you guys dropped our study."

"That was one of Todd's cost-cutting moves. He signed up

for Conover Data Source instead because it was cheaper." Carmen flashed a look of annoyance, prompting Judith to quickly add, "But none of us even bother to look at it because it doesn't have enough detail."

"Not to mention enough accuracy," Priscilla added, her voice dripping with cynicism.

"He bases everything on proxy data," Judith noted, hoping she hadn't said something stupid.

"That's why his numbers are unstable," Carmen explained. "But most of the little agencies don't see that, and they think something is better than nothing. If they can't afford the TDG study, they'd be better off not getting anything."

"Which is why no one in our shop uses it," Judith said, delighted to get Carmen's nod of approval.

"Smart girl."

Sofia nonchalantly speared yet another shrimp on Judith's plate. "So you like working with that segment? You're a lesbian, right?"

"Yes, I am." Judith was glad to get that declaration out of the way. "And I do like working with that segment. It was more fun when we had the resources to bring in big groups and do the escorted tours. I'm afraid that era's over, though."

Carmen nodded her understanding. "The margins are just too small." Obviously, she knew the industry inside and out, even though she had never worked at an agency.

"That's true, but if you use special events like escorted tours or charters to cultivate a clientele, you have the chance to win their business for everything else."

Sofia set her fork down and picked up her purse. "That's how we operate at Zeigler-Marsh, Judith." She plucked out a business card and laid it on the table between them. "Good. We're talking business. Now I can write this off. So when you're ready to move on, why don't you give me a call?"

"Wow, thanks." Carmen had hinted there might be a possibility, but Judith hadn't wanted to get her hopes up, especially after realizing this really was just a dinner among friends. "Here, have another shrimp."

Everyone at the table laughed.

"She always says it tastes better if she steals it."

"You speak so badly of me, Carmen."

"Just the truth."

Over more gossip and good-natured ribbing, the women finished their dinner. Judith then traded places with Sofia when Carmen offered to share tiramisu for dessert. She loved watching these friends tease each other with such open affection. All four of them were relaxed and unguarded, and she felt totally at ease in their company. It had turned into a fantastic evening, one she knew she would never forget.

"Right here is fine," Judith told the taxi driver, who stopped suddenly in the middle of Fifteenth Street.

"Which one is it?" Carmen asked, curious to see what sort of place Judith called home. The buildings here weren't as tall as those in midtown, and the street-level shops around the corner gave it more of a neighborhood feel.

Judith pointed up. "I live there, in that middle brownstone. Fifth floor."

"Elevator?" Sofia asked.

"You're kidding, right?"

"I love it. You're so close to the Village, it's practically bohemian."

"Among other things," Judith agreed, gripping the door handle. "I really appreciate you asking me along. It was wonderful. And thanks for dinner, Sofia."

"It was the least I could do after eating everyone's food." Sofia held out her hand and tugged Judith toward her for a peck on the cheek. "Take care, dear."

Carmen followed suit, leaning across Sofia to trade kisses. "I'm really glad you could join us. Be sure to come to Sofia's session tomorrow morning. And bring old fruit."

"I would never do something like that," Judith told Sofia seriously.

"I know. You're far too nice to associate with scum like Carmen."

"I think that surly exterior of hers is all for show."

"No, it isn't," Sofia answered.

The three yelled "goodnight" several times and Judith disappeared through a glass door into a dimly-lit stairwell. As the taxi continued toward the Grand, Sofia scooted over to sit beside the other window.

"Since when do you like tiramisu?"

Carmen had known she would get the third degree from her old friend as soon as they were alone. "I told you she was nice. Was I right?"

"She's very nice. And I have to admit, after sitting close to her, she doesn't look as much like Brooke as I thought at first."

"No, she doesn't. Her hair's a lot darker and she has hazel eyes. Brooke's are bright blue."

"And she doesn't have any of Brooke's mannerisms. You know how Brooke always talks with her hands."

"That's from hanging around with a bunch of Italians for thirty years."

"How come we've never seen Judith at one of these conventions before? Surely one of us would have noticed her."

"She told Cathy she'd only been to one, the one in Boston."

"Wasn't that the year you all skipped because of your niece?"

Carmen nodded solemnly. "Susanna. Hard to believe that's been three years."

Sofia patted her hand as her mind wandered back to that devastating time when leukemia had claimed her brother's youngest child.

"So what happens next with Judith?"

"I don't know." Carmen exhaled loudly. Now that she knew her better, Carmen wanted to ask her out, but having her sanity called into question by her friends was something she didn't need. "I thought I might ask her to go get a drink or something tomorrow night after the reception."

They were almost at the hotel, which would get her out of this conversation for now, since Sofia was headed to her apartment on the Upper East Side.

"You know, Carmen, there's nothing any of us would like better than to see you move on from Brooke Healey." The cab came to a stop in front of the hotel and a valet opened Carmen's door. "I'm just worried you're not really doing that with Judith."

"I'm not doing anything with Judith right now." She looked up at the cab driver, who was slumped against the console. Conversations this inane probably bored him out of his mind. "But if I do, it isn't going to be a big deal. That's not what happens at conventions."

Chapter 7

Art Conover was making the most of his opportunity for Carmen's ear. He had prepared a short list of talking points, all designed to secure a stronger foothold in the business. " . . . and given all the services we both provide for this industry, don't you think there ought to be something we could work on together? It would be good for both of us to present an image of cooperation."

Carmen didn't see it that way. She already had the lion's share of clients, along with twenty years of experience and the respect of industry professionals. TDG had nothing to gain from teaming up with Conover Data Source on a project. It would only lend Art credibility.

"I don't know, Art. We don't really provide the same kinds of services."

"Sure we do. Both of us inform the agencies on how best to

market themselves and reach new customers."

"Right, but our products are so different. You merge market-level media usage data with credit card expenditures. We interview four thousand people a month. Your focus is on where agencies ought to advertise. Ours is advertising, destinations, promotions, packaging and up-selling. And we're trending everything." Carmen knew exactly what kind of data her clients needed because she asked them again and again.

"We both know your operation's bigger—"

"It isn't just bigger, Art. It's richer. I put out sixteen reports a year for each client. And I've got five people on my staff whose only job is to help them put all that data to work."

"And it works quite well. You wouldn't believe how hard it is for me to convince your clients to drop you and come with me." Art chuckled and made a big display of pushing aside his breakfast plate so he could fold his hands on the table. It was meant to demonstrate his humility, but Carmen wasn't buying it. "That's why I think we should work together instead of against each other."

Carmen couldn't believe her ears. He wanted her help and had nothing to offer in return. "I'm just not seeing this, Art."

"Look, it's simple. You know about our real estate division, right?"

"Real estate?"

"That's growing into a bigger pie for us than any other segment, but it dovetails nicely with travel. You and I have been watching this industry shrink for fifteen years because of the Internet, and now the baby boomers are pouring their travel dollars into second homes."

"If real estate is where you want to go, you don't need me."

"But if you bring what you've done at TDG to our real estate division, we can triple our revenue and yours. That's a lot of money on the table for both of us."

If Carmen wanted to grow her business, she had plenty of

opportunities for branching out. TDG Syndicated was the sort of turnkey operation that could easily be adapted to any industry. But she wasn't interested in other industries. "You know exactly what we do at TDG, Art. You've had a good enough look at our methodology and reports to replicate them for your real estate clients if you want to."

He started to object but Carmen cut him off.

"Neither of us would be doing our jobs if we didn't check out the competition. I've seen what you provide your clients, and I'm sure you've seen what we give ours."

Art refused to take no for an answer. "It would take CDS two or three years to get to where you are now. You could help us make the conversion in a matter of months."

"Except I don't care about real estate."

"This is an incredible opportunity," he pleaded, unwilling to accept that she could just turn her back on promises of riches. "Do you have any idea where we could go with this? The sky is the limit."

Carmen grabbed the check from the waiter and charged it to her room. "Shoot for the sky then, Art. But you're going to have to do all the work up front to get there. That's what we did, and we're right where we want to be."

Art sighed in frustration. "You know I'm not going to just give up that easily, don't you?"

"You'd save yourself a lot of time if you did."

"Promise me you'll think about it," he called as she walked away.

"I just did."

From her seat on the back row, Judith had a view of the entire room. Sofia was on stage taking part in a panel discussion on customer satisfaction. Carmen was nowhere to be seen, despite her playful threat last night to heckle her friend at the session this morning.

Judith was still floating from her night out with Carmen and her friends. Unable to sleep when she had gotten home, she had surfed the Internet to learn more about Zeigler-Marsh, possibly her next employer. Their Careers page was loaded with information on jobs and benefits, but nothing about salary or commissions. It didn't matter, though. They couldn't pay less than what she made at Rainbow Getaways.

Her ruminations about a new job at Zeigler-Marsh were all that was keeping her feet on the ground this morning. When she wasn't forcing herself to focus on that, her mind filled with giddy thoughts of Carmen. She could still feel that simple kiss on the cheek they had shared last night when she left the cab. The sweet, subtle perfume had surprised her, but she would never forget it.

All night, she had pored over the conversation at dinner, searching for hints about Carmen's personal life. There was nothing to suggest she was involved with someone, nor any indication she was straight. None of that was iron-clad proof of anything, but it left all the doors open for Judith to imagine what she wanted.

Ten minutes into the panel, the door opened quietly and Carmen and Priscilla tiptoed up the aisle to sit a few rows in front of Judith. When Carmen turned to whisper to the man behind her, Judith caught her eye. Both smiled immediately, and Carmen signaled for Judith to meet her outside later.

The session might as well have ended then as far as Judith was concerned. She barely heard another word that was said, so intent she was on guessing what Carmen wanted to see her about. This was the last day of the convention. If they were going to keep in touch after this weekend, one of them had to make an overture soon. What would it hurt for her to tell Carmen she hoped they could get together next time she was in town?

When the speakers finished, Judith waited nervously by the complimentary coffee stand in the hallway as the room emptied.

Through the open door, she could see Carmen, still inside and talking to practically everyone in the crowd. At last she exited, breaking away to head in her direction.

"Thanks for waiting. I wanted to ask a favor."

"Whatever you need."

"If you have other plans, I understand, but—"

"If I have other plans, I'll cancel them."

Carmen responded with an enormous grin. "In that case"—she handed Judith an envelope—"here's an invitation to a reception we're hosting tonight at Tavern on the Green. I'd love it if you could come."

"Of course I'll come. But what's the favor?"

"I have some new clients from Japan and this is their first trip to New York. If you could talk to them about the city and give them ideas for things to do while they're here . . . I don't want them just standing around feeling out of place because they don't know anyone."

Judith was touched by Carmen's thoughtfulness. "I'll be sure to make them feel welcome."

"Thank you. I'll have somebody find you after the business meeting."

"Can I go like this?" She gestured at her pantsuit, a dark gray pinstripe with a peach-colored silk shirt. A dress might be better, but she would have to cut out of the conference and buy one this afternoon.

Carmen smiled and eyed her head to toe. "I think you look great."

Her mouth agape, Judith simply stared as Carmen walked away.

Carmen surveyed the room with pride, satisfied her guests were enjoying themselves. Tavern on the Green had laid out a lavish spread of hors d'oeuvres and desserts, one that said TDG valued its loyal customers. The money she spent on this reception each year—over fifty thousand dollars—was insurance that her clients would renew their contracts with TDG. No one wanted to miss out on this tradition, which, in only six years, had become one of the most prestigious social events of the convention. Attendance was by invitation only, and reserved for her full-service customers.

One good thing about hosting an exclusive party was Carmen didn't have to worry about wining and dining her competition while they lured her customers away. But the specter of Art Conover was here tonight in the form of Bob Durbin, who was headed toward her right now.

"Carmen, good to see you."

"How are you, Bob? Sorry I didn't have time to talk earlier. Lenore said she had a nice lunch with you today."

"We did have a nice lunch. I like Lenore, but she's kind of hard-headed."

"What do you mean?" She flinched inwardly as Durbin put his arm around her shoulder.

"Just that you and I probably could have come to a deal of some sort, but . . . well, I guess she probably doesn't have the authority to make deals for TDG like you do."

"She's my vice president, Bob. She speaks for the company." Carmen stepped to the side to grab a glass of wine from a passing waiter, freeing herself from Durbin's faux embrace. "We debriefed on it this afternoon, and I'm with her a hundred percent."

"Then I hate to be the one to tell you, but you're going to see your business go down the tubes here in the next couple of years, three at the most. I was proposing a way you could save it and help all the agencies at the same time."

"I know where you're going with this. We're not interested in scaling back our study."

"Then unbundle it. Let people buy just the monthly reports

without all the seminars and consultation and charge a lower price. That way, you're going head to head with Conover with a better product."

"I'm not competing with Conover Data Source, Bob. We don't provide the same service."

"No, but I know he's skimming off some of the agencies that are cutting back on their budgets. He's even offering to drop his price for first-year customers so he can dip into your business. But every single agency I've talked to would rather work with you. All you have to do is downscale your product and offer it at a lower price. Anyone who wants to get the premium package with all the extras can pay more, but the point is that Conover won't survive if you undercut him. You'll own the whole market."

Durbin was right that a less expensive product from TDG would wipe out the threat of CDS once and for all. Unfortunately, it would also take an enormous bite out of TDG's bottom line because half of their customers would drop the premium service if they could get the monthly reports without it. But if they didn't have the expertise to apply the findings, they might soon find the information unwieldy and drop the service altogether. "That's not the kind of market I want. The Delallo Group didn't get its reputation by doing things halfway. The bottom line is that our service gets results."

"I think you're making a big mistake, Carmen. You're taking our business for granted, and I'm not speaking just for myself. There are plenty of us who feel this way."

Outwardly, she maintained her cool, but she bristled inside at Durbin's patronizing attitude. She would rather do business with someone like Bill Hinkle, who at least was honest about his flaws, than a conniving sleazebag like Durbin. She had half a mind to get word to Conover that Durbin was selling him out to pressure a better deal at TDG. "Let's do this, Bob. I'll let you out of the balance of your contract effective today and you go ahead and make the switch to Conover. If"—she held up her hand to stop him from interrupting—"if you come back within three years, I'll waive your setup fee. If not, then I'll assume you're getting your money's worth from CDS."

That wasn't what Durbin wanted and she knew it. But he had backed himself into a corner with his big talk, enabling her to wash her hands of him once and for all. Some customers weren't worth keeping.

"Excuse me, Carmen." Cathy came up from behind and tapped her on the shoulder. "You wanted me to let you know when Judith arrived. She and Sofia just walked in."

"Thank you, Cathy. Sofia's so lucky Judith O'Shea decided to go with Zeigler-Marsh. I bet she brings them a million dollars in new business next year." Carmen threw that in as a parting shot at Durbin. "Excuse me, Bob."

Judith had never been to a party like this in her life. The tables were piled high with delicacies like fresh seafood, pâté and imported cheese. A carving station offered rare roast beef and turkey breast, and waiters worked the crowd with trays of wine and champagne. Practically everyone in attendance was a decision-maker in their agency—everyone except Judith.

But tonight, she had a purpose, and without delay, she went straight for the small group of Japanese visitors and introduced herself. Just as Carmen had predicted, they had many questions about museums, shows and galleries throughout the city, and she spent more than two hours offering tips on getting around. From time to time, she shifted her position so she could watch Carmen interact with the crowd. Everyone seemed to want her ear, and she obliged.

The Japanese guests finally took their leave, and Judith grabbed a glass of white wine from a passing waiter. Carmen suddenly materialized in front of her. She was gorgeous tonight, wearing a tailored, olive green pantsuit with a mother-of-pearl necklace and earrings. In Judith's eye, she was easily the most attractive woman in the room.

"Are you having a good time?" Carmen asked.

"I'm having a wonderful time. Thank you so much."

"No, thank you. I really appreciate your entertaining my clients. They said they enjoyed talking with you and that's good for TDG."

"Oh, it was no problem at—" Before she could finish her sentence, a man she recognized as the CEO of a time-share company walked up to Carmen and put his arm around her waist. More people, including Lenore Yates, joined the group, and soon Judith found herself outside the circle. It was awkward, but she didn't feel at home in high-powered company like that anyway. She turned toward the buffet table and filled a small plate with snacks, then found a table in the corner.

Cathy joined her within moments and kicked off her shoes under the table. "My feet are killing me."

"When are we ever going to learn to wear sensible shoes?" Judith joked.

"Never." They looked over at Carmen and the time-share people. "That's Bill Hinkle. Every time Carmen has to go to his office in Philly, we have to practically shove her out the door."

Judith was surprised by the remark, since, from where she was sitting, Carmen seemed to be having a wonderful time. "It looks to me like she's enjoying herself."

"It's business. She knows how to make people feel good. Besides, she's one of the nicest people you'll ever meet."

"That I can believe. All of you have been so nice to include me in your plans. It's made this whole weekend something I'll remember for a long time."

Cathy looked at her seriously for an instant, then smiled as if she had wanted to say something but stopped herself. "I guess I should go run interference for Carmen and see if I can move those folks along."

Judith watched as Cathy filled a plate with hors d'oeuvres. She then entered the circle and handed the food to Carmen, directing her to another cluster of customers standing near the bar. Cathy always seemed to know exactly what Carmen needed and when, and that went well beyond the typical duties of an administrative assistant. Clearly, she was very devoted to her boss and friend.

Another half hour passed and the crowd began to thin. Carmen broke free from a discussion and made her way to where Judith was sitting. Without a word, she stretched across the table and snatched Judith's wineglass. In two gulps, she drained it. Then she shook herself from head to toe and blew out a frazzled breath. "Thanks. I needed that."

Judith laughed, delighted to get a glimpse of Carmen's playfulness. "You look like you could use a whole bottle."

"I'll manage. It's almost over." She looked at her watch. "They're kicking us out of here in a half hour. If you're up for it, I could use a walk to unwind."

"I'd love it."

Carmen grinned and saluted before returning to her clients.

Judith's stomach fluttered as she watched her walk away. Whatever might be brewing between them would reveal itself soon.

Judith closed the snaps on her down parka as Carmen tied the sash of her raincoat. "Are you sure you're going to be warm enough to walk in that?"

"It has a flannel lining." Carmen opened the coat to show her. "I zipped it in this afternoon."

They stepped out into the crisp night air, immediately tightening their scarves and burrowing their gloved hands into their pockets. Their pace was moderate, as fast as either could walk comfortably in dress shoes.

"It was a great party, Carmen."

"Yeah, it looked like everyone had a good time. I'm just glad to have it over with for another year."

"You do this every year?"

"We try to. We missed Boston because my niece died that year and I didn't go."

"I'm so sorry."

"Thank you." Despite the heavy emotion that sort of topic always brought to bear, the lull that followed wasn't the least bit awkward. "Did you ever lose someone close to you?"

"My dad was killed in a construction accident when I was eleven. I don't remember much about it, but I know I cried a lot back then."

Carmen nodded as though she understood. "Do you have other family?"

"My mom's still living. And I have a brother. He's two years older."

"Which makes him . . . ?"

"Forty-six." Judith laughed softly to herself at Carmen's not-so-subtle way of learning her age. "They both live over in Brooklyn."

"It's nice having family close."

"Yeah."

As they turned from the walkway onto Central Park West, Judith could feel the sparks between them. Since her own cards were already on the table—she had told everyone at dinner last night she was a lesbian—it was up to Carmen to take the next step if she was interested.

"I suppose I should have asked you already if you were seeing anybody," Carmen said quietly, looking out into the night.

"I'm not."

"Good." Carmen chuckled. "That saved us both from an embarrassing moment or two."

"All you had to do was ask."

"I've been flirting with you for three days." Carmen reached over and took her hand. "Didn't you notice?"

Even through their gloves, Judith could feel a warm connection. They slowed to a stroll. "I noticed that . . . well, you've been very nice to me. But if that's your idea of flirting, I prefer the sledgehammer approach."

"I have a mortal fear of being shot down," Carmen said, her teeth chattering against the cold.

It was impossible to tell if she was being serious or not, but the idea of Carmen Delallo being shot down by anyone was incomprehensible. "I find it hard to believe that happens to you very often."

"Happens all the time. It's . . . what can I say? It's just devastating." She managed to keep a straight face for all of three seconds.

"You're a terrible liar."

Carmen nodded toward a bench on the sidewalk ahead. "Want to sit for a few minutes?"

"It's pretty cold."

"What if I promise to keep you warm?"

"That sounds like an offer I can't refuse."

She took a seat on the cold bench and Carmen squeezed close, wrapping both arms around her shoulders. "People who live in Chicago have to learn to snuggle."

"I bet you're pretty good at that."

"I am." Carmen rested her forehead against Judith's temple. "I should tell you that this isn't something I usually do."

Judith nestled her cheek against Carmen's cold nose. "What is?"

"I don't usually hook up with women at conventions . . . and I never fool around with clients."

"Then I'm glad I'm not a client anymore."

"So am I."

Carmen tilted her head forward and tipped Judith's chin toward her.

When they came together, Judith forgot all about being cold. The only sensation she knew was the silky touch of lips to hers. Carmen's tongue lightly raked her teeth, seeking more with each stroke. In all her life, Judith had never been kissed like this, not by someone who seemed determined to bring pleasure to her mouth with warmth and softness. She parted her lips, gently sucking Carmen's tongue inside.

Approaching voices shattered the moment and they pulled apart. When the people passed, Carmen kissed her temple gently. "Will you come back to my room?"

Judith never considered saying anything but yes.

Moments later, they were in a taxi speeding toward the hotel. As they pulled into the valet circle, Carmen tossed a twenty into the front seat and told the cabbie to keep the change. Together, they rushed inside and strode quickly toward the elevators, oblivious to the people who milled about. They grabbed the first elevator and Carmen pushed the button before anyone else could board. The instant the door closed, she pinned Judith to the wall with a crushing kiss. "I want you everywhere," she murmured. Her hands snaked inside Judith's parka to massage her breasts.

Judith gave herself up completely to the hungry assault. If Carmen's lovemaking was as fierce as her foreplay, she was about to go somewhere she had never been. She clung to Carmen's arm as they exited the elevator and hurried to the room. Carmen swiped her key card and the door opened into a suite, where cardboard boxes lined the entry.

"Hi, Carmen."

They froze in the entryway. "Raul."

Judith instantly recognized the programmer from his bio on the Web site. It was obvious Carmen had not expected him to be here.

"I was just packing up the last of the terminals. A bellman's going to pick them up tomorrow morning."

Carmen nodded numbly.

"Hi, Brooke," he said, smiling in Judith's direction.

She whirled around, thinking someone must be behind her. When there wasn't, the truth was slow to grip her.

"Raul, this is Judith . . . Judith O'Shea . . . from here in New York." Carmen's voice was shaking slightly, and Raul looked as if he had swallowed his foot. "Judith, this is Raul Sanchez. He works for me."

"Pleased to meet you, Raul," she said stiffly, shaking his hand.

"Same here. Sorry about the mistake. I didn't have my glasses on. I always wear glasses."

"No problem." The unfolding scene was almost too bizarre to comprehend, but Judith thought she had the whole, humiliating picture now. "I'm going to get out of here and let you two finish your work."

"No!" Carmen said, her eyes pleading. "Raul was just leaving, weren't you?"

"Yes . . . yes, absolutely. Out of here." He dashed by her and out the door, leaving behind the most awkward scene imaginable.

"I can explain."

"I doubt it." Whatever had sparked between them had nothing to do with her. She should have known someone like Carmen Delallo wouldn't simply choose her out of a crowd.

Carmen took her elbow and nudged her toward the sofa. "Please sit down. This isn't what you think."

Judith felt the urge to just turn and leave it all unanswered, but a small part of her held out hope that Carmen really could explain it away. So she sat.

"Yes, you look like Brooke. But other than that you're nothing like her."

"But why would you—?" Judith didn't like the only answer

that made sense. "Are you in love with her?"

Carmen sighed. "It's complicated."

"It's a yes-no question. How hard can it be?"

"There's never been anything between us. She's married . . . and very straight. You know how that is."

"In other words, you couldn't have her, so you wanted me." She started to get up, but Carmen stopped her.

"It isn't like that. Please don't make this out to be worse than it is."

"You all must have had a spectacular laugh last night after dinner."

"No, we didn't." Carmen grabbed both her hands and squeezed them. "I promise you, no one laughed at you. Sofia did ask me in the taxi if I might be insane—which under the circumstances was probably a fair question."

As uncomfortable as things were, Judith appreciated Carmen's efforts to lighten things up. Carmen wasn't some evil, manipulative person, but no amount of charm would fix this mess. "This is too weird for me. I'm sorry."

"Me too . . . sorry, that is. Not weird . . . well, maybe I am a little." She slumped against the back of the couch and sighed heavily. "I bet you're too principled to just go have mind-blowing sex anyway."

Judith couldn't help but chuckle. "I'm afraid my libido left town about five minutes ago. Besides, I have this thing about wanting to hear my own name called out in the throes of passion."

"That's kind of old-fashioned, don't you think?" Carmen got up and walked over to the mini-bar. "I usually have a drink or five when I feel like shit. Would you like one?"

"No, thanks."

Carmen turned back and looked at her with genuine regret. "I'm sorry, Judith."

"So am I."

"Just out of curiosity"—Carmen emptied a mini-bottle of scotch into a glass—"was there any way I could have handled this better, or were we doomed from the start just because you happen to look like Brooke?"

"Would you have given me your raincoat if I hadn't looked like Brooke?"

"Probably not."

Judith wanted to ask if they could just back up and start over. But this wasn't about them getting to know each other and forging a relationship. It was an affair at a convention between two virtual strangers. The only thing left to do now was get out with her dignity intact. "I had a good time this weekend, thanks to you. Obviously, things didn't turn out the way either of us would have liked, but I'm still glad I met you."

"I hope you mean that."

"I do." Judith closed the distance between them and kissed her lightly on the cheek. "Take care of yourself. I mean that too."

Chapter 8

" . . . added two more intercept sites so that's going to make the Asia contingent happy. Richard thinks we could pick up China within eighteen months if the contacts are there," Lenore said.

Standing behind her desk, Carmen peered through smudged reading glasses at her notes, the ones she had scribbled on the plane last Monday in an attempt to focus on anything but the debacle on Sunday night. They had put this meeting off for two days so Cathy could return to Chicago by train. "Whose idea was it to add sites?" There was a belligerence in her voice that she was powerless to stop.

Lenore shuffled her papers. "I, uh . . ."

"It was yours, Carmen," Cathy said evenly. "I have it in my notes from the meeting on the third."

"I don't remember anything about it."

"Yes, you do. And you thought it was brilliant at the time. You said you had been looking for a client to pay for picking up Portland and San Jose. Both have flights to Narita, so you suggested adding it to the Asia budget."

Carmen sighed and dropped the folder on her desk. Yes, it had been her idea. And no, she didn't feel like having this meeting. She didn't feel like being in this office at all.

"So . . . should we go ahead with setting this up?"

Lenore was saying something.

"Carmen?"

"Yes, yes. Go ahead." She waved her hand as if shooing a fly. "It's yours. I want you to take over all of Syndicated from this minute on, okay? I'll handle the custom side, but I can't deal with both anymore. That's why you were promoted." She glanced up to see Cathy tip her head toward the door, urging Lenore to leave.

Lenore closed the door on her way out and Cathy set her folder on the coffee table.

Carmen knew what was coming next and she didn't want to hear it. "I don't want a lecture."

"Okay, fine. Can we just talk one friend to another?"

Carmen came around the desk and dropped onto the sofa in the spot Lenore had just vacated. Leaning forward, she massaged her temples. "Do we have any aspirin?"

Cathy ran her hand gently along Carmen's shoulders. "I'm sure I can find you some. Do you have a headache?"

Carmen nodded.

"Do you want to lie down?"

"No. Not here, anyway. I wouldn't mind lying down in front of a bus."

"Maybe you should spend a couple of days at home relaxing. I don't think anybody here would begrudge you a little time off."

Carmen leaned back against the sofa and closed her eyes. Going home wouldn't do her any good. She couldn't outrun what was eating her. "What the fuck was I thinking, Cathy?"

"Does this have anything to do with what Raul told me this morning?"

"Shit. It's all over the office, isn't it?"

"No, as far as I know, it's just you, me and Raul. He said he's been avoiding you since he got back because he thought he was in trouble."

"He's not."

"I know. I told him that."

"So what was I thinking? Was that just the stupidest thing I've ever done in my life, or what?"

Cathy chuckled. "Nah, you've done way stupider things than that. Besides, I didn't think it was stupid for you to have a good time with somebody you liked. I was glad to see it for a change. You haven't even had a date since when?"

"Robin, two years ago."

Cathy nodded. "I never cared for her. But I have to admit, she had you looking buff."

"She worked my ass off. Thank God she dumped me."

"That'll teach you to hook up with a personal trainer. Next time, go for a massage therapist or a gourmet chef."

Carmen didn't want to think about next time. What she was feeling right now was worse than getting dumped, because this was all her fault for being an idiot. "I'm such an asshole."

"Why? You didn't try to pretend Judith was Brooke, did you?"

"Of course not."

"Then what was it you did that was so wrong?"

"I embarrassed her and I hurt her feelings."

"So what bothers you more, the fact that you're an asshole or that Judith had her feelings hurt?"

"She didn't deserve it." She leaned forward and clutched her temples again as the blood pounded in her head.

"I'll be right back."

Alone for what seemed like the first time all day, Carmen sat and stared out the window across the city. Work was her solace, the one place she always reaped rewards for her efforts. But this time, TDG gave her no refuge from her sense of shame, or the compulsion she felt to talk to Judith again and try to make things right.

"Here you go." Cathy returned with two aspirin and a small glass of water. "Do you want me to shoot off an e-mail to Judith? I could just say it was nice to meet her and that I hope we'll run into her again. Maybe that would—"

"She'd see right through it."

Cathy sighed. "Too bad, because it really is true. I thought she was nice." She handed Carmen a pink note. "I suppose this would be a bad time to tell you Brooke called. She wants you to meet her for dinner tonight."

"I can't very well do that if I'm in bed with the covers over my head."

"There's an interesting idea—telling Brooke Healey no."

"Don't start, Cathy." The last time they had a discussion like this it ended with Cathy telling her she always listened least when she needed advice most. Not that she ever took anyone's advice when it came to Brooke. No one else knew Brooke or cared for her the way she did.

"Then how about this one?" She handed Carmen a second message. "Sofia wants you back in New York next Friday to sit in on a planning meeting at Zeigler-Marsh."

Judith squeezed aboard the F-Train for the short trip to Brooklyn and staked out her square foot of space in the aisle. Transfer passengers were already jockeying for position for the next stop at Broadway and Lafayette. Many of those now standing would find a place to sit, but Judith always stood when she made this trip during the week, yielding the few seats to commuters who worked on their feet all day.

She was lucky to have her brother only a few stops away across the river. It had taken nine years to secure Victor's placement at the Wyckoff Center for Independent Living, a therapeutic group home for mentally retarded adults. Just a two-block walk from the Bergen Street station, she could get there from work in less than thirty minutes. She was proud of her brother's progress since coming to Wyckoff two years ago. He now held a part-time job cooking fries during the lunch shift at a fast-food restaurant. That was an extraordinary accomplishment for a man doctors said might not live to see his tenth birthday.

She was looking forward to seeing him after missing their usual Sunday jaunt to their mother's house in Greenpoint. Victor sometimes had difficulty adapting to variations in his routine, and a Wednesday visit like this one could be disruptive if it happened to fall on one of his "agitated" days. But she had called the shift supervisor this afternoon to confirm he'd had a good day so far, and they promised to have him ready to go out with her for a walk.

The weekend couldn't come soon enough for Judith. She needed some downtime to get her head back together. Her return to work after the convention had been difficult, and not just because of the incident with Carmen. That was enough to ruin her whole week, but it wasn't her only letdown. All three of the positions she had found on the job board were filled over the weekend, probably through personal contacts at the convention. Her best prospect, Zeigler-Marsh, was now out of the question, thanks to Sofia's part in Carmen's charade. That left her stuck at Rainbow, which felt like a sinking ship now that Celia had won the job at the network.

She had tried not to dwell on the fiasco with Carmen, pushing it out of her mind as quickly as it would enter. The whole episode had gotten deeply under her skin. When she woke up on Monday morning, she had a whole new perspective, and her head was full of things she wished she had said. She had even toyed with the idea of sending an e-mail to get it off her chest.

But Carmen probably hadn't given her another thought since returning to Chicago, so nothing she had left unsaid really mattered now. A part of her wished they had just gone ahead and screwed their brains out and let that be all there was to it.

Lost in her rumination, Judith almost missed her stop. At the last moment, she darted off the train and climbed the stairs. The group home was inconspicuously situated two blocks south among a row of apartments.

Knowing the tile floor inside would be spotless, she wiped her feet on the bristled mat at the front door and rang the bell. A crackly voice answered and she leaned into the box to announce herself. "Judith O'Shea. I'm here to see Victor."

When the lock clicked, she opened the door and entered. The reception counter was vacant, but there was plenty of activity in the common area. To her left was a large day room, where several staff members and residents watched a game show on television. The staffers seemed to be in a heated competition to see who could guess the puzzle first. There was no sign of Victor, but he didn't care much for television, preferring instead to sit in his room at night and color.

A thirty-ish man emerged from the office with an armload of papers. "Hi, Judith."

"Hi, Russ. How's it going?"

"Not too bad. We just finished dinner." He dropped the papers in a plastic recycle bin and handed her a clipboard. "You and Victor going out?"

"Yeah, maybe just down to the arcade." She spun the clipboard around and filled in the required information. "Is he doing all right?"

"Yeah, he got a small burn on his arm today from the grease at the restaurant, but we put some salve on it."

A black woman joined her at the counter. "Have you come to

get my boyfriend?"

Judith grinned at the woman's brashness. She appreciated the way Stacey fussed over her brother. "Yes, but I'll bring him back before he misses you too much." She followed Stacey down the hall to the room Victor shared with two other men. He was sitting at a small desk meticulously coloring in a book.

"Victor, look who's here."

More than any sight in the world, Judith loved her brother's smile, especially the first one when she hadn't seen him in a few days. "Hi, Vic. I missed you."

Victor blushed and looked back at his coloring book, still grinning.

"Want to go for a walk with me?"

He looked to Stacey for an answer.

"You can go, Victor."

Still smiling, he began the arduous process of returning his crayons to the box. He was particular about getting each one into a certain slot.

"You can do that when you get back, honey. I'll save it for you. Go get your coat from the closet."

The preparations took almost ten minutes, but finally they walked out the front door. Their gait was slow because Victor's left foot was turned inward. Judith hooked her arm through his to hold him close. He usually liked the physical contact of hugs and pats, though he had no understanding of how to reciprocate.

"I missed you this week, Victor. Did you miss me?"

Another bashful smile was her answer. Judith liked to imagine that he understood her words, even though he had never spoken. He was generally mild-mannered, but capable of physical rage if he stayed agitated for more than a few hours. Of all the people close to Victor, Judith was best at keeping him on an even keel.

"I went to a convention last weekend for work. That's why I didn't come on Sunday." If her absence had mattered to her brother, she couldn't tell.

"I met some very nice people. One of them sort of played a trick on me that wasn't very nice, though." Victor seemed to like to hear her talk, and since he never judged her or offered advice, he made a great sounding board. "I guess it wasn't really a trick. She was nice to me and acted like she wanted to be my friend, but I'm not sure it was me that she liked. I think she only liked me because I looked like somebody who was already her friend."

They stopped at the corner of State Street, where Judith instructed her brother to wait at the crosswalk. "Now watch for the white stickman to blink." She hung back and allowed him to respond, which he did when the signal flashed. Then she praised him profusely as they crossed the street, prompting a proud grin.

Gamers Arcade was jumping with its usual crowd of adolescent boys, a few of whom snickered as they walked in. Judith shot them a stern look before walking Victor to the back where an alcove housed two auto racing games side by side. "Which one do you want?" Having him choose from two options and demonstrate his choice by sitting down at the controls was a complex task, the sort of thing she worked on every time they were together. Victor had come a long way from responding to simple one-step commands in order to receive a piece of a cookie. He now performed many of his hygiene and room care tasks on his own, and he no longer required primary reinforcement.

He slowly climbed into the seat on the left and she took the other one. Both grasped their steering wheels and pretended to drive. Victor was mesmerized by the video screens, which showed rapid lane changes, obstacles and a blurred landscape.

"That woman I told you about, she was really pretty." That word always made Victor blush. "She had big brown eyes, even darker than yours. I bet you would have thought she was pretty too."

She dropped three quarters into his machine, knowing he would wreck his race car in no time flat. But he liked the sounds of the rumbling engine, the screeching tires and the horrific crashes.

"Her name was Carmen and she was a big shot at the convention I went to. Everybody there wanted to talk with her. I felt lucky because she wanted to be with me."

When his last vehicle slammed into the wall, he fingered the coin slots, clearly hoping she would add more money so he could play again. Instead, she handed him the quarters one at a time and guided him through the process of inserting them.

"We talked about things, like back when Daddy died. And I told her you were my big brother and you lived in Brooklyn."

He finished the game and touched the coin slot again.

"I don't have any more quarters. But I brought you something else you like." She held out a candy bar and smiled as his face lit up. "We have to walk back to your house. Are you ready to go?"

He followed her outside, and she gave him the candy after they had crossed the street so he could enjoy it without distractions.

"I wish I could tell her just one more thing but I probably won't ever see her again." When he finished the candy, she hooked her arm in his again. "Anyway, thanks for listening. I'm lucky to have a big brother like you to talk to."

Carmen shed her coat and slid into the booth at La Cantina across from Brooke. "Sorry I'm late. I had to run home and take the princess out."

Brooke shook her head and laughed. "No one buys your shtick about not loving that dog. You spoil her like a child."

"I do not. If I hadn't gone home she would have found the thing I love most and chewed it up."

"I told you to get a child gate and close her off in the kitchen."

"I did. She gnawed on the bottom of my cherry cabinets. Cost me six hundred dollars to get them refinished."

"She doesn't do things like that when Healey's there."

"That's because she's saving up to punish me when I get home."

The waiter appeared to fill her wineglass from the bottle Brooke had already selected. Carmen didn't bother with the menu, ordering a chicken Caesar salad.

"Cathy isn't here, you know. I won't tell her if you order a steak."

"I had a big lunch." That wasn't true. Carmen hadn't had much of an appetite since coming back from New York.

"I'm so glad to get out of the house. Geoffrey's driving me crazy."

Lately, it seemed the only times they talked were so Brooke could dump about Geoffrey. Carmen liked being the friend Brooke turned to when she needed to vent, but she enjoyed it more when they got together just for fun. "Everybody needs a break once in a while."

"I'm starting to need them more than just once in a while. If I could, I'd go out every night."

That didn't sound good, but it was old news. Brooke and Geoffrey practically lived on the rocks. Carmen would listen to the rants, but she drew the line at giving advice, because her advice would be to leave him. She couldn't say something like that without worrying she was doing it for selfish reasons.

"He comes to dinner every night and hardly says a word to anyone. Then he has the nerve to whine about . . ."

Brooke's hair looked blonder than usual, as if she recently had it colored. Carmen might not have noticed except it was so much lighter than Judith's, which had a soft reddish tint. Judith's hair was also shinier, and Carmen would bet the color was natural.

" . . . at least I think so. It's not my job to keep him entertained."

Carmen nodded, realizing she hadn't heard a word Brooke had said. "What did he say about you taking the job?"

"I haven't even told him. I think I'll just wait and see how long it takes him to notice I'm gone all day."

The waiter delivered their dinner, and Carmen was surprised to discover she was hungry. As he set Brooke's dish in front of her, he accidentally tipped over her near-empty wineglass, spilling a small amount on the tablecloth.

"I'm so sorry, madam." He covered the spill with a napkin and soaked it up. "I'll bring another glass."

Carmen smiled and thanked him, but Brooke never even acknowledged his presence. It wasn't exactly rude, just dismissive, and it brought to mind how Judith had handled her mishap at lunch. There probably weren't many people who would have been as nice about that as she was.

" . . . and Geoffrey only has two reactions to everything. Either he doesn't care, or the way someone else is doing it is wrong. So it doesn't matter what I do."

Carmen considered telling Brooke about her weekend, including the whole sordid tale of Judith, but she feared where that conversation might lead. If it turned serious, she might find herself having to explain to Brooke why she found herself sexually drawn to her near-twin. And if it turned frivolous, they would end up laughing about it, and she didn't want to laugh at Judith's expense.

A lot of their conversations were like this one tonight—one-sided, with Carmen listening as Brooke bared her soul. It wasn't anything new, nor was it something Carmen worried about. She liked listening, and when they talked about Brooke's feelings and not hers, she didn't have to guard her words. Cathy and Sofia said they knew how she felt about Brooke long before the night she got drunk at Brooke's first wedding and told them. But Carmen had convinced herself that Brooke didn't know, and that's the way they would keep it.

" . . . and then he comes to bed when I'm half asleep and wants to fuck."

Carmen was jarred from her thoughts. This was a consequence of never wanting to talk about her feelings. She had to let the conversation go wherever Brooke decided to take it, and her intimate relationship with Geoffrey was territory she abhorred. Twenty-five years ago, it was both fascinating and devastating to hear Brooke talk about having sex with men, but Carmen had heard enough details since then to render her numb. Now it was something she simply stored in the recesses of her mind, where she could almost pretend it didn't exist.

"At least we still do that well. Seems like the only time we really get along is when we're fucking, but that's because we don't even talk anymore. As long as we both get off, who needs the afterglow? I sleep well."

The waiter came to ask if everything was all right, which made Carmen notice she had barely touched her dinner after all. She allowed him to take it away, though, hoping it might bring an early end to their evening. She was tired and wanted to be alone.

"If I ever start talking about getting married again, please just slap me upside the head and tell me that people don't have to be married to fuck." Brooke snatched up the bill when it came. "I invited you, remember?"

Carmen chuckled when she saw Brooke squinting at the small print. Brooke was too vain to admit she needed reading glasses.

They stood and Carmen helped her with her coat. "When do you start work?"

"Monday."

When they stepped outside, Carmen started to wave for a cab.

"I have my car. I'll drop you off."

"Okay."

As they started down the sidewalk toward the parking garage,

Brooke hooked her arm in Carmen's. "The girls are busy this weekend. Are you doing anything?"

Carmen folded her other arm across her chest so she could cover Brooke's cold fingers with her gloved hand. It immediately brought to mind her walk with Judith along Central Park on Sunday night. "Nothing that requires getting out of bed and getting dressed. I'm so tired all I can think about is sleeping for two days."

"You poor thing. What if I bring over some groceries and make you dinner on Sunday? We can sit in bed and watch movies all day."

Carmen usually loved days like that but she didn't feel deserving of human company. "I appreciate the offer, but I think that might require more brain cells than I plan to use."

"Are you sure? I could throw in a backrub."

Carmen sometimes wondered if Brooke knew exactly the effect she was having, and did it just to be a tease.

Chapter 9

Judith cradled the phone underneath her chin as she filled in the fields on the Key West booking form. "No, you'll like Irene's. The whole house is women only."

From the corner of her eye, she saw Todd emerge from his office, a stack of forms in his hand. "All right, people. Huddle up," he yelled.

She had come to detest that phrase, which Todd used every time he called an impromptu meeting. His appropriation of sports idiom was probably meant to make them feel like a team, but he undercut the concept by pitting them against each other for bonuses and plum clients. She ignored him, turning her attention back to the woman on her phone. "Your friend's right. Key West is mostly male, but it's very lesbian friendly. And Irene knows all the best places. She'll give you a calendar of events when you check in."

The woman on the phone, Antoinette, was one of her best clients, having booked a trip with her every year since her first all-lesbian cruise seven years ago. If Rainbow Getaways had more repeat customers like her, they wouldn't have to spend so much on national marketing.

"I'll find out. I think she has eleven rooms. Do you know that many couples who might want to go?" Another reason to like Antoinette was she had lots of friends. "I'll call her and see. But we'll need to book all of it this week to guarantee Memorial Weekend."

His impatience mounting, Todd began slapping the rolled-up forms in his hand.

"I'll call her this afternoon and get back to you . . . e-mail okay?" She scribbled herself a note and began to group the papers in her folder. "Bye now."

When all eight agents had gathered around the entrance to Todd's office, he began to hand out the forms.

"What you're looking at is the new commission structure. You'll notice that we've decreased the rate for bookings that come in over the Web site, the eight-hundred number or in response to special promotions. That's because we consider those the result of agency expenditures, not agent sales."

Another annoying habit Todd had was to use "we" instead of "I" so he wouldn't have to feel solely responsible for being an asshole. Judith glanced over at Celia, who was rolling her eyes. It was hard not to envy her status as a short-timer. After giving her two-week notice last Friday, she was ready to get out of here and start making more money.

"The good news is that if a client books again—and asks to deal directly with you—we'll bump that rate back up on the second transaction. Any questions?"

"I have one." Judith reread the provisions to see how her existing clients would be handled. "I already have a client base. Does this mean I continue to get the higher rate for their bookings when they ask for me?"

"This policy goes into effect today. As of right now, no one has a client base, but if a customer asks for you, you'll earn the higher rate on the second transaction."

"That isn't fair, Todd. I've had some of these clients for seventeen years. A lot of them are personal friends."

"Nobody said life had to be fair. We're trying to give everybody here an even playing field. If these folks are your friends, they'll ask for you and you'll be back up to the higher rate before you know it."

"Todd, I have over six hundred clients. If you cut my rate on their next trip, that's going to be thousands of dollars out of my pocket, and I'll never make it up."

"But you'll be eligible to pick up new clients from the same pool as everyone else. That should offset some of the drain."

Technically, the asshole was right, but practically, it meant working more for less. As she walked back to her cubicle, she envisioned Celia's hands around Todd's scrawny neck. It had a certain primal appeal.

A faint chime from her lower desk drawer signaled a missed call on her cell phone, probably her mother anxious to confirm her visit on Sunday with Victor. It was hard sometimes to tell who was more upset by a change in routine, her mother or her brother.

Her stomach did a flip when she saw the area code, definitely not her mother's. As she dug in her purse for the business card that would confirm the caller's identity, the phone beeped to announce a message.

Carmen dropped the phone back into its cradle as if it were on fire. She should have hung up without leaving a message. No, she had to say something, because Judith's cell phone would have a record of her call and she would have looked like a stalker if she had just hung up. Damned technology!

She had even planned for the possibility of reaching voice mail and practiced what to say. But once she heard Judith's voice, all she could manage was gibberish about paying Zeigler-Marsh a visit at the end of the week. It was all true, but way too formal for a woman whose breasts she had fondled in an elevator a week ago.

For the life of her, Carmen didn't know why she couldn't just chalk up her encounter with Judith O'Shea to an embarrassing blunder and let it go. She didn't like the idea that Judith probably thought she was an asshole, even though she had behaved like one. But that didn't explain why she felt so desperate to right things.

Cathy entered the open door with Carmen's travel portfolio. "I wasn't able to get you back in the Grand, but I booked you into the Marriott Marquis for Thursday night."

"Fine." Carmen shuffled the papers on her desk, pretending to be absorbed in her work. She hadn't accomplished much in the last week.

"Do you want me to set up dinner with Sofia on Thursday?"

"No . . . breakfast on Friday, maybe."

"Okay, I'll ask her. And what about the return? Seven or nine on Friday night?"

What she really wanted was to stay over on Friday night in New York in hopes of seeing Judith again. "I'm not sure. Why don't you leave it and I'll call them back when I decide? And, uh . . . leave me the info on the hotel too . . . in case I want to change something."

Cathy looked at her skeptically. "Since when do you make your own travel arrangements?"

"Since maybe I might not want everybody in my business," she snapped. As soon as the words left her lips, Carmen wanted them back. Cathy's look was a perfect cross between anger and hurt as she turned to leave. "Wait. I'm sorry."

"You should be."

Carmen sighed and tossed her pen across the room in frustration. "I finally called her." By the look on Cathy's face, her cryptic explanation wasn't enough to justify her rude behavior. "I wasn't going to say anything to anybody because I've already made a big enough fool of myself."

"You called Judith?"

She nodded sheepishly.

Cathy shut the door and returned deliberately to the couch, where she made herself comfortable. This was going to turn into a heart-to-heart and there was nothing Carmen could do to escape it.

"You know, your capacity to commit foolishness is unlimited as far as I'm concerned."

"What's that supposed to mean?"

"It means you get to make mistakes over and over and I'll forgive you because you're my oldest friend and you'd do the same for me."

"Maybe it's time I got my due."

"What did she say?"

Carmen shook her head. "She wasn't there. I left a message that I was going to be in town and asked her to call me. Who knows if she will?"

Cathy kicked off her shoes and put her feet up on the coffee table. "Have you been thinking about that question I asked you last week?"

"Which one was that?"

"I don't remember exactly how I put it, but I wondered what bothered you most—the fact that she was upset or that you were responsible?"

"I don't see what difference it makes. I'm responsible for hurting her feelings."

"But do you want to fix things so she'll feel better, or so you'll feel better?"

"If she feels better, I'll feel better."

"Let me put it a different way. What if what makes her feel

better is for you to get lost? Will you be okay with that?"

"No."

"Then what is it you want from her?"

Carmen heaved a deep sigh and gazed out the window, unable to look her friend in the eye. "I want her to go out with me. I want to show her that I'm not the biggest asshole that ever lived. I want another chance to earn her respect." She could feel Cathy's eyes burning into her.

"Listen to yourself, Carmen. Everything's about you and what Judith thinks of you."

Cathy was right, but only because Carmen wasn't coming clean about what she really wanted. The truth was she was drawn to Judith. She wanted to spend time with her and get to know her better. She just didn't want anyone to think it was because she couldn't have Brooke. "Would you believe me if I told you I cared about her? I don't really know why, but I do."

"I've never seen you kick yourself this long about anyone."

Carmen got up and walked around her desk to join Cathy on the couch. "I can't stop thinking about her. And it isn't just because I feel bad about the Brooke thing. I really thought she was nice—one of the nicest people I've met in a long time. And I fucked it up."

"What did you fuck up?"

"That's just it. We'll probably never know."

They sat in silence for almost a minute. Cathy finally pushed her feet back into her shoes and stood. "I forgive you for being a bitch about the travel reservations. But I don't trust you to make your own arrangements so I'll hang on to them."

Carmen chuckled and shook her head.

"You have until Thursday at two to let me know what you want to do. Once you're out the door, you're on your own."

"Fair enough." Carmen followed her to the door. "Thanks . . . for everything . . . as usual."

Cathy squeezed her shoulder. "You're welcome . . . as usual."

When they opened the office door, the receptionist waved in their direction.

"Can you hold, please?" Looking up at Carmen, she announced the call. "I have Judith O'Shea on the line for you. She says she's returning your call."

Carmen felt a surge of panic, but Cathy gave her a reassuring look as she pushed her back into the office and closed the door behind her.

Judith pulled up the collar on her wool blazer to stave off the cool breeze creeping down her neck. The late winter sun made it too warm for her parka, but a scarf would have been nice had she known she would be sitting on a bench in Washington Square Park in the middle of the afternoon.

One of the great things about New York was that one was never alone, and yet, there was privacy in crowded anonymity. Judith needed that privacy today, and that's why she had walked out of the agency with her phone in her hand, stopping only to tell Todd she had to tend to a personal matter. If he had an objection, she hadn't stayed to hear it.

On the way to the park, she had listened to Carmen's message four times, looking for a clue about why she was calling. Her first thought was it had something to do with her not following up with Sofia at Zeigler-Marsh. That's why she said she was coming to town, so maybe Sofia had asked about her.

Even after more than a week, Judith was unable to forget the events of her encounter with Carmen. No matter why Carmen was calling, Judith planned to seize this chance to tell her the one thing that had been eating at her, something so important it was keeping her awake at night.

The familiar voice finally answered the phone, sending a quiver down Judith's spine. "Judith."

"Hi."

"I'm glad you called."

"I got your message . . . except I didn't quite understand it."

"Yeah, I'm afraid the senior moments have already started. My brain has a tendency to shut down whenever I'm talking to a machine."

Carmen didn't sound much like the self-assured CEO who had swept her off her feet and almost into bed. This Carmen was definitely more reserved, a sure sign she was dragging baggage from their ill-fated night.

"I was calling—"

"I'm glad you—"

They chuckled at trying to talk at the same time.

"You first," Carmen offered.

Judith relaxed against the back of the park bench. With a conscious effort, she let go of her image of Carmen as the beautiful, dazzling, sophisticated bigwig from the conference. Right this minute, she was just Carmen, and she seemed as nervous as Judith. "I was going to say I was glad you called because I wanted to tell you something important . . . something I wish I had thought of that night at the hotel."

"Okay," Carmen said slowly, her voice filled with apprehension.

"I realized I was just as much to blame as you were, so I should apologize too."

"That isn't true, Judith. It wasn't your fault at all. I should have just told you that you looked like a friend of mine. Then it wouldn't have been such a shock to hear it from someone else."

"Yeah, that part was your fault, but it happened and you said you were sorry. What I did was just as bad if not worse, because I didn't even realize it at the time." Judith sighed in frustration. "Why is it that I can go over this in my head and get all the words just right, but when I finally get a chance to say them, nothing comes out like it's supposed to?"

Carmen laughed, breaking the tension. "I think that's called real life. I did the same thing before I left that stupid message."

Judith smiled, completely disarmed by Carmen's admission. "Anyway, what I did was let myself get caught up with feeling like Cinderella. You were thinking about me looking like Brooke, and I was thinking about you being my Princess Charming."

"Princess Charming? Me?" Carmen snorted. "You have no idea how far from reality that is."

"Are you saying the real Carmen Delallo isn't charming?"

"I wish, but lately I think everyone would say the real Carmen Delallo is a jerk."

"You certainly charmed the hell out of me."

"Then maybe I haven't totally lost my touch after all."

Now it was Judith's turn to laugh. "No, I'd say you still have it."

"Good to know."

Judith blew out a breath. "Okay, that's all I wanted to say. Your turn."

"Great. Time to speak clearly and not sound stupid."

"The pressure's on."

Carmen cleared her throat. "I'm going to be in New York on Friday. I have a meeting with Zeigler-Marsh that should last all day. I was hoping you might be interested in having dinner on Friday night . . . and maybe seeing a show."

The giddy feeling she got from the surprise invitation was exactly what Judith had experienced at the convention, but she needed to keep her feet on the ground this time. "I'd love to, but only if I get to see the real you."

"The real me?"

"Not Miss Fancy Big Shot, just you."

"What if the real me isn't all that interesting?"

"I can't imagine that would be the case."

"Now the pressure's really on. I have to be both charming and interesting. I guess that means I can't talk about work."

"I'm willing to grant you a little leeway on that, but I can read all about The Delallo Group at your Web site."

"I'm in trouble then. I have only three days to completely invent a pleasing personality."

"Just be yourself and I promise to do the same." Judith already was catching glimpses of what she thought might be the real Carmen, a woman who conveyed nothing but confidence among professional colleagues, but hid her personal insecurities with self-effacing humor. She couldn't wait to unravel the enigma.

"Okay, but remember, you asked for it."

Judith checked her watch. Todd would be pacing the hallway outside her cubicle by now. She didn't care. She hadn't felt happy since last weekend and she was in no hurry to get back to work. "Where shall we meet?"

"I'm staying at the Marriott Marquis in Times Square. I can send a car if you like. Is six o'clock okay? That'll give us time to eat."

Judith was thrilled at the lavish notion of Carmen ordering a limo for her, but she wasn't going to let herself get swept up again. "The subway works fine for me, especially at rush hour. Why don't I just meet you in the lobby at six?"

"That works too. Is there anything in particular you want to see, or shall we take potluck with the concierge?"

"It doesn't matter to me. I can even pick up tickets if you like."

"You don't trust me? You're afraid you'll end up at *Logistic Regression: The Musical*?"

"I hope not, because I don't even understand what you just said."

"I'll find something light and frivolous. We can turn off our brains and relax."

"That sounds terrific. I could use a little relaxation."

"So how are things at work? Sofia said she hadn't heard from you."

"I'm trying to stick it out at Rainbow. It's hard to leave a place after seventeen years, especially one that's just six blocks from my apartment." That wasn't exactly true, but Judith didn't want to get into all her reasons for not following up with Sofia. She just didn't feel comfortable calling, especially after the way things had turned out. And if she and Carmen eventually became friends, she wouldn't want to take advantage of that.

"She'll be disappointed to hear that."

"I should call her and tell her what I've decided."

"She'll try to change your mind."

"Does she . . . know about . . . what happened?"

"No, I don't usually trumpet my embarrassing moments. I have Cathy for that. She keeps my head from getting too big."

"I liked Cathy."

"She liked you too. In fact, she was glad to hear I was calling you. I think she was afraid I was going to keep stomping around here and eventually fire the whole staff."

Had Carmen really been that upset about last weekend? "That doesn't sound very charming."

"I warned you."

"So you did."

"You can rig one of those emergency plans with a friend. You know, you send her a text message from the bathroom and she places an urgent call ten minutes later telling you to come at once because there's been an accident."

"I get the feeling that happens to you a lot."

Carmen laughed. "It probably should."

"I'm not worried. In fact, at the risk of sounding overly excited, I'm not dreading dinner with you at all."

"That's the spirit."

Judith was, in fact, ecstatic about their plans. They could start again, this time with everything out in the open.

"I guess I should be going," Carmen said, interrupting her daydream. "Cathy's probably getting ear strain from standing outside the door."

"I'm glad you called."

"Me too, and I can't wait to see you."

They said their good-byes and Judith started to pocket her cell phone. Instead, she called Todd to say something had come up and she would need the rest of the afternoon off. A date with Carmen Delallo called for a new outfit.

Carmen walked the length of their offices to a climate-controlled room humming with computers and servers. This was Raul's domain, and she rarely ventured this far from her corner office.

"Hey, boss," he said, jumping up to open the door.

"Everything okay down here in the cave?"

"Couldn't be better. What can I do for you?"

"Nothing. I just wanted to see how things were going and try to make you feel appreciated. I've heard that social reinforcement is a better motivator than a raise or time off." She shot him a grin before turning back toward the staff offices.

"Don't believe everything you hear!" he shouted.

She laughed and stuck her head into a workroom shared by four research assistants. "You guys doing all right?"

"Lenore's working our tails off."

"I'm sure it's good for you . . . builds character . . . that sort of thing."

One of the young men handed her a report. "Here's that data run you wanted for Durbin Dreams."

"Great. Now all I have to do is put a bow on it and kiss his ass good-bye." She stopped next to speak to Richard, then to Kristy, commending both on their recent work. She ended her circuit in Lenore's doorway. "You're doing a fantastic job. I know because all the research assistants look haggard and underfed and Raul has his door locked."

Lenore looked up wearily. "Our deadline on the time-share conversion is going to be very close."

"Do you want me to tell Hinkle it won't be ready until the fall?" The idea of sucking up to Bill Hinkle and asking for an extension was distasteful, but they wouldn't take shortcuts to get the job done on time.

"Lord, no. I don't want to owe him anything special. He might want to take it out in trade."

"So we'll make the deadline?"

"Yes, but like I said, it's going to be close. Can you clone Raul?"

"You need another programmer? I posted an ad at the conference but we didn't get any bites."

"If he had somebody to do the routine data runs, he could concentrate on this."

"Are we talking temporary?"

Lenore bobbed her head from side to side as she considered the question. "For this, yeah. But we're taking a big chance having Raul be the only one in the company who knows how to read this data. We should think about bringing someone else on board."

Carmen ran some numbers in her head. "The new revenue should more than pay for it. See if Raul knows anyone from UC and let's do some interviews. If the temporary gig works out, we can make it permanent."

"Just like that?"

"Isn't that what you wanted?"

"It's exactly what I wanted, but I'm not used to getting it."

Carmen grinned. "I'm having a good day." She continued on to Cathy's office and rapped gently on the door jamb.

"I hear laughter down the hall. Are you sick?"

"No, but I'll need an extra night in New York. And can you get me an open return on Saturday"—Carmen glanced over her shoulder to make sure no one was listening—"in case I decide to sleep in?"

Chapter 10

Judith slowed her gait to study her reflection in the window on Forty-Second Street. She had lucked into a sale at Marshall's where she found gray slacks and a black sweater that looked . . . well, like they were off the rack at a discount store. But she didn't buy much she couldn't toss in a washer and dryer. Besides, she was through with pretense. Carmen needed to see the real Judith O'Shea, a woman who lived on a tight budget.

At the corner, she turned onto Broadway, where foot traffic was heavy, typical for a Friday night. She loved the theatre, but hadn't been to a show in almost a year. That had less to do with her budget than her social life. Tonight was her first real date in almost three years, if she didn't count the times she went out to the clubs with Celia, where both had been on the prowl and returned home alone, discouraged by the scarcity of women their age in the club scene.

As she closed in on Times Square, she checked her watch. She was four minutes early, which would seem like an eternity waiting at the Marriott, where the ground floor was like a fishbowl.

She was anxious about what her first moments with Carmen would be like, if there might still be chemistry between them after their awkward parting. Last time had been raw and spontaneous, but tonight was orchestrated—dinner and a show. Civilized. Formal. There would be no going back to Carmen's room tonight, no matter how big the temptation.

As she crossed the valet drive-through, she spotted a dark-haired woman leaning casually against a wall inside the brightly-lit enclosure of the first floor. Her doubts about whether there would be sparks dissipated immediately as her nervousness was replaced with anticipation. Walking closer, she confirmed it was Carmen and studied her through the glass. She was elegantly dressed in black slacks with a high-collared white shirt, and her calf-length Burberry raincoat. She looked fabulous, easily the prettiest woman Judith had ever gone out with.

"Hi! Have you been waiting long?"

"No, I just got here."

Both of them smiled broadly and greeted one another with a light hug and kisses on the cheek. It wasn't exactly awkward, but it was clear they weren't sure where they stood with one another.

"You look nice," Carmen said.

"Thank you. So do you." Judith couldn't help but blush a little, and she briefly regretted not splurging for something classier to wear. "I love that shirt."

Carmen tugged at the collar. "There's enough starch in here to stand up a corpse."

"You never know when you're going to need a good neck brace."

"Let's hope it isn't tonight. My luck, these tickets will turn out to be obstructed view." Carmen's arm went around her waist as they exited the building.

"What show did you get?"

"*Mama Mia*. I've seen it five times already, but I love it."

"I haven't seen it, but it sounds like fun. Are you going to sing along?"

Carmen laughed. "No, I'm really trying to make a good impression here. I don't think my singing would help that."

Judith liked that Carmen wanted to impress her, but it would be too easy to fall into that trap again. "You know what? I'm already impressed by you. You promised me you'd be yourself tonight."

"So you're giving me permission to sing?"

"As long as we don't get kicked out. It's so embarrassing when they shine that flashlight and people point at you."

"Ah, so you're shy when it comes to public spectacles."

"I didn't say that," Judith answered with a chuckle, her mind going back to two weeks ago when she and Carmen were making out on the sidewalk next to Central Park.

Carmen stepped in front of her and blocked her path. "Are you flirting with me? Because I respond very well to flirting."

Judith instantly recognized that she, not Carmen, was responsible for their drift in conversation. "So where are you taking me for dinner?"

Carmen squinted at her as though scolding her for changing the subject. "Trattoria, if that's all right. I guess I should have asked."

"It's good. I happen to like Italian."

"But does a sweet Irish lass like yourself like Italians?"

"I like some Italians."

"I would take that as encouragement if I weren't so insecure."

In spite of herself, Judith snorted at the remark. If there was one thing Carmen wasn't, it was insecure.

Carmen took her hand and hooked it through her elbow, guiding her into a turn at Forty-Fourth Street, and through the door of the restaurant. Judith was impressed with how well she knew her way around New York and said so.

"I get here about four or five times a year on business. I usually stay in midtown because Zeigler-Marsh is on Forty-Sixth, so I've found a few places around here I like." She paused while they were being seated at a table for two. "Speaking of Zeigler-Marsh, Sofia asked about you today. She's still interested if you change your mind about where you're working."

"I, uh . . ." Judith scrunched her mouth. The topic of two weeks ago was like an elephant in the parlor, one they were going to have to at least acknowledge if tonight was going to be a new start. "To tell you the truth, I'm too embarrassed about what happened to follow up with her."

"I told you not to be."

"I know. But it really made me uncomfortable to realize that everyone was in on the private joke but me."

The smile Carmen had been wearing since the Marriott was gone. "I'm really sorry about all that. For what it's worth, I didn't tell anyone about what happened on Sunday night . . . except Cathy. And I only told her because I fired everyone and she hired them all back. She's so insolent."

Judith couldn't help but laugh. "You fired everyone?"

"I was in a foul mood. My doctor says I have to turn stress outward."

"You fired everyone?"

"Not really. But they were all using the back stairs so they wouldn't have to pass by my door."

"And you looked like such a happy crew."

"An illusion." They paused to place their order with the waiter. When he left, Carmen leaned forward and folded her hands on the table. "Now, would you like to talk some more about the last time I was here? Because I can probably apologize for at least another hour without saying the same thing twice."

"I don't think I could stand to listen to that for an hour.

Besides, I told you already I wasn't exactly innocent myself."

"That's right, the Cinderella thing. I didn't really get what you were saying. Did you expect it all to disappear when I left town?"

"No, it wasn't that." Judith fingered her linen napkin nervously. "I felt as if the glass slipper just happened to fit me of all people. And then I got caught up with you being so beautiful and important. I was paying more attention to what you were than who you were."

Carmen looked at her seriously before breaking into a small smile. "You think I'm beautiful?"

"Of course you are." Judith couldn't stop her own embarrassed smile. "And no, I'm not flirting."

"Pity."

"But like I told you on the phone, I want to know the real you, not the Carmen Delallo everyone at the conference knows."

Carmen sighed and leaned back. "What if I told you the real me is that person you already met?"

"Is it?"

"Pretty much. I know we weren't going to talk about work tonight, but it's a very big part of who I am. Outside of my family, most of the people I'm close to are people I'm connected to through work."

"Except Brooke."

"Except Brooke," Carmen said quietly.

Judith studied Carmen's serious expression and weighed whether or not to make Brooke an issue tonight. Her specter had already ruined their first weekend, and if tonight turned out to be their only real date, there was no point in stirring it up again. "Tell me about your family." She was instantly glad for her decision, as the question produced a broad smile.

"My twin sisters are the youngest, and I have three brothers. I'm the third oldest."

"Your poor mother had six children?"

"We're Catholic. Blame it on the pope."

The waiter interrupted again with their salads and warm bread. Judith took her cue from Carmen, filling her bread plate with olive oil and a dash of balsamic vinegar. It wasn't her usual habit, but Carmen made it seem like the proper way to eat Italian bread.

"Is your whole family still in Chicago?"

"Pretty much. My oldest brother, Paul, lives in Milwaukee, but that's close enough for Sunday dinner in Evanston, which we aren't invited to unless we've been to Mass."

"Sounds like your folks and the pope are pretty tight."

"Just my mom, really. I'd like to think seventeen years of Catholic school earned me a lot of credits for down the road."

"If that's the case, I'm in deep trouble. The public schools in Brooklyn didn't offer much in the way of spiritual development."

"Don't worry. I probably got enough for you too."

Judith set her bread and salad aside to save room for her main course. Had she been with Celia down in the Village, she would have asked the waiter to wrap it to go. "What was it like growing up in a family that large?"

"I was spoiled because I was the only girl for a while. And I never had to share a room because I was seven when the twins came along."

"Are all of you still close?"

"We try to get together on holidays and special occasions. We even have a message board on the Internet so we can keep up with everyone. We're now at nineteen grandchildren and three great-grandchildren."

"How do you even remember all their names?"

"It's funny you say that. I'm so bad with names." She laughed and took a drink of her wine. "Sometimes I have to fake it. If there's one I can't remember, I hang back and wait for someone else to call them."

Judith wasn't having much success separating the charming

woman before her from the one she thought was merely an illusion. Carmen sounded every bit as animated tonight as she had at dinner with her friends. "Are the rest of your siblings as busy as you?"

"Busier, I'd say. Angie's the only one who doesn't have kids, but she's an OB-GYN, so babies rule her life anyway."

"Your sister's a doctor?"

"Both of my sisters are doctors, and so are two of my brothers."

No wonder Carmen was so driven to succeed. "You have four doctors in your family?"

"Five, counting Dad. He was on the faculty at Northwestern."

"How did you manage to end up in the travel business?"

Carmen shrugged. "Medical school didn't really appeal to me. I studied behavioral science at DePaul thinking I might go into psychiatry. But I took a couple of business courses my senior year and decided that was more fun."

"Did you break your dad's heart?"

"I don't think so. Every couple of years I send him and Mom on some great vacation and tell him he has to take notes on everything. He always comes back with a big report and tons of pictures."

"So he takes you seriously?"

"Who says I'm not serious? Nothing like a destination review from a source I trust."

"Your family sounds like so much fun."

"They are. What about yours? Do you see them a lot?"

"I try to get over to Brooklyn every weekend. But it's just Mom and Victor and me."

"Your brother isn't married?"

"He's . . . no, he's—" The waiter returned with their entrees, postponing a discussion of Victor. Judith was looking forward to telling Carmen about her brother and his accomplishments, but she didn't want to rush through it. Victor was a big part of her life, and anyone who knew her needed to understand why.

"This is the best Alfredo sauce in New York," Carmen said, wasting no time digging into her linguine.

"I bet if Cathy were here, she'd tell you that was too heavy to eat in the evening."

Carmen waved a hand dismissively. "Cathy would have me eating fish and salad at every meal. You can't do that to an Italian. It's against our nature."

"But she's Italian too, right?"

"Oh, she can eat whatever she wants. It's all about my deprivation, not hers."

Judith knew people like Cathy, women who had children and began mothering all of their friends. Carmen didn't seem to truly mind it. Rather, it was as if both were playing a familiar game, with Carmen trying to sneak things by.

They dug into their dinners ravenously, mindful of the clock. The curtain was going up at eight, whether they were in their seats or not.

"Italians don't just eat," Carmen explained. "They have relationships with food. No offense, but I really don't think the Irish understand food."

Judith chuckled. "No offense, but I'm not Irish."

"Excuse me? O'Shea isn't the greenest name in all of Ireland?"

"It might very well be. All I know is it was easier to spell than Kowalczyk."

"Than cola what?"

"Kowalczyk was my maiden name. Very Polish."

She laughed aloud as Carmen froze for several seconds before dropping her jaw in exaggerated shock.

"Your maiden name?"

"But I take your point about food. Kevin didn't care what or where we ate, as long as he got enough. He wasn't really fond of seafood, but he liked—" Carmen's expression hadn't changed at all. "What? Did I forget to tell you that I used to be married?"

"To a man?"

"Well, doh! I guess deep down I knew I was making a mistake. I just didn't know I was making one of that magnitude."

Carmen's face finally returned to normal and she eyed her plate again. "I think I'm going to sit here quietly and enjoy my dinner while you tell me all about that."

"Well, I—"

"Just answer me this. Are you definitely a lesbian?"

Judith made an X across her chest with her fingers. "Cross my heart."

"I'm very glad to hear that. Do you have any more surprises?"

She almost mentioned Victor, but she never played him for laughs. "I can't just dump out all my surprises at once. If you want to know them, you're going to have to discover them one at a time."

Carmen's face brightened. "That sounds like an invitation."

Judith ignored the flirtation. "Do you really want to hear about my ill-fated marriage, or can you do what I do and just pretend it never happened?"

"Oh, no. I want the details." Carmen leaned across the table and lowered her voice. "And don't leave anything out."

"You don't get those details, because there are some things I just don't want to experience again, thank you. But Kevin really was a nice guy. He was from Boston. I met him at a friend's wedding here in New York and we started seeing each other. We went back and forth on the weekends, but then he got a job here in the city and we got married."

"How old were you?"

"Twenty-three. And we were married for three years."

Carmen took one last bite and pushed her bowl away, apparently satisfied. "What happened? I mean, besides the obvious."

"Believe it or not, it wasn't the obvious. I had no clue there was more to sex than what we had, but that's another story altogether."

"Now if you're going to talk about sex, I may need a cigarette."

Judith was momentarily stunned. That didn't fit her image of Carmen at all. "You don't smoke, do you?"

"No, but I could start."

"Please don't do that on my account."

"So if it didn't have anything to do with sex, what happened?" The waiter brought their check and Carmen quickly handed over her credit card. "We need to go or we'll be late."

Judith couldn't tell the whole story of Kevin without talking about Victor, so she gave a quick version as they headed out. "Kevin never liked New York. He talked about moving back to Boston, but I couldn't leave. Finally, he just got another job there and that was the end of it."

"You chose staying in New York over your marriage?"

The way Carmen put it sounded pretty cold. "It's more complicated than that. He knew I wouldn't leave, so getting a job in Boston was the same as asking for a divorce." They arrived at the theater, effectively ending the conversation before she could fully explain.

Carmen adjusted the settings on her cell phone as the lights went dim. "Remind me to turn this back on when we go out. I never remember."

Carmen clapped absently along with everyone else, glad the show was ending. If she had it to do over again, she would have suggested something different for their date tonight, something that would have let them talk more. The dinner conversation had been rushed, she realized, and she hadn't learned much about Judith, something she definitely wanted to do.

Judith wasn't anything like the usual women whose pleasures

Carmen enjoyed. She might have been, had they gone through with their frolic a couple of weeks ago. A few nights with someone pretty would have made a nice distraction, just like that other woman—Meara something or other—she had met a few years ago on one of her trips to the Big Apple. But she wasn't thinking of Judith as a sexual conquest anymore. Correction: She wasn't thinking of Judith as *only* a sexual conquest.

"I didn't hear you sing," Judith said, taking her arm as they walked out.

"You scared me into silence. All I could think about was those people coming for me with a flashlight." They reached the corner at Broadway, where the lights of Times Square pulsed as if the lifeblood of the city. "This sight always gets to me."

"I think it gets to everyone," Judith said, stopping to gaze at the kaleidoscope of electronic stimuli. "Oh, I'm supposed to remind you, turn your cell phone back on."

Mindlessly, Carmen reached into her pocket and activated the device, not taking her eye from Judith's profile, which was stunningly reminiscent of Brooke's. "Do you want to get a drink or dessert or something? Or have you had enough of me?"

"I'm not really sick of you yet, if that's what you're asking." Judith's hand found hers and squeezed.

"I didn't exactly ask it that way."

Judith turned and faced her, ending the inadvertent masquerade. "I'm enjoying my evening with you very much. I'm not ready for it to be over."

"Admit it. The real Carmen Delallo is infinitely more charming than you ever imagined." And Judith O'Shea was prettier than Brooke Nance, she decided.

"By far."

"Let's get out of this circus. Where can we go to talk?" The obvious choice was her hotel, but Judith would probably think that was presumptuous. She would be right.

"How about your hotel?"

"You just read my mind."

"I was thinking of the bar."

"That would probably be best. I have a feeling I'm going to need plenty to drink." She wrapped an arm around Judith's waist and steered her toward the Marriott. "Are you really having a good time or are you just being polite?"

"I haven't used my fake phone call yet."

"Right. I'll take that as a good sign." They entered the hotel's ground floor lobby and she pushed a button for the elevator. When the door opened, she nudged Judith through and pressed the button to close the door so they wouldn't have to share their ride. Her fingers hovered over the control panel. "Let's see . . . I think my room is on the forty-first floor."

Judith reached across her and pressed the one that said Broadway Lounge.

"Oh, you meant the main bar," she said with a teasing grin. Unable to resist, she closed in on Judith and kissed her full on the lips, just as the elevator rose into the open atrium where anyone looking could see. It wasn't wild and steamy like the last time they had kissed in an elevator, but it was very pleasant.

"You're turning me into a public spectacle again," Judith said when they pulled apart.

"We're in an elevator. It's our tradition."

The door opened and they exited into the lounge, securing a table for two by the glass wall that overlooked Times Square. Carmen waved to the cocktail waitress as she draped her coat over the back of her chair.

"What can I get you ladies?"

"Chivas on the rocks," she answered, helping Judith with her coat.

"And I'll have a Tia Maria, straight up, with black coffee."

Every tidbit of information Judith offered was a revelation into who she was, and a stark reminder to Carmen that she wasn't like Brooke at all. "I would never have guessed that in a million years. You don't strike me as a Tia Maria type."

"Is there a profile?"

"Certainly not somebody from New York."

"It's my island side. The first time I had it was about sixteen years ago on my first escorted lesbian cruise. Come to think of it, I managed to keep most of the habits I acquired that week."

"That was after Kevin, right?"

"Oh, yeah. He'd been gone a couple of years by then. I went to work for Myrna after he left and she kept teasing me that I was batting for the wrong team. Then we came back from that cruise and she crowed like she had presented me at the lesbian debutante ball. My face was red for a month."

"And that's your coming out tale?"

"Pretty much. It was the first time I consciously considered whether I belonged with a woman or a man. But once I had a comparison, it was a no-brainer."

The waitress quietly deposited their drinks and left after Carmen signed the room charge.

"So how has a pretty woman like you managed to stay single all these years?" Carmen asked. She was satisfied to see Judith's face take on a pink hue, visible even in the dim light of the lounge.

"I could ask you the same question."

She chuckled. "Yes, you could. But you'd have to wait your turn because I asked you first."

Judith sipped her drink and set it down. "Most of the lesbians I know are in relationships. If they aren't, there's usually a good reason."

"I know what you mean there. But what does that say about us?"

"Well, we're different," Judith said coyly. "And I haven't always been single. I bet that's true for you too."

"Unh-unh." She swung her finger from side to side as she shook her head. "We talked about me all through dinner. It's your turn now. I want to hear about all the fools that let you get away."

"Just one, really. And I'm not sure you could say she let me get away." Judith picked up her drink again and sipped, swiping an errant drop with her tongue. "We were together for seven years."

"That's like . . . married."

"Not really. This is a terrible thing to say, but I don't think there was ever a time when I thought Noelle and I would stay together . . . or even felt like I wanted us to."

"That's a lot of marking time." Carmen bit her tongue during a lengthy lull, hoping Judith would tell her more.

"Marking time is a good way of putting it. Noelle was French—not like you're Italian and I'm Polish. I mean she came to New York from Paris to work on a project for her company. She didn't know how long she would be here, so I guess neither one of us ever really expected things to be permanent. Once you get a mindset like that, I think it's only natural to hold back a little."

Carmen drained her drink and set the empty glass on the table. "You apparently have a thing for out-of-towners."

"So it seems." Judith raised her glass with a smile that told her she was officially included in that list.

"You're in luck then, because it so happens I have a thing for New Yorkers."

"You don't say."

"It's true. I just discovered it a couple of weeks ago."

"You're flirting again."

"I can't help myself. I think I'm showing unusual restraint for a second date."

"Are you calling that last disaster our first date?"

"It wasn't a total disaster." She leaned across the table and lowered her voice. "Admit it—the ride up in the elevator was at least memorable."

Judith gave a half smile before looking down to focus on her drink. Clearly, she was uncomfortable with the turn in conversation.

"Okay, so it wasn't that great."

"Of course it was."

"Then what's wrong?"

Judith polished off what was left of her drink as if for courage, still not making eye contact. "You wouldn't believe how close I came to pressing forty-one in that elevator."

Carmen shuddered at what that would have meant. "What stopped you?"

"This." She held out her hand to indicate the scene in the lounge. "I wanted to talk to you. I can't imagine we would have done much of that in your room."

Carmen chuckled. "I guess talking and crying out in passion aren't really the same thing." She reached over and took Judith's hand. "I'm glad we came in here instead too. I know . . . you don't believe that for a minute. But I wanted the chance to get to know you better."

Judith's lips were smiling but there was doubt in her eyes.

"I think you're a very sexy woman, Judith, but I'm not out for a conquest. I didn't feel like shit for the past two weeks just because we didn't get to f—have sex."

"I guess if we had, that would have been it."

"Maybe, maybe not. But since it didn't happen that way, why don't we just go with what we've got?" She squeezed Judith's hand. "Spend the day with me tomorrow. We'll do something fun."

"I thought you had to go back to Chicago."

"I do, but I can take a late plane. Let's spend the day together. You decide what we do."

"I have to meet a client in the morning to go over her itinerary. But maybe after that we could—"

"I'm so glad you said that. I almost forgot I have a conference call in the morning. What is it with you people who work on Saturdays?"

"I work with the public. What's your excuse?"

"My excuse is I work with a bunch of nerds. Raul—I think you met him at the hotel." The circumstances flooded back to her and she slapped her forehead. "Of course you did. How could I forget that? Anyway, we need to hire a new programmer and he's lined up one of his buddies for a phone interview in the morning."

Judith stood and picked up her coat. "Why don't you meet me for lunch?"

"Name the place."

"What will you eat besides Italian?"

"I'll eat Polish." The stunned look on Judith's face was priceless, and Carmen couldn't resist lofting her eyebrows lasciviously.

"Pierogi it is, then. Meet me at Washington Square at noon, and wear your walking shoes."

Carmen held her coat while she put it on. "Do you want me to ride home with you in a taxi?"

"No, I'll just take the subway. I'll be fine."

"But it's nearly midnight. Please let me get you a taxi."

"Carmen, I've lived here all my—"

"Please," she said, as emphatically as she could without shouting. "I'm sorry. If you go off on the subway, I'll worry from the time you leave until I hear that you're home safe with your doors locked. I simply can't endure all that stressful waiting on only one drink."

"Fine, I'll take a taxi, but you don't have to escort me home. You should get some rest and get ready for your call tomorrow."

They stepped into the elevator and pressed the button for the ground floor.

"I'll wait with you downstairs, at least." The car abruptly stopped and a young woman got on. She pressed the already-lit ground floor button to continue their descent, and leaned against the rail on the opposite side from where they stood holding hands.

Carmen looked at Judith and smiled, reading her mind. Oblivious to the other passenger, she dipped her head and stole a kiss.

"I knew you were going to do that."

"It's tradition."

Chapter 11

" . . . and you'll get forms like these on the plane before you land. You have to declare everything you buy in Europe. Just try to keep it under four hundred dollars a day." Judith folded the documents and stuffed them into the travel portfolio.

"Is that four hundred each or between us?" Carla Person asked.

"Each."

"Like it matters. We're going to spend every last nickel to do stuff, not to buy it and bring it home."

Judith handed over the documents, stealing a glance at the wall clock. It was ten till twelve. "It's going to be a fabulous trip, Carla."

"Thanks. I really appreciate all you've done to put this together at the last minute. Laura's going to have the time of her life." Tears rimmed Carla's eyes as she gathered her belongings.

"I hope you both enjoy every minute," Judith said, near tears herself. She enveloped the young woman in a hug. "And make sure you keep all your medical documents with you in case Laura has an emergency."

"We will."

When she had gone, Judith took a tissue from a box on her desk and blew her nose.

Todd appeared in the doorway. "What was that all about?"

"She and her partner are leaving Monday for a three-week tour of Europe."

"And you're both crying about it?"

"Her partner has ovarian cancer and isn't expected to live much longer."

"Oh."

"They just found out a couple of weeks ago. This was a trip they'd always talked about, but they kept putting it off." This sort of thing—a personal relationship with her customers—was just the thing Todd didn't seem to understand.

"That's too bad." He turned around and went back into his office.

Judith grabbed her fleece jacket from the back of her chair and pulled it on. She was looking forward to her escape from the office, especially after the sorrowful meeting with Carla. A brisk, four-block walk over to Washington Square was just what she needed to clear her head. She put the last of her papers away and started for the door.

"Judith?" Todd was standing in his office door.

She gave the clock another glance. "Something else?"

"I have these . . . they're upgrade coupons. I got them at the trade show last summer. What airline are your friends using?"

"Continental."

He handed over two first-class upgrades. "They're supposed to be good for any time if they have seats available. And here's one for a free night at the Ritz-Carlton . . . any city in Europe."

Judith was overwhelmed at the gesture, and felt her eyes filling with tears again. "Todd, this is wonderful. Thank you. It's just so . . ." She kissed him on the cheek and spun back into her office to make the ticket changes.

Carmen would have to wait a few minutes.

Carmen peered through the fare sticker in the taxi window at Washington Square Park. She had strolled around this part of the city a few years ago with Sofia. She appreciated the casual feel, a contrast to the high fashion, bustling crowds of midtown she usually encountered on her visits to New York.

"Right here's fine," she said, pushing a ten through the small window. "Keep it."

She got out at the curb and scanned the area for a place to wait. Judith's call that she would be a few minutes late had come only ten minutes ago, so Carmen had at least a few minutes to kill.

Dozens of people were gathered around the animal runs, where spirited dogs pranced, dug in the dirt and sniffed one another. Prissy would never stand for sharing a space that small with other animals. She growled if another dog came within thirty feet.

Carmen turned and wandered across the park, noting the diversity of the crowd. There were yuppies with elaborate strollers, tattooed teenagers lying in the grass and homeless people. Tourists documented it all with their cameras. It was interesting to think of this as Judith's territory, where she relaxed and mingled. Carmen could almost picture her at the fruit stand or sitting on one of the benches eating a bag of popcorn.

A familiar figure appeared at the corner and entered the park, and Carmen smiled with delight. Judith was wearing faded jeans, a pale yellow V-neck sweater and a blue jacket, unzipped. A scarf was wrapped loosely around her neck, prompting Carmen to envision pulling it off and attacking the skin underneath it. She watched as Judith stopped to speak to a homeless woman and hand her a small paper bag.

"Hey, pretty lady," Carmen said, eyeing Judith brazenly from head to toe as she walked closer. "Don't you look cute!"

"Right. I should have known you'd still be dressed up." Judith leaned up and gave her a peck on the lips.

"It's all I had." She was wearing gray wool slacks, a matching cashmere turtleneck and the ever-present Burberry raincoat. "That woman you just talked to . . . you know her?"

"That's Agnes. She lives in the neighborhood. Whenever I have a little extra from eating out, I always try to find her."

"That's really nice of you." And not at all surprising, she thought, remembering the incident with the waiter.

"I can't believe you wore those shoes."

Carmen lifted up her foot to show the bottom of her pumps. "I wear them all the time. They're comfortable."

"But you don't walk for miles every day, do you?"

"Are you going to make me walk for miles?"

"You wanted Polish food, right?"

"Well"—she drew out the word—"that's not exactly what I said."

Judith smacked her arm gently. "I heard what you said. And I'm taking you to Teresa's and force-feeding you borscht."

"That's beets, right? I can handle beets." She offered her elbow to Judith, who steered them through the park and out the other side. "Your boss must be a slave driver to keep you late on Saturday."

"Normally, I'd say yes, but my opinion of him skyrocketed today."

Carmen heard the story of the two women making a final, poignant trip. When Judith's voice cracked, it stirred Carmen so much she instinctively pulled her closer and wrapped an arm around her shoulder. "That's very sad. And I'm sorry it's hurting you."

"I'm just glad I was able to help them out."

"Of course you are."

Judith went on to talk about her boss's gesture, but Carmen was still caught up with the sensation of wanting to give comfort, to hold her close. It was strange to feel that way, because it wasn't Judith's tragedy, just something that moved her and made her sad. And for that reason, it made Carmen sad too.

They walked several blocks, stopping finally at a diner on First Avenue.

"This is probably the best traditional Polish food you're going to find in Manhattan," Judith said as they were shown to a booth. "I can't believe we're getting a table so fast. Usually, they're packed."

"Hope that doesn't mean the cook quit." She studied the menu. "Look at all these porcine delicacies . . . pig's feet, pig's knuckles. Can't they just serve ham?"

"Where's your sense of adventure?"

Carmen closed her menu. "It's sitting across from you. Order whatever you think I should have."

"If Cathy were here, she'd probably make you get the borscht. But I think you ought to try the pierogi too. Do you want meat or vegetables?"

"I probably should get vegetables. I don't usually eat a heavy meal in the middle of the day."

"It's better for you than eating it at night, you know. Let's get some of both . . . with a cucumber salad and some potato pancakes."

An obviously harried waitress slid two overflowing glasses of water across their table and pulled an order pad from her apron. Carmen kept expecting her to say something, but she took the order from Judith and left without a word.

"Not very friendly."

"Really? I didn't notice," Judith answered. "Did you have

your conference call?"

"I did. I probably would have forgotten it even after we talked about it last night, but Cathy called a half hour ahead of time to remind me."

"She really keeps you organized, doesn't she?"

"I don't know what I'd do without her . . . or actually, what I will do without her. She wants to retire."

"Aren't you two the same age?"

"Yeah, but she's got grandchildren she wants to play with. She hates traveling to conferences because she won't get on an airplane." She took a sip of her water and wiped the excess drops off the table with her napkin. "At least she's willing to work my schedule. Where else am I going to find an administrative assistant who'll call me on a Saturday morning?"

"Your whole staff seems to be like that."

"They are. I'm lucky to have every single one of them. I know if we had an important deadline, they'd all be in the office on a Sunday afternoon."

"And I bet they stay with you because you take care of them," Judith said.

"I try to. But I've come to depend on Cathy so much that I don't keep up with things like I should."

"No one can do it all."

Cathy said the same thing every time she persuaded Carmen to hire more help and delegate responsibility. "Speaking of not having to work on Saturday, have you thought any more about Sofia?"

"You mean while I was sleeping? We just talked about that a few hours ago."

It was impossible not to appreciate Judith's quick wit. "I plan to nag you until you call her."

"Fine. At least give me a couple of weeks to see if this being able to stand my boss is permanent."

The waitress interrupted to deposit an armload of plates and bowls. Carmen was surprised when she actually spoke, pointing out which of the dumplings contained meat, and which contained vegetables.

"Why don't we set these in the middle?" Judith rearranged the plates so they could share. "My brother likes the potato pancakes."

"You started to tell me about him last night. He lives in Brooklyn, right?"

"That's right. Victor . . ." She swallowed a bite of pierogi and took a sip of water. "Victor lives in a group home for adults with mental disabilities. He's classified as severely retarded, but he's able to do a lot of things for himself. He even has a part-time job at McDonald's."

The information came as such a shock that Carmen floundered for a response. "So he . . . lives in a group home." What was the right response?

"Yeah, he's been away since he was twelve. That's when he got too big for Mom to handle. He was violent sometimes, and she was afraid he would hurt somebody."

Carmen hoped her reaction had seemed more normal than it felt. She had never been confronted with the issue before, at least not with someone close to her. The only thing she could do was follow Judith's lead. "Is he still violent?"

"Not often, but he gets very agitated if his routines are disrupted. Then he's more dangerous to himself than he is to someone else."

"What does he do?"

"Mostly, he just tries to run away."

Carmen absently took a bite of the potato pancake, her mind reeling with questions and things she thought she should say.

"But he hasn't done that in a long time."

"Do you see him often?"

"I usually go every Sunday. We take the subway up to Greenpoint where Mom lives. She has a big lunch and then we all take a walk together or something."

"That's nice."

"Yeah, he looks forward to it every week. If I can't make it, he gets confused about what day it is and they have a hard time getting him ready to go to work the next day."

"What happens when your mother goes?"

"Mom can't bring herself to go, not even for his annual review. She's been like that ever since I turned fifteen and started going by myself. I think she still feels guilty for having to put him somewhere."

"That's too bad. I'm sure it was best for everyone."

"For Victor, especially. He's healthy and happy, and he does more for himself now than anyone ever thought he would."

Suddenly aware she had stopped eating, Carmen scooped another pierogi onto her plate. "So Victor is why you said your husband knew that asking you to move to Boston was the same as asking for divorce."

"And why Noelle knew I wouldn't consider coming with her to Paris."

And why their own relationship would probably be limited to occasional weekends in New York, Carmen realized. "It's wonderful that you're so devoted to him."

"I've loved him as long as I can remember. I was probably four or five years old before I understood that he wasn't like everyone else."

Carmen loved her siblings too, but with a family of overachievers, everything had always been easy. Perhaps it was growing up with a brother like Victor that had made Judith the way she was—a woman who seemed to care more about others than she did about herself.

Judith waited solemnly on the sidewalk, granting Carmen all the time she needed to view the World Trade Center memorial site. On the way from the restaurant, she had described her memories of that awful day, watching the smoke billow as sirens wailed throughout the city. But the physical site of the disaster was something people had to experience for themselves.

When Carmen joined her on the sidewalk, there were tears in her eyes. "Every time I come to New York, I think about doing that. I'm glad I finally did."

"What was it like in Chicago?"

"They evacuated our building—we're in the Sears Tower—and the Hancock Building. Most of us just went back home. I called everybody that day and talked about it. It was like I needed to touch everyone I knew."

She took hold of Carmen's hand as they started walking away from the site. "It was like that here too. I wanted to go be with Mom, but the only way out of Manhattan was on foot."

"What did you do?"

"We all hung out in the hallways with our doors open. That night, a bunch of us sat out on the steps."

"People got closer, even with strangers."

"Yeah, we aren't all that close anymore, but I think we all feel like we went through it together. At least we know each other's names now." Following Carmen's lead, she slowed her pace to a stroll, noticing a slight limp in Carmen's gait. "You okay?"

Carmen hesitated, but finally muttered, "I hate being wrong, almost as much as I hate admitting it."

"Your feet hurt."

"Just the left one. I think I'm getting a blister on my little toe."

"That's enough walking for today, then." She felt a wave of disappointment that their time together was almost over, and that this would probably hasten Carmen's departure. "Do you want to go back to your hotel?"

Carmen checked her watch. "I should head back there about four, but it's only three. Why don't you invite me to your place?"

"Of all the places in New York, surely we can find something more interesting than my place."

"I didn't hang around today to see New York. I stayed to be with you."

Though she loved hearing that, Judith wouldn't let herself read too much into it. In the back of her mind, this whole weekend had been about erasing the ugly memory of what had happened at the convention. That was done, as far as Judith was concerned, no matter what happened next. She genuinely liked the person underneath Carmen's corporate persona, and she felt assured that Carmen now saw past her resemblance to Brooke.

"We can go to my place if you promise not to make fun of how small it is."

"Would I do something like that?" Carmen asked, her voice tinged with mischief.

The subway was out of the question with Carmen's foot hurting, since it meant walking a couple of blocks on each end. Judith stopped at the corner and dropped Carmen's hand. "Stay put. I'll get us a cab." Three taxis passed before one lurched to the curb. She held the door while Carmen slid into the backseat. "Eighth Avenue and Fifteenth Street, please."

Carmen kicked off her shoe and examined her injured toe.

"How is it?"

"It feels good to sit."

"Are you familiar with the term walk-up?"

"You mean an apartment without an elevator? Sure."

"And the term fifth-floor walk-up?" She laughed evilly at the look of horror on Carmen's face. "Sure you don't want to go back to your luxurious hotel?"

"I've already checked out. They're just holding my bag." She looked at her toe again. "Can you bring me oxygen on the third floor landing?"

"It's a pretty good setup for never having to entertain. People find out where I live and say 'forget it.'"

"Do you really not want me to come?"

"No, I do. But you should know that I don't show my place to just anybody."

"Are you saying I'm special?"

The taxi stopped suddenly at the corner, saving Judith from having to answer what was becoming obvious.

She counted out a small stack of ones to cover the fare, and held out her hand to help Carmen from the backseat. "Remember, you promised not to make fun."

"After hauling my ass up all those stairs, I probably won't have breath to speak."

Judith started up the steps of her brownstone. "These don't count because they're outside."

"Yippee."

She was glad to see the hallway had been swept this morning and cleared of debris. The super, who lived in the building next door, was better than most. Though slow to fix things inside the apartments, he usually kept the common areas clean and in good repair, and cracked down on nuisance tenants. On this street, one couldn't ask for much more than that.

"Nice floor," Carmen said, eyeing the worn black-and-white tile of the stairs. "Some of the older buildings in Chicago are like this."

"Do you have a house?" They reached the second floor.

"No, a condo next to Lincoln Park. It's by the lake."

"In that case, you aren't allowed to make fun of my view, either," Judith said as she reached the third floor. "Only two more to go."

Carmen waved her on. "You run on ahead. Get the oxygen ready."

By the time they reached the fifth floor, Carmen was feigning exhaustion, but Judith guessed it was all for show, because she wasn't even out of breath. "You're a faker."

"I was hoping I'd get you to carry me. Then I could just drape my arms around your neck and look all dreamy and helpless."

"You don't strike me as the helpless type."

"I'm not really. But you know how much I like elevators," she said, leaning forward in search of a kiss.

Judith let her purse fall to the floor and wrapped her arms around Carmen's neck as she was pressed against the door to her apartment. Not caring that any of her three neighbors on the floor might suddenly open their door, she luxuriated in the familiar sensation of Carmen's mouth on hers. The woman could kiss.

"I think I'm going to regret us not getting here sooner," Carmen murmured, nipping gently at her earlobe.

Judith felt the same surge of desire, especially since their bodies were in contact from their heads to their knees. "I might not let you leave."

"Will you at least let me use your bathroom?"

Judith sighed. "Are you always this romantic?"

"Just when my bladder's full."

She spun in Carmen's arms and put her key in the lock. Unable to bend down because of the arms that still surrounded her, she kicked her purse into the apartment as she opened the door. "Yes, I know it's small, but it's perfect for one."

She was proud of her home, especially the creative ways she maximized her space with the loft and built-in cabinets. But Carmen would probably be shocked to imagine anyone living in such a small place, and dubious about her claims that she actually was quite comfortable.

Inside the kitchen, Carmen was immediately drawn to the corner window, where a table for two was flush with the windowsill.

"Is this the view you were talking about?"

"One of them." A courtyard garden was visible in the back. "The woman on the first floor tends that. She just put the flowers out last week."

"It's nice."

"It's right outside her window. She started it a few years ago to keep people from dumping their junk out there. Now we all look forward to it every spring."

Carmen looked around the tidy room, clearly impressed. "Do you mind?" she asked, grasping the handle of the narrow pantry door.

"Help yourself. That's for food and groceries. I also have some space under the sink." She gestured to the cabinet and counter, only three feet in length. "Dishes are up here. Pots and pans are down below."

"It's everything you need. Do you cook a lot?"

"Nothing elaborate. I just don't have the counter space to pull it off."

"So no romantic dinners for two?"

"I didn't say that." But she could have. Only one of the women she had dated since moving into this apartment had ever visited here.

Carmen walked through the doorway into the other room. "You have an upstairs?"

"Just a loft. I keep my clothes up there, and a few boxes of things I don't use much." She waited nervously as Carmen inspected the room, taking in all the details of her home.

"I hope you don't take this the wrong way . . ." Carmen stuck her head into the tiny bathroom and turned back around to face her. "This reminds me of those guys who come in and organize your closets. But you've done it for your whole apartment."

"Everyone in New York does this."

"I bet you pack a suitcase like a pro."

"Technically, I am a pro."

Carmen smirked and disappeared into the bathroom. "I can reach everything in here from where I'm sitting," she shouted from behind the closed door.

"I'm a strong believer in efficiency."

A few moments later, Carmen emerged and walked over to the futon. "I take it this is your little love nest."

"Yeah, I'm surprised there was no one in it already when we got here."

"It's the stairs."

"Do you want something to drink?"

"I just got rid of something to drink. I need to look at my poor little foot again." She sat down and pulled off her shoe and nylon sock. "Just as I thought. You abused me making me walk so far."

"I can fix it."

"You'll kiss it?"

"I'll put a Band-Aid on it."

"That'll have to do."

Judith found a bandage in the bathroom cabinet and presented it.

"You said you'd do it. I can't bear to look."

"You're a big baby." She knelt down and touched her lips gently to the blistered toes before wrapping the bandage around it.

"See? That wasn't so hard." Carmen grasped her hand and tugged her onto the futon beside her. "I have a great idea. Why don't you demonstrate your superior packing skills by coming to visit me in Chicago next weekend?"

Judith was stunned by the invitation. Even though their weekend had been fun, she never expected to be more to Carmen than someone to spend time with when her work brought her to New York, even if that developed into intimate time. "I can't."

"You can't pack? You can't visit me?"

"I can't come next weekend. It's Victor's birthday."

"Oh. Then it will have to be the weekend after that. But I suppose I should look at my schedule before I just throw out open invitations. I'd hate to have you show up and me be in Tokyo." She opened her cell phone and accessed its calendar function. "No, I'm home."

Judith still couldn't believe Carmen was inviting her to Chicago as casually as she had for dinner and a Broadway show.

"You will come, though . . . won't you?"

"If you want me to."

"Of course I do." Her voice was surprisingly serious, but then she smiled. "I'd invite myself back to New York, but I'd feel guilty for leaving the princess with the dog sitting service again. That's another reason you have to come. Once you meet Prissy, you'll know how I got to be this way."

"What way is that?"

"Nuts."

"I can't believe you're blaming your personality disorder on a poor animal that isn't here to defend itself."

"Be sure to bring shoes you don't like because she'll chew them up."

All Judith had to do was find someone to cover for her at work, and make arrangements to see Victor when she got back. "I'll look for a cheap ticket. Friday after next?"

"Yeah, through Sunday night. Think you can stand me that long?"

Judith swore she heard uncertainty in Carmen's voice. It amazed her to think such a beautiful, accomplished woman was insecure about anything, but she had glimpsed that in Carmen several times. "I'm sure I'll manage."

"Good." Carmen leaned forward for a peck on the lips and looked again at her watch. "I have about five minutes before I need to get a cab back to my hotel. Can we kiss that long?"

Judith fell into Carmen's embrace, meeting her lips for a long, slow kiss. Finally they broke and she leaned back nearly breathless. "The hardest thing about kissing you is stopping."

"No, the hardest thing is to stop at kissing," Carmen said. "It would be easier to let go of your lips if I could move on to something else."

She told herself not to ask, but the words came out anyway. "What would you do next?"

Carmen lunged for her again, this time crushing her with a kiss as her palm wandered up to cover Judith's breast. "I'd kiss it all . . . every inch."

Judith blew out a frustrated breath and shook her head to clear it. "I swear, my whole body reacts to every word you say."

"Does your body want to come to Chicago?"

Carmen's other hand was now massaging her ass, and all she could think was that she wanted to come in New York. "Definitely."

"I promise you a trip to remember."

"I have no doubt." She met Carmen in another fervent kiss, gasping as cool fingers snaked beneath her sweater and bra to find her nipple, which hardened instantly. "Are you sure you have to fly out tonight?"

"Believe me, I would never leave this if I didn't have to."

Judith hissed as she sucked cold air between her teeth. She clutched Carmen's forearm and pulled it out of her shirt. "You have to stop, Carmen. I won't let you leave if you don't stop now."

"I know." She rested her forehead on Judith's shoulder. "But I'm going to think about that nipple for two whole weeks . . . Judith's pointy nipple."

She looked down at what Carmen was seeing. Indeed, her nipple strained against her sweater. "Let's . . . forget about my nipple for the moment . . . if we can. It's a little after four. If you're going to miss your plane, tell me now."

"I can't."

"Then we should go. Let's walk out to Eighth Avenue and I'll get you a cab."

"And you promise to come see me in two weeks."

"I will." It was the only way she could let Carmen walk out of her apartment.

Carmen leaned back in her first-class leather seat and sipped a scotch with her left hand. With her right, she rolled her thumb and index fingers together, trying to recapture in her mind the feel of Judith's nipple as it became erect. The next two weeks were going to drag by, despite the hectic schedule she faced at work.

She would have to let Cathy know first thing on Monday to reschedule her meeting in San Diego for another day. At present, she was scheduled to land at O'Hare at eleven thirty on Friday night, the same night Judith was due to arrive in Chicago. No way was she going to give up even a minute of time they could be together.

Judith O'Shea had gotten to her. Not like Robin, the personal trainer, or Kim Tau, the magazine editor with whom she had spent five years. Or any of the other women who had piqued her sexual interest and hung around until she was forced to admit it was a relationship. Only one other person had gotten to her the way Judith had—Brooke Healey. And that realization both terrified and thrilled her.

Chapter 12

Judith loved Sundays. While most people looked forward to languishing in bed on this day of rest, her habit was to get up early and head out for a hot, buttery croissant and a strong latte. Then she would return to her apartment to devour both her breakfast and the Sunday *Times*. Most Sundays, she followed that with a leisurely shower and the trip to Brooklyn.

She had an extra task today—making a reservation to Chicago for the weekend after next. It was a popular route, which meant virtually all airlines would offer it at the same price. As her laptop booted up, she watched through the window as the sun broke through the clouds for the first time in almost a week. It was too bad Carmen wasn't still in town.

That thought drew her eyes to the futon, where she had fantasized before falling asleep last night about Carmen's hands and mouth all over her . . . every inch, she had said. That mystery would undoubtedly be revealed in a couple of weeks, and Judith's greatest fear was that she would disappoint. Carmen was overtly sexual, and while Judith knew her body would respond, she wasn't as confident she could reciprocate, at least not on the level Carmen might expect.

She logged on to the wireless network, which she shared through an informal arrangement with her neighbors on the other side of the wall. A quick check of her e-mail yielded a delightful surprise—a note from Carmen. She read quickly, just to make sure things were as they had left them yesterday afternoon. Her eyes went wide as she realized Carmen had already made her reservation out of LaGuardia at six thirty on Friday, arriving at O'Hare at eight that night. She would have dinner waiting . . . and hoped Judith would accept her invitation to stay at her home rather than a hotel.

Judith almost laughed at the last bit. She had never even considered staying in a hotel, especially after their heated session on the futon. That struck her as yet more evidence of Carmen's insecurity, something that made absolutely no sense.

She typed her reply, chiding Carmen over purchasing the ticket already, but thanking her just the same. A six thirty departure would squeeze her a bit, but she could make it, and yes, she wanted to stay in Carmen's home. This insecurity needed to be put to rest.

If she lived to be a hundred years old, Carmen would never regret naming Lenore vice president of The Delallo Group. The young woman would be running her own company someday unless Carmen found a way to bring her on as a partner.

"So this is our timetable for conversion," Lenore explained, standing at the head of the conference table by the glossy white erasure board. Her prop was a multi-colored PERT chart outlining a work plan to complete the time-share transition for Bill

Hinkle and Franklin Resorts. "Obviously, this is the first critical piece." She circled a marker that read "hire additional programmer."

"I liked your friend," Carmen said, spinning in her chair to face Raul. "But his salary demands are a little high."

"He's worth it, Carmen. He's one of the best."

"He's asking for almost as much as you make, and you've worked here six years. Does that seem fair to you?"

"You could pay me more if it would make you feel better."

She rolled her eyes dramatically. Her employees were well-compensated, but worth every penny.

Cathy entered the conference room carrying a cardboard box. "Lunch is here." She set the box on the desk and began to take the items out. "Here's a Greek salad for Lenore . . . roast beef for Raul . . . and a roast beef for Carmen."

Carmen's mouth was watering already. The only thing rarer than the Quincy Street Deli's roast beef was the occasion for her to eat it. Cathy seldom let her order—"Hey! This is turkey."

"They were out of roast beef," Cathy replied nonchalantly.

Carmen glanced at Raul, who quickly tucked his sandwich beneath the table. "He has roast beef."

"They ran out right after that." She picked up the box and left the room, with Carmen in pursuit.

"Do you have to do this all the time?" she demanded, dropping the turkey sandwich on Cathy's desk.

Cathy set the box beside it and reached inside, pulling out another sandwich, which she slapped into Carmen's hand. "For your information, I don't enjoy policing your diet, but you won't do it yourself. I happen to care about you. I figured you probably didn't pay attention to your cholesterol this weekend and thought you ought to get back in the habit of eating right."

Carmen scowled, remembering the Alfredo sauce on Friday, the rich pierogi on Saturday, and the London broil at her mother's yesterday. Though it pained her, she tossed the roast beef back into the box and picked up the turkey. "Sorry."

"When are you going to start taking better care of yourself?"

"You didn't even ask about my weekend."

"And you didn't ask about mine."

Carmen was startled by the sharpness of her friend's tone, but the words nailed her. "I'm sorry. That was selfish."

"It's okay."

"You're always too quick to forgive me when I act like a shit. You should let me wallow in it for at least a few minutes." She sat in the chair opposite Cathy's desk, putting aside the meeting that continued without her in the other room. "Tell me about your weekend."

Cathy rummaged in the box for a salad before carrying the rest of the items out to the receptionist's counter. When she returned, she sat in the chair beside Carmen. "I had Ramona and Simon for the whole weekend. We met up yesterday with Priscilla and her granddaughter at the zoo in Lincoln Park. We thought about stopping in to say hi, but I figured you wouldn't want three screaming kids running out on your balcony."

"It would have been okay, except I wasn't home. Paul brought his new girlfriend to Mom and Dad's for lunch. It was a big deal for everyone to finally meet her."

"Is this the one?"

"Who knows? He's fifty-six years old. I'd say he's not the marrying type."

"It only takes one. Did you like her?"

"Yeah. She seems like a good person. She runs some kind of literacy foundation that teaches adults to read."

Cathy took a bite of her salad and mumbled, "You want to talk about Judith?"

"I will if you like, or we can talk some more about your grandkids."

"They wore me out. But I'd rather make you listen later when I bring pictures. Go ahead and tell me what you did this week-

anyone until you fall out of love with her." She leaned over and picked up a small stack of pink messages. "Speak of the devil, guess who called?"

"Did she say what she wanted?"

"She wants us all for a girls' night this Sunday at your place."

"My place?"

"She said there weren't any men at your house."

"Are you coming?"

"Sure. Hank's two brothers are staying with us for the whole weekend and I'll be ready for a night without men."

"Why aren't all of you lesbians?"

"Men aren't that bad. All you have to do is find one who listens to you even when his mother's in the room."

"Does Hank do that?"

"In spades."

Carmen chuckled. "I suppose I could cook something for all of us . . . veal scaloppine maybe." She caught a stern look from her friend. "What I obviously meant to say was some kind of whole grain pasta tossed with vegetables and tofu."

"That sounds delicious. I'll bring cheesecake." Cathy got up to go back to her desk.

"Wait a—" She could only shake her head. "Thank you for my lovely lunch. I assume you paid out of petty cash since we're technically in a meeting."

"I did."

"Good. I need to get rolling on hiring that new programmer. And I'm going to have to give Raul a little raise to put some distance between them."

"Good help is expensive. I try to keep my job performance in line with my salary so you won't ever have to give me a raise."

"Sometimes I think I should just fire you all and go back to working out of my house."

"You'd have a heart attack within a month. Now go call Brooke and tell her we're on."

Carmen walked out, fantasizing again that this was her company and she was in charge.

"No, Victor. That's too big for one bite." Judith got up from her chair and went around the table. "Switch your fork to this hand." She tapped his left wrist. "Now take your knife and cut your meat. You remember how to do that."

This was a difficult task for her brother, one he didn't practice much at the group home, since the food was always presented in bite-size portions.

"Tell her kielbasa's your favorite food, honey. That's why you try to eat it so fast." Judith knew, for Halina Kowalczyk, there was no better feeling in the world than having her daughter and son at her dinner table on Sunday. And this week was extra special because it was Victor's forty-seventh birthday.

"Doesn't he look handsome in his new shirt?" Judith grinned joyously as Victor smiled and blushed. "I bet Stacey likes it."

The mention of his favorite staffer made his smile even wider.

"Good job, Victor." She returned to her seat to finish her meal. "I'm going to be out of town next weekend, Mom."

"Will you be back in time to bring Victor on Sunday afternoon?"

"No, I'm going to Chicago to visit someone. I won't get back until Sunday night."

"So I won't get to see Victor next week," her mother said dismally.

It had been at least a year since they last talked about her mother going to the group home on her own. But with Carmen in the picture—and the hope for Judith that she might visit Chicago on a regular basis—it was a good time to raise the issue again.

"You know, you could go on your own very easily."

Halina shook her head. "You know I don't like to go to that

place."

"It's a very nice facility, very comfortable."

"But it's still a facility," she hissed.

"It's Victor's home, Mom. He likes it there and he's doing very well." She hated to talk about her brother as if he weren't there. "Isn't that right, Victor? You like living at Wyckoff, don't you?"

He gave a weak smile and began to rock forward and back in his chair, a sign he was getting agitated at the tone of the conversation.

"It's okay. Everyone's okay," Judith said in her most reassuring voice. She looked at her mother, who was also smiling and patting Victor's hand. "Why don't we walk to McCarren Park before we come back and have dessert?"

"That's a great idea," her mother said with exaggerated enthusiasm. "And guess what we're having for dessert, Victor."

"I bet it's someone's birthday cake," Judith answered, relieved to see her brother growing calmer. "Let's go get our coats on."

She put on her fleece pullover before helping Victor with his Windbreaker.

"Do you have another convention in Chicago?" Halina asked as they walked out.

"No, I'm going to visit a friend." Moments like these always made Judith squirm with discomfort. Telling the whole truth—that she was romantically involved with another woman—wasn't an option where her mother was concerned. Judith had imagined the hysterical scene a thousand times. Yet, she couldn't resist the chance to talk about the fascinating woman who filled her thoughts. "I met her at the convention a few weeks ago. She's a research consultant and knows everybody in the travel business."

"Are you still thinking about changing jobs?"

"I wouldn't say no to better commissions." Her mother understood how her job worked, but she had no idea of her agency's clientele.

"I hope you're not thinking about moving to Chicago."

"No, Mom." Judith took her brother's arm as they neared Bedford Street. "Victor, show Mom when you're supposed to cross the street."

She and her mother grinned with pride as Victor led the way when the pedestrian light flashed white.

"You're so smart, honey," Halina gushed.

"Tell her you learn a lot at Wyckoff, Victor." She said that just to get under her mother's skin. No, she wasn't moving to Chicago, but she wouldn't mind visiting—a lot. That meant being gone on weekends, though, and her mother would have to step up for Victor.

Without speaking, they followed the path through the park to a bench, where they settled with Victor in the middle. Halina fussed over the zipper in her son's jacket. "You need to keep warm, honey."

"Mom, I have an idea for when I get back from Chicago. What if I come by here on Monday after work and we both go down to Wyckoff? That way, he gets to visit with you and show you some of his new pictures. We don't have to stay there long. We can take him out for a walk." She rubbed her brother's back as she talked about him. "He likes going out in that neighborhood too." She held her breath while waiting to see how her mother would handle the invitation.

"I can miss a week without seeing him here and there."

"But what about him? He wants to see you."

"I know that. That's why I think you should come back early on Sunday. He gets to walk around in that neighborhood all the time, but he only gets to come home when you bring him."

The guilt trip was an old routine, but Judith had learned how to play that game too. "Why can't you go get him on Sunday and bring him back here by yourself? They can have him ready to leave and all you have to do is drop him at the door when you go back."

This time, her mother wouldn't answer.

"I bet Victor would like to show you his room and how nice he keeps his things. And he has a lot of new pictures up. Isn't that right, Victor?"

Her brother began to rock again.

"He likes it better when you bring him home and we can all be together. Don't you, honey?"

Judith was on the verge of losing her temper, but she had been the one to start this. It was clear they couldn't have this conversation with Victor present. She smiled at her mother in an effort to quell his anxiety, but her words were on point. "All I'm saying is that I can make time to go to Wyckoff and see him at least once a week, but that might not mean every Sunday if I start traveling more or doing things with my friends. I don't want you to miss out on seeing Victor just because I might be busy."

"You could always invite your friends to come along to Sunday dinner if you want to spend time with them. If they're real friends, they'll want to know your brother too."

Judith bit the inside of her cheek, holding back a burst of anger. As long as she could remember, her mother had discouraged her from bringing friends to the house because it interfered with her attention to Victor. Now she suddenly wanted to be the Welcome Wagon.

Victor suddenly stood and spun around. No matter how much they tried to disguise the tension in their voices, he picked up on it with uncanny acuity.

"Looks like someone I know is ready for his birthday cake, Mom."

"I think we should get ice cream too. Would you like that, Victor?"

Judith was glad to see her brother's smile return. This was his special day, and not a day for him to get upset. But the door to getting her mother down to Wyckoff had been opened. They would talk about it again, but not in front of Victor.

ᕦ

"Prissy, no!" Carmen dropped her basting brush and took off in pursuit of the dachshund, who had appeared briefly in the kitchen doorway to taunt her with a slipper between her teeth. "Give me that!"

The dog dashed into the guest bedroom and under the bed.

"Come on, Prissy. Don't do this to me right now. Mommy doesn't have time to play." Actually, the salads were tossed and the bread was buttered and ready to go into the oven. "Oh, fine."

She retrieved a squeaky toy from the living room and gave it several sharp squeezes. As always, the sound drew Prissy out to play. "I can't believe how spoiled you are. Who did that to you?"

Prissy barked and pranced, demanding she throw the toy. She did, and in a flash, the dog was back in front of her, dropping it at her feet for another toss. Carmen threw it a few more times before kneeling to cover Prissy with a playful hug and force her onto her back for a belly rub. "You better not tell a soul I treat you like this. You're such a big baby, but you're Mommy's girl, aren't you?"

The doorbell rang.

"Someone's here. Act aloof."

No such luck, as Prissy barreled toward the door yapping. Carmen opened it to Priscilla.

"Prissy!" Priscilla dropped to all fours as Carmen had to lavish the dog with attention.

"I'll be up here whenever you're ready to say hello."

"Your mommy's ill-tempered, isn't she? Come to Auntie Priscilla and let me love you."

Carmen rolled her eyes at the love-fest on the floor. "Be sure to wash your hands with antibacterial soap because I think she has worms."

Priscilla stopped suddenly and withdrew her hands. "Are you serious?"

"No."

"You're mean to everyone, aren't you?"

"I cooked."

"Here, I brought wine."

"Any sign of the others?"

"What? You think I spotted them on the street and raced to the elevator to get here first?"

"Knowing you?"

Priscilla tugged her coat off and tossed it onto the guest bed. "I wish Sofia could be here when we have nights like this. It was fun getting together in New York."

"Except Brooke wasn't there."

"No, but we had a reasonable facsimile, didn't we?"

Carmen decided to ignore that crack. "I saw Sofia again last week in New York."

"I hear you saw Judith too."

"Great. You're all talking about me behind my back. What else have you learned?"

"Now don't get all paranoid. I wanted to stop by with the grandkids last weekend and Cathy said you were staying over in New York to see her. I thought it was nice."

The doorbell rang again. "Do me a favor, Priscilla. Don't say anything about Judith in front of Brooke, okay? I haven't decided how to handle that one yet." She started for the door.

"Does it need to be handled?"

Carmen stopped and turned back, whispering, "She's coming next weekend. Now open the wine."

Before she could reach the door, Cathy and Brooke let themselves in. "You need to keep this locked if you're going to keep out the riff-raff," Brooke proclaimed with a wide grin.

Carmen froze in the entryway, momentarily stunned by the physical resemblance between Brooke and Judith. She had gotten past that with Judith, but this was different. For once, it wasn't Brooke who was pushing her buttons and causing her to well up with emotion.

From their confused expressions, she had been staring too long. "Don't just stand there. Come on in. Priscilla's pouring the wine."

"Make mine a double," Brooke said, bussing Carmen's cheek as she strode past her into the living room. "Priscilla!" She held her arms wide. "I haven't seen you in ages. I'm so glad you and Cathy said yes."

"And me?" Carmen asked.

"I see you all the time."

"In other words, how can you miss me if I won't go away?" Carmen was teasing, but she knew Cathy and Priscilla were probably weighing the merits of her question.

"I never want you to go away, silly. You're the easiest one of all my friends to talk to because you don't put up with men." Like Priscilla, Brooke got down on the floor to play with Prissy. "You don't like men either. Do you, Prissy?"

Cathy took a glass of wine from Priscilla and sat at the end of the L-shaped leather sofa. "When you said you wanted a girls' night, I figured that meant you were fed up with Geoffrey. What's he done?"

"Just the same old, same old. I was so jealous when I talked to Carmen in New York and heard all of you were going out. I wanted to be there too."

Priscilla joined them in the living room and sat next to Cathy. "You were there . . . in spirit, anyway. At least it seemed like that to all of us."

Carmen shot Cathy and Priscilla a stern look as they chuckled.

"I left Roger at home doing laundry," Priscilla said, patting the couch so her namesake would join her.

"All the men at my house were watching the basketball tournament. They didn't mind me coming over here, but Hank nearly threw himself under the wheels of the car when he saw me trying to leave with the cheesecake."

"You brought cheesecake?" Priscilla's face lit up.

Cathy looked away sheepishly. "No, I left it with them."

"You're such a sucker!" Brooke squealed.

"They were pitiful. What if one of them had starved while I was gone? I would have felt terrible."

As Carmen sank onto the couch, she thought she noticed Brooke wiping a tear. "You okay?"

Brooke nodded hastily. "Just something in my eye. I'll go see about it." She jumped up and disappeared into the bathroom, not the guest bath in the hallway, but Carmen's bath in the master suite. Carmen liked that Brooke felt completely at home.

The three women sat silently until Brooke joined them again. "It was an eyelash. It's okay now."

"So how do you like your new job, Brooke?"

"It's fantastic!"

Carmen went into the kitchen to put the bread in the oven. "Why don't you tell us about it while we eat all this delicious food that isn't cheesecake?"

For the next two hours, the four friends ate, laughed and talked, all reveling in their conspiratorial freedom from men. Even Prissy celebrated, secretly scoring pieces of mozzarella cheese from each of the visitors. When the food was gone, they retreated to the living room for coffee, which Carmen splashed with Bailey's since they didn't have dessert.

"I guess I should be getting home," Cathy announced. "That cheesecake will be gone by now and they'll all be starving again."

"Me too," Priscilla said. "I have to get to bed early. I have a seven o'clock breakfast with His Honor to go over his top secret ideas for bidding on the Olympics."

"You must mean the Winter Olympics, right?" Carmen asked, feigning innocence.

"Can't you see them bobsledding at the Eisenhower interchange?" Cathy quipped on her way into the guest bedroom to get their coats.

"You guys are funny. I'll be sure to share your thoughts."

"I'm glad you could make it over. We don't get to do this often enough," Carmen said, slinging her arm around Brooke's shoulder.

"We could do it again next weekend if you're free," Priscilla said, undoubtedly knowing it would get a rise out of Carmen. "Oh, never mind. I think I promised Roger we'd go to The Dells."

Cathy returned to distribute their coats, but Brooke tossed hers over the couch. "I'm not quite ready to go, unless you need me to."

"No, you can stay." All evening, Carmen had felt as if something was bothering Brooke. Now that the others were leaving, she would encourage her to talk about it.

"Cathy, I'll see you tomorrow."

"You have a conference call at eight thirty and another at nine fifteen."

"Great way to start a Monday." She held the front door as Priscilla followed Cathy out. "And you be sure to give His Honor my warmest regards."

"Should I tell him you think he's an asshole?"

"Sure, why not?" She closed the door behind her friends and turned to face Brooke, who looked as if she was on the verge of tears. "What's up with you? Is something wrong?"

Brooke suddenly wrapped her arms around Carmen's neck and began to sob.

"Brooke?" Carmen held her for several minutes while she cried, gently stroking her back and swaying slightly to soothe her. "Let's go sit down."

She led Brooke to the couch and let go of her.

"No, sit beside me."

"I will. Do you need anything? Do you want something to drink?"

Brooke shook her head.

One by one, Carmen turned out the lights in her apartment until they were in total darkness. Then she flipped a switch to turn on the gas log fireplace. In their thirty years as friends, this was how they talked, how Carmen rendered comfort. To her, the quiet repose was as intimate as sex, and the darkness helped hide her face from revealing her true feelings.

"Okay, now tell me what's wrong." She returned to Brooke's side and pulled her close. "Is it Geoffrey?"

"No . . . yes . . . God, I feel like such an idiot." She pushed away new tears. "Why did I ever marry him?"

"You loved him. I remember how you felt, how happy you were."

"Why didn't we just leave well enough alone? I would have been so much happier living with you and going over to his place for sex. That's when I loved him most, when we didn't have to try so hard to get along all goddamn day. And it's when he loved me too."

"But that wasn't what you wanted. You wanted to build a life together. You couldn't do that living with me." And Carmen couldn't have endured all those nights alone knowing Brooke was with Geoffrey.

"I can't seem to build a life with anybody, Carmen. I fucked up with Anthony and now I'm fucking up with Geoffrey. What is it about me that turns men into cold-hearted bastards?"

"You didn't do that to Anthony. He had to be born that way to be so good at it."

"But Geoffrey used to be such a nice guy. We used to laugh and make love all day."

Carmen hoped this wasn't going to turn into another conversation about Brooke and Geoffrey fucking. "Why don't you laugh now?"

"Because nothing's ever funny. It's all just pathetic." She leaned into Carmen's arms and sighed. "When Cathy said that about leaving her stupid cheesecake with Hank, it just made me cry. I can't imagine what it would feel like to love Geoffrey that much."

Carmen wished she would leave Geoffrey once and for all. It was obvious he didn't come close to giving her the kind of love she needed. He was too selfish, too wrapped up in his own needs. But she couldn't be the one to say that. Brooke would have to take that step on her own. "You two need to talk to somebody. If he won't go, then you'll have to go by yourself."

"Can't I just talk to you?"

"You know you can. But I can't help you."

"I don't know if I even want help anymore. Sometimes I think I just don't want to be married, not ever again."

Carmen tilted her head to rest against Brooke's. Her heart was filled with love and concern, and her arms ached to offer protection from that which caused her beloved friend pain. Brooke Healey had known enough pain in her life.

"Let's do something next weekend," Brooke said. "What if I pick you up on Saturday and take you on a tour of all the places I've decorated for the realtors? I'd love for you to see my work. You're the only one who really cares about it."

"We all care about it. Didn't you see how excited Cathy and Priscilla were when you were telling us?"

"I know they were interested. But that's not the same as caring about it like you do. That's why I want you to see it."

"I can't. I'm busy next weekend." It wasn't unusual for her to be busy with her work or her family, so she hoped Brooke would simply accept her vague excuse.

"Are you working? We could do it Sunday."

"I'm having company, someone from New York."

"Sofia?"

"No." Why was Brooke so interested in her personal life all of a sudden? "A woman I met at the convention last month."

Brooke sat up straight and turned to face her. "You're seeing someone? Why didn't you tell me?"

"We just met a month ago, that weekend I went for the convention."

"Did you see her again when you went back?"

Getting the third degree from Brooke was unusual. "Yeah, we had dinner and went to a show."

Brooke's face took on a confused look and she slumped against the couch.

"What's wrong?"

"Nothing. I'm just surprised you like somebody enough to invite her here for a weekend, but you don't tell your friends about it. What's with that?"

"We just started seeing each other." Carmen could almost feel her insides roiling. Hiding the truth about Judith from Brooke betrayed both of them. "Not everybody I go out with is lucky enough to meet my friends."

"And I'm not letting you fall for just anybody. She better be something special if she wants my seal of approval."

Chapter 13

"Hold on . . . almost ready." Carmen juggled a cardboard box filled with groceries, shifting it to one hip as she slipped her key into the lock. Prissy whimpered impatiently, tearing through the door as soon as it cracked open. Carmen dropped the leash and caught the falling box. "Thanks for your all your help," she said sarcastically.

She lugged the box into the kitchen and dropped it on the counter—all the ingredients for a romantic candlelight dinner, something she hadn't orchestrated in over a dozen years.

So what was it about Judith O'Shea that had her obsessed with pulling off the perfect evening? Considering where they had left things in New York, this seduction scene probably wasn't even necessary. A hello kiss would probably send them straight to the bedroom. But she didn't want a night like the one Raul had interrupted at the hotel. She was adding the romantic element to officially undo that clumsy start, to recast their relationship as more than just a fling.

Ironically, that was Brooke's doing, because it made her think all week about what she wanted from Judith. All along, they had talked about being themselves, and Judith had shown her personal side in New York. Carmen needed to do that too.

"Please be good this weekend, Prissy. Mommy likes Judith very much and we want her to like us so she'll come back and see us again."

She got out the cutting board and cleaver to prepare the chicken. It needed to marinate for two hours, and that would put it just about right for Judith's arrival. By the clock on the stove, she would be getting to the airport in New York soon.

Unable to resist, Carmen plucked her cell phone from her purse and dialed the familiar number. It was answered after only two rings. "I hope you're in a taxi . . . No, a bus isn't sort of a taxi. I can't believe you'd endure all of that, especially dragging a suitcase." She hadn't thought fast enough to keep from saying that. It made her sound snobbish to suggest that only a fool would take mass transit. Judith did it all the time, as did millions of other people in New York. "You're welcome. I know you would have been fine in coach, but I wanted you to be relaxed when you got here. And I'm sending a car for you so you won't have to worry about a thing on this end . . . Because I'll be here cooking you a wonderful dinner, so don't eat on the plane. Mine will be better, I promise . . . Besides, I don't drive much. People tell me I'm not very good at it."

Judith's laugh brought an instant smile to Carmen's face. That's what she wanted for the weekend, a chance for them to relax and enjoy each other's company. Among other things.

Prissy began to bark at a bird on the rail of the balcony.

"Yes, that's my little precious now. Once you meet this dog of mine, you may never want to come back . . . She knows I'm talking about her . . . She'll probably run under the bed as soon as you walk in. That's how she usually handles strangers." It was also how she handled their shoes, but Carmen didn't add that. "Okay, fly safely . . . I can't wait to see you."

She hung up and sighed. Besides dinner, there wasn't much else to do to get ready for her arrival. The cleaning lady had come this morning, and Carmen had put the finishing touches on the place with fresh flowers in the dining room and sandalwood incense when she first got home. Now if she could only get the clock to move faster.

A half hour ticked by as she prepared the chicken and put it in the refrigerator to marinate. She was about to draw a bath when her phone rang.

"Hello . . . You're kidding." Judith's plane was late, something about the weather in Miami delaying the inbound flight. Then she remembered the day. "This isn't an April Fool's joke, is it?" The estimate was forty-five minutes late, which would put dinner at around nine—ten for Judith, since she was on Eastern Time. "Why don't you go ahead and eat on the plane? I don't want you to have to wait so long . . . If you're sure . . . Okay, I'll have it ready as soon as you get here."

They said good-bye and Carmen studied the clock. Lots of time. Too much time. How was she going to kill three and a half hours? Why had she left work so early? She should have worked late to pass the time and brought something in for dinner. This was going to be torture.

No, it wouldn't. She would soak in the tub and go over that report Richard had given her at lunchtime. She had brought it home only to justify tearing out of the office at a quarter to four because she couldn't concentrate anymore. She had planned to read it Sunday night.

No sooner had she settled in the tub than her cell phone, which was on the kitchen counter, began to chirp. Not wanting to miss an update from Judith, she wrapped herself in a towel and raced to answer it.

"Hello . . . That's fantastic!" The airline had miraculously produced another crew and plane, one that was leaving at seven. She would be only a half hour late after all. "Nothing important, just bathing away the grime of the day. You know how dirty office work can be."

That laugh again. She wanted to hear it all weekend. Well, not all weekend. A little screaming and moaning mixed in would be nice.

"Call me when you're in your seat . . . Prissy's very excited. I've told her all about you."

She took the phone into the bathroom this time, and climbed back into the tub. The water had cooled, so she let some out and added more hot. Only an extra half hour. That wouldn't be so bad. She could shave her legs . . . maybe even trim a little of her pubic hair. She expected that particular section of her anatomy to get a good bit of attention over the next couple of days.

She smiled immediately when the phone rang again. Judith was buckled in and on her way, for sure.

"Hello . . . No fucking way . . . I don't believe you." A security scare at LaGuardia was prompting an evacuation of the entire concourse. "I smell a conspiracy. Who did you piss off at the airlines?" Judith had no idea how long the process would take, but all outbound passengers would have to be rescreened. "Call me again when you know something."

So much for the perfect evening. There was probably no way Judith would arrive before eleven. She would be exhausted and wound tight from her ordeal. There would be no romantic candlelight dinner tonight, and no breath-stealing seduction scene.

If they were lucky, they would have tomorrow to try again.

"Thank you very much." Judith tried to hand the driver a twenty, but he waved her off.

"Ms. Delallo already took care of it. You have a nice evening."

"Thank you," she said again, turning to the building's doorman. He was smiling his welcome and ready to help her with her bag. "Hello, I'm Judith O'Shea."

He stopped suddenly as if surprised, then smiled again. "I'm Luis. You're Miss Delallo's guest. She's expecting you."

"I think she's been expecting me for quite a while. My plane was late."

"I'm so sorry. Where were you flying in from?" He led her to the elevator and pressed the button.

"New York."

"I hope you have a pleasant stay. Miss Delallo is on the fifteenth floor, unit A in the corner."

"Thank you," she said as the doors closed. It was nearly eleven o'clock, but she was too keyed up to be tired. If all those calls from Carmen were a clue, she was excited too.

When the elevator stopped, she stepped out with her bag and looked around in the hallway before knocking on the door. Her place in New York was a ghetto compared to this building. At least, that's probably what Carmen had thought. She knew she shouldn't feel this way, intimidated by Carmen's hard-earned prosperity. Carmen said she wanted to share her world this weekend, and this marvelous home was part of it, just like the first-class ticket and the limo at the airport.

Standing before unit A, she took a deep breath and gently rapped on the door. Inside, a dog began to yap frantically. She could hear Carmen trying in vain to shush the animal before she finally opened the door.

"Welcome, finally."

The wait was definitely worth it, Judith decided instantly. Gone were the stylish silk suits and cashmere sweaters she had seen in New York. This Carmen looked sensational in faded jeans and an oversized denim shirt.

"Hi." They embraced in the doorway, a hug that seemed to grow stronger every second until Judith dared to wonder what it meant. She had missed Carmen too, but she hadn't expected a welcome like this. "I'm sorry it took me so long to get here."

"I'm sorry too. I bet you're exhausted."

Prissy barked and lunged forward, demanding attention.

"Look at this little sweetheart!" She tore herself from Carmen's embrace and knelt down, holding out a hand for the black-and-tan dachshund to sniff.

Prissy sniffed, barked and jumped back. Then she edged forward to lick the outstretched hand.

"That little sweetheart only likes you if you've brought beloved possessions for her to destroy. I expect her to run under the bed any second to lie in wait."

But Prissy didn't run. She dropped to her side to expose her belly, wagging her tail excitedly.

"She looks pretty friendly to me." Judith scratched Prissy's tummy, delighted with the idea that this little one likely had Carmen wrapped around her paw. "She's still a puppy?"

"A little over a year. She's a miniature, though, so she won't get much bigger. Thank God for that, or she'd be turning over the furniture."

"She's precious, Carmen. I can't believe the way you malign this sweet dog."

"You'll believe it when she eats through the strap on your purse." Carmen rolled her suitcase in and closed the door before dropping to the rug beside her. "And whatever you do, don't feed her any people food while you're here, no matter how much she begs. Priscilla did that last weekend and she threw up on my bed in the middle of the night."

Judith looked up to take in her surroundings. The apartment looked like something out of a decorator magazine. The floors were dark oak, which matched the wainscoting and door frames. Expensive-looking artwork adorned the dark green walls of the foyer. "This is gorgeous, Carmen."

"Thank you. Prissy likes it, and that's all that really matters."

With Carmen beside her, she gave herself a tour of the modern kitchen and dining room. "I already have square footage envy, and I haven't even seen the other rooms."

"But you have an upstairs."

Judith looked down at Carmen's bare feet and kicked her own shoes off.

Carmen leaned over and picked them up, placing them on the third tier of a bookshelf in the hallway, next to her own. "Don't ever leave your shoes there. You won't recognize them the next time you see them." She shoved her hands in her pockets and led her across the foyer to an alcove that served as an entry to the guest bedroom, the guest bath and her office. "If it makes you feel better about the space, the office is the only part of this whole apartment that's mine. The rest belongs to Prissy."

Carmen looked nervous, Judith thought.

Next, they entered the living room, which was dominated by an enormous leather sectional sofa. Across from that, a fire burned low in the gas log fireplace. From the small balcony, Carmen explained, she had a distant view of the lake across Lincoln Park.

From there they strolled into the master bedroom, which held a king-sized bed in rich mahogany, with a matching dresser and nightstands. The fireplace from the living room opened into this room as well. Carmen wrapped up the tour by showing off the master bath, with its marble shower and oval tub, and enormous custom-built closet.

"See what I mean about my closet reminding me of how you organized things at your place?"

Judith noted with irony that the closet was roughly one-third the size of her place. "Would you like to hear again how jealous I am?" As she looked around, she gave in to the urge to yawn, covering her mouth. She always yawned after flying, her body's way of equalizing the pressure in her ears.

"You shouldn't be. Your apartment's perfect for you. This is perfect for Prissy. See how the shelves keep things off the floor so she can't reach them. I highly recommend dogs with very short legs."

Prissy had followed them from room to room, wagging her tail each time Carmen said her name.

"Let's go sit in the living room. Could I get you something to drink?"

"No, thank you." Their words sounded so formal, not at all what she had expected after their good-bye kiss two weeks ago in New York. That should have gotten both of them past their insecurities. "I'm glad I'm here, Carmen."

"So am I." They sat on the soft leather couch, where Prissy jumped between them, determined to disprove her reputation as unfriendly. "Make that we. She's usually shy and neurotic around new people, but she's decided to be normal for a change."

Carmen seemed determined to use Prissy as a buffer until her awkwardness dissipated. "Maybe she thinks I'm somebody else." She laughed at Carmen's scolding look, and took her hand. It was their first physical contact since the hug when she first walked in.

"I think dogs are supposed to be smarter than people."

"You mean smarter than your doorman? You should have seen the look on his face when I introduced myself." She caught herself covering another yawn.

"Please don't say he called you Mrs. Nance."

"No, but I think he was about to. You're going to have to show me a picture of Brooke so I can see for myself."

"I will . . . but not tonight." Carmen looked directly into her eyes for what seemed like the first time and said softly, "I want tonight to be about you and me."

"That sounds like a great idea."

"But my plans for sweeping you off your feet with a candlelight dinner went all to hell."

Judith was dismayed by the look of genuine disappointment.

"You swept me off my feet already, remember? And we agreed you didn't have to do that anymore."

"I know. But this wasn't about impressing you with anything. It was about me being romantic for a change instead of my usual horny self." Carmen's nervous demeanor had gone from casual to serious.

"I'm not sure you could get any more romantic than sitting here in front of a fire telling me tonight is about us."

"That was kind of profound, wasn't it?" Carmen leaned closer, her lips poised to make contact. She hovered, sharing a breath. Finally, her mouth slid gently over Judith's. The kiss was sweet and tender, the kind that warmed from the inside out.

Something was wrong. This wasn't how they kissed. Where was the hunger? The heat?

As if confirming her worries, Carmen suddenly pulled away. "You should get your rest tonight. I have a big day planned tomorrow."

Rest? Judith hadn't come all the way to Chicago to rest. Was Carmen having second thoughts? That's all it could be. Why else would she be pulling back? "You're going to kiss me like that and expect me to sleep?"

Carmen smiled and gave her a peck on the nose. "You don't have to sleep alone unless you really want to." Before she could respond, Carmen clarified, "If you leave your door open, I guarantee Prissy will visit you in the night."

"Fine, you go sleep with her. I'm trying to take the high road here," Carmen said to Prissy as she prepared for bed. "She thinks you're adorable."

Judith had showered in the guest bath and was now blow-drying her hair.

If ever Carmen had needed a cold shower, it was tonight. Restraint had never been her strong suit. All the excitement, the anticipation about taking Judith in her arms—and into her bed—had given way to something else the moment they hugged in the doorway. It wasn't as if her desire had just flown out the window. She wanted Judith even more tonight than she had that first night in the hotel. The difference was that it mattered to her now what happened next, and she wasn't going to screw that up by pretending it was only about sex.

"I can't be in love with her already," she whispered. "She'd think I was nuts."

Though falling in love didn't seem to follow any sort of rational progression, at least for Carmen. She could remember the very instant her feelings for Brooke Healey had vaulted to that realm, and there hadn't been any logic to that either.

The hair dryer stopped and the bathroom door opened. Judith was going to bed.

Carmen settled between her sheets and turned out the light, not feeling the least bit sleepy. Her head was full of questions. What had happened at the front door to spin her insides out of control?

As her eyes adjusted to the darkness, she noticed a faint glow of light in the living room, probably coming from Judith's room. "She's waiting for you, Miss Priss." She nudged the dog gently, but Prissy was already comfortable by her feet. "Go on so you can report back. I want to know what she sleeps in."

The living room suddenly flooded with light and a silhouette filled her doorway.

"Carmen?"

"Yes?" She threw back the covers and sat up. "Is everything all right?"

"That's sort of what I wanted to ask you."

"Wha—?"

"Things seem kind of, I don't know . . . different."

Things were different, but not the way Judith probably thought. And not in a way that Carmen was ready to talk about.

"There isn't anything wrong at all. I'm very glad you're here."

Judith came in and sat at the end of the bed. "Can we talk a little while? I'm not really sleepy."

"Sure." Nothing like having the object of your lust sitting at the end of your bed. "You want to go back in the living room, or is this okay?"

"This is fine with me. You have a nice room."

"Let me turn the fire back on." She got up and flipped the wall switch, bringing the flames to life. Judith was wearing long flannel pants and a tank top. "I can't believe you're not zonked out. It's after one in New York."

"I know, but I drank a triple latte at the airport. I may be awake all weekend."

That's why she thought something was wrong, Carmen realized, because she had hurried her off to bed before she was ready. Judith thought she was being pushed away, when all Carmen was doing was making sure she didn't start something she couldn't finish. They'd had enough false starts between them.

"Cathy doesn't let me drink caffeine. She's afraid I'd never sleep." She caught herself staring at Judith's nipples, taut against the fabric of her top. She had touched one of those. "Are you warm enough? You want to get under the covers?"

To both her horror and delight, Judith came around the bed and got in on the other side. Caffeine or not, her blood pressure was headed to the red zone.

"Prissy came in and checked out my purse. I took your advice and put it up on the dresser."

"Good thinking." She fluffed her pillows and leaned against the headboard, holding out an arm in invitation. The feel of Judith's body as she nestled against her ignited a flame of arousal, and she struggled to still her hands from their desire to wander.

"I've been so excited about this weekend." Beneath the blanket, Judith rested her hand on Carmen's thigh. Only thin pajamas separated them. "What kind of big plans do you have for me?"

Carmen had been holding her breath so long she feared her voice would squeak when she answered. "The first order of business is a walk through Lincoln Park with someone's spoiled rotten sausage dog." She nudged Prissy with her foot, but the dog merely sighed. "Then I thought we'd take a boat tour of downtown and have lunch at a jazz café on Rush Street."

"Sounds like a nice day."

"I want you to have a good time so you'll come back. Prissy and I already talked about it. She's actually thinking about behaving herself."

Judith turned toward her and smiled. Apparently, the invitation to come back was just the ticket to quell her worries that something was amiss between them. "And you? Are you thinking about behaving yourself?"

Carmen swallowed hard. Her resolve was slipping fast, but at this point, she couldn't have cared less. "I was thinking about it earlier, but it's losing its appeal."

"Why were you thinking about it earlier?" Judith's hand was creeping across her stomach.

"I forget . . . but I'm sure it wasn't a very good reason."

Chapter 14

Judith fell back on the bed under the onslaught of Carmen's demanding lips. This was how they were supposed to kiss, with tongues and hands that couldn't be still. She squirmed to turn, positioning herself beneath Carmen's body. Already, their hips were writhing in a quest for contact.

One hand swarmed her body, from the back of her thigh over the curve of her hip. Subtly, Carmen teased the elastic of her pants to slip inside and caress her ass. The fingers crept lower before they suddenly darted away, only to slide underneath her shirt.

Judith thrust her chest forward, all but begging Carmen to touch her breasts. Too many clothes . . . too hot. With a heave, she kicked the covers to the foot of the bed, sending Prissy scurrying to the floor.

"Mark my word, we'll pay for that," Carmen murmured,

finally brushing her fingertips across a nipple. "I haven't forgotten about this pointy nipple . . . how it rolled in my fingers . . . how the more I flicked it, the harder it got."

Judith couldn't think of anything but that nipple either. She wanted to rip off her shirt, but Carmen had her pinned to the bed. So she slid her hands under Carmen's top to stroke the smooth planes of her back. "I haven't forgotten it either."

Carmen abandoned one nipple for the other, teasing both into rock-hard peaks. Then she sat up to straddle Judith's hips, massaging both breasts at the same time. "I bet these are gorgeous. Are you warm enough to start giving up some of these clothes?"

If Judith got much warmer, she would spontaneously combust. That nearly happened anyway when Carmen suddenly lifted her own top above her head and tossed it to the floor. She was thinner than she appeared in her clothes, and her breasts were high and round, with dark brown nipples as hard as her own.

Judith raised her arms above her head as Carmen helped her out of her tank top. Then she held her breath for several seconds under a firelight appraisal.

"Stunning," was the verdict. Slowly, Carmen lowered her hips between Judith's legs, bringing their nipples together as they kissed again. Her hands then snaked underneath to clutch Judith's back and she began a slow grind.

Judith's body was pounding with need as Carmen pressed rhythmically against her clit, which felt as big as a grape. Judith spread her legs wider and wrapped them around Carmen's thighs. Then she gripped Carmen's butt and pulled her closer. "God, you feel good."

Carmen nipped her earlobe before whispering, "I've been having fantasies about you." Then she scooted lower and took a nipple in her teeth.

Judith hissed, suspended in ecstasy on the precipice of injury.

Carmen immediately released her bite and licked the nipple gently.

"Sorry. I can already tell I'm going to have trouble controlling myself."

Judith took her head with both hands and drove it back down. "Don't even try." Carmen sucked and nibbled her nipples until she thought she might scream. Her breath hitched as Carmen's lips left her breasts and traveled slowly down her abdomen. When Carmen tugged on the elastic of her pants, she raised her hips to allow them to be removed.

"I believe there's excitement in the air."

She didn't know whether to be embarrassed or proud. Either way, it was Carmen's doing, not hers. "What did you expect?"

Carmen removed her own pants and knelt between Judith's knees. "Lovely," she said, trailing her fingers along Judith's thighs to the edge of her pubic hair and back. "I'm very glad I skipped dessert."

And Judith was glad she had loaded up on coffee. Not that she was worried about falling asleep. She was thinking ahead to how many times they were going to make each other come before giving in to exhaustion. Whatever had been her personal best was going down tonight.

Carmen was going down too, inhaling her scent as if committing it to memory. Judith waited with tingling anticipation for the touch of her tongue. When it finally came, it teased her lips apart gently before swirling inside her.

Judith tried to take her deeper, instinctively raising her knees to open herself more.

"You know just how I like it, don't you?" Carmen said.

Carmen's shoulders molded to the backs of her thighs and pushed her hips up off the bed. Hands wrapped around her waist and parted her lips, exposing her clit to hot breath. Every vision of Carmen's skill as a lover was proving true.

Judith felt a quiver inside her, the precursor to her climax.

Each time Carmen's tongue crossed her clit, it grew stronger. She tightened her cheeks as if to force it out, knowing the release would match the intensity of her effort.

Suddenly, Carmen stopped her motions. "If you're going to do that, I want to feel it too." A finger slid in and out of her vagina several times before it pressed to Judith's tight rim. "I want you to throb all around me and suck me inside."

Judith moaned and thrust her hips forward to impale herself on Carmen's fingers. She gasped for breath as she felt one digit slide into her ass at the same time another plunged deep into her vagina. Carmen returned to lick her clit, matching the rhythm of the steady thrusts inside her.

Judith blindly gripped the sheets as she fought to hold her climax at bay. Suddenly, her walls erupted in spasms and Carmen filled her, sucking her clit in short bursts to make the ecstasy last.

When she opened her eyes, Carmen was smiling at her, her lips poised just inches above her clit. "Are there more where that one came from?"

"Am I still alive?"

Carmen chuckled and slid her hand out before scooting back to lower her hips to the bed. "For the moment, but I'm not finished."

"Aren't there laws against necrophilia in this state?"

"Only if you get caught." Carmen crawled up to lie alongside her. "You ready to let go of the bed?"

"Are we still moving?"

"No, but we can fix that." She returned her fingers to Judith's still-throbbing clit, but Judith covered her hand to hold it still.

"I need a little break . . . I'm just starting to feel my legs again."

"And I can feel my tongue again."

Judith hooked a hand behind Carmen's neck and pulled her face down. "Let me have that tongue." This kiss was neither tentative nor hungry. But it was intimate and unwavering, as if an acknowledgment of their new status as lovers.

"I'm very glad you decided to ignore being sent to bed. We're both going to sleep so much better now."

"We're not going to sleep now, Carmen."

"We're not?"

"Not until we trade places."

"You want to sleep on this side?"

Judith put a hand on Carmen's chest and pushed her back, rolling over on top to face her. "I get to have my way with you now."

"I was hoping you would."

For the first time since they'd known each other, Judith initiated a kiss, taking her time to explore Carmen's mouth, her teeth, tongue and lips. Satisfied that she had touched every corner, her mouth traveled down Carmen's slender neck to her pronounced collarbone, and out to her shoulder. "You could stand to gain a few pounds, you know."

"Could you put that in a memo and send it to Cathy?"

"Maybe later." Judith lowered her mouth to Carmen's breast, sucking a wide brown nipple between her lips.

Carmen threw her arms over her head as though offering herself. With her eyes closed and her mouth parted, she was the picture of total concentration. Judith watched her face as best she could while fondling and sucking her breasts. The expression never changed until she traced her hand into the dark triangle between Carmen's legs. As her fingertips met wet flesh, Carmen's face contorted and she moaned.

Judith felt her own loins buzz with excitement when Carmen opened her legs. Leaving the breasts, she ducked between her legs to explore the treasure her hand had found. Even in the dim light, she could see the glistening lips. "I'm going to love this," she said, burying her mouth in the slippery slit.

"You're not the only one," Carmen groaned.

"Tell me what you want."

"You obviously don't need my help to figure that out."

Five—possibly six—orgasms later, they both collapsed, with Judith climbing up to cover Carmen's body with hers. Warm fingers tickled her back as they both caught their breath.

"You're so beautiful, Carmen."

"Looks can be deceiving."

"What does that mean?"

Carmen heaved her chest, causing Judith to roll off to her side. "It means you weigh a ton. Who knew you were so heavy?"

"Must you always be so serious?"

That earned her a chuckle. "I have lots of chances to be serious. This room should be fun."

"It's certainly living up to that tonight."

Carmen turned on her side to face her. "Please don't think it means this isn't real for me. I love this with you."

Judith's stomach fluttered at Carmen's choice of words. "So do I."

Another kiss followed, this one filled with heat as Carmen once again began to caress her body. "I'm about to show you how much. Let's hope that coffee works. I don't think my ego could handle it if you fell asleep."

"I wouldn't worry if I were you. I plan to stroke that ego of yours all weekend."

Carmen flinched when Prissy's wet nose brushed against hers. The dog seemed to know how annoying that was, and made it a point to do it every morning.

But Carmen wasn't ready to get up. She and Judith had stayed awake half the night making love. If she woke up for anything, it would be for more of that.

A noise from the kitchen interrupted her dozing and she automatically stretched an arm across the bed beside her. Empty.

"What's she doing, Prissy?"

She threw the covers back and swung her legs over the side of the bed. Her first steps toward the closet for her robe reminded her of muscles she hadn't used in a while—over two years in fact.

Carmen donned her robe and padded out of the bedroom. When she reached the kitchen doorway, Judith was bent over peering into the refrigerator. She was wearing the denim shirt Carmen had worn last night, and from the looks of it, nothing else.

"Why are you up already? I thought I killed you."

Judith turned and grinned. "I'm afraid it's going to take a lot more than that."

"But I kept you up doing unspeakable things until three in the morning. That was just five hours ago."

"I'm starving."

Carmen enveloped her in her arms and kissed her firmly. "How can that be? You ate all night."

Judith wriggled loose and reached for something on the kitchen table. "Speaking of eating . . ." She held up one of her socks, now riddled with chew holes.

"Welcome to my world. I warned you about that when you kicked her off the bed last night."

"I think she did this because you have nothing in this house to eat."

"I never eat breakfast here. I usually wait until I get to work."

"What do you do on the weekends?"

"Starbucks is around the corner. So you can cover that beautiful ass of yours and come with me to walk Prissy, or you can leave that beautiful ass just as it is and I'll bring something back."

"I'm going with you. You might go out there and meet some cute thing and not come back." Judith headed for the bedroom, and Carmen grabbed her shirttail and pulled it up.

"Not a chance. She might want to have sex with me and I'm too sore."

"What a sob story."

Twenty minutes later, they emerged from Starbucks with breakfast. Prissy, who was tied to the leg of a café table, was the center of attention for a small group of children and their mothers.

"How can you leave Prissy tied up outside like this?" Judith asked. "She's so cute. Somebody's going to steal her one of these days."

Carmen shrugged. "Whoever got her would bring her back the next day and tie her to the table."

"You liar. You'd be heartbroken. I saw you two cuddling when I got up."

"We were not cuddling. She hogs the bed. I was just holding her in place so she wouldn't keep pushing me over." She untied the leash and hooked it through her hand.

"I would have given anything for a camera. One picture would have cracked that charade once and for all." Judith sipped her latte and took a bite of her bagel.

"I'll admit she's pretty good company when she isn't eating something expensive. She's gone through shoes, throw pillows, furniture, you name it. Healey says it's because she doesn't like to be left alone."

"Healey's Brooke's daughter, right?"

"Her oldest, my goddaughter. She's the one who told Priscilla I needed a dog."

"Why would she do that?"

An honest answer would launch a discussion of her relationship with Brooke and her daughters, something that probably needed to happen eventually. There was no escaping the fact that Brooke and her girls were an important part of her life, and it wasn't fair to Judith to try to push it all under the rug after the problems it had caused for them already.

"I got the girls a puppy from the pound back when we were all living together. But I'm the one who ended up taking care of him, and I missed him when they all moved away."

"You used to live with Brooke?"

"Yeah, about ten years ago. Let's cross here and go into the park." Carmen wished they had better weather to show off her beloved Chicago. It was nippy and threatening rain. That didn't bode well for a boat ride, but she was game for whatever Judith wanted.

Judith finished her bagel and hooked her free hand through Carmen's elbow. "So tell me about when you lived with Brooke."

Carmen let Prissy set the pace, and they slowed to a stroll as the dog stopped and sniffed the grass along the path. "She came to me one night and said she was scared of Anthony. He was her husband, and I knew they were having some problems, but I didn't know things were that bad. I told her to go home and get the girls and come back to my apartment. She did, and all hell broke loose."

"He snapped?"

"He never got violent, but he got mean. He went to court to get custody because he didn't want his daughters being raised by lesbians. But we were never lovers, no matter what anyone thought."

"But she got custody."

"Yes, but Anthony tied her up for two years before settling on support. She had nothing to live on and nowhere to go, so I bought a four-bedroom house near where my folks live in Evanston and we all moved up there."

"You really came through for her."

"It made me happy . . . in my own demented way. Then she met Geoffrey. They went to Vegas one weekend and came back married. That was the end of it." Her efforts not to sound morose probably failed, because Judith gripped her arm tighter and leaned a head on her shoulder.

"Does she know how you feel about her?"

"She knows I love her. I suppose she'd have to be stupid not to have figured out what that means, but we've never talked about it. I know she considers me her best friend."

"You've been friends for that long and never once told her how you felt?"

Carmen sighed. "I always thought it would make things awkward. There wasn't anything either of us could do about it." The first raindrops began to fall and she turned them back to her building. "This might not be a great day for a boat ride."

"What do you like to do on a rainy day?"

She wrapped an arm around Judith's waist and pulled her close. "Lie in bed with a pretty woman."

Judith stripped off her wet coat in the elevator. "Did you see your doorman do that double take?"

"Next time we go through the lobby, I'm going to say something about the cloning experiments. That'll get the grapevine buzzing." She leaned over and delivered her traditional elevator kiss. "Sure you don't mind missing the boat tour?"

"If you're nice to me, I'll come back and we can do it another time."

"So you aren't mad about the sock thing?"

They stepped off the elevator and turned toward Carmen's apartment. Prissy led the way, dragging her leash along the floor.

"The sock thing was my fault. I should never have left my suitcase unlocked."

"I'm glad you understand. Lock it and keep the key in your bra." Carmen opened the door and immediately tossed their coats over a chair in the foyer. "Although I predict I'll be helping you out of that soon."

Judith was more than ready to return to bed, but something else was on her mind, left over from their conversation in the park. "Can I see a picture of Brooke?"

Carmen gave her a half smile. "I was hoping you might forget about that."

"If you don't want to—"

"No, I'll show you. Let's go in my office." She nodded downward. "But don't leave your shoes there."

Judith chuckled and placed them on the shelf beside Carmen's.

As her computer booted up, Carmen retrieved a framed photo from the credenza. "This is all of us. It was taken about seven years ago, just before Brooke married Geoffrey."

Judith's breath caught as she got her first look at the woman Carmen called her best friend. Brooke's hair was lighter and wavy, and she was trim and fit. Otherwise, they could have been sisters. "No wonder everyone you know stares at me."

"It's just a first impression."

"She works out, doesn't she?"

"Constantly." Carmen grabbed her hand and pulled her close to the computer screen. "But I've seen that body of yours up close and personal, and you're no slouch."

"Mine's from hauling things up four flights of stairs."

Carmen clicked a folder to display a set of thumbnails. "Here's a close-up."

"Wow." The resemblance wasn't as obvious in this photo. But Brooke was a dazzling beauty, with crystal blue eyes, perfect teeth and dimples. "She's very pretty."

"You're prettier."

"Yeah, I bet." She hadn't meant to say that aloud.

"Thank you, Carmen. What a lovely thing to say."

Judith laughed, leaning over to wrap an arm across Carmen's chest. "Thank you, Carmen. What a lovely thing to say."

"That's better." She clicked on another thumbnail, which showed Brooke in Carmen's kitchen. "She came over last weekend and the first thing I thought was how much she looked like you. It was weird after thinking you looked like her. I've gotten used to you."

"I should hope so." Judith hadn't even considered that

Carmen might still be thinking about Brooke, but she should have realized that the issue hadn't simply vanished.

Carmen must have read her look because she closed the photo folder and stood to face her. "This is all about you and me. I hope you believe that."

"If you say it, I believe it."

"Does that go for anything?" It was said seriously, as though Carmen had more truth to tell.

"Yes." She waited with anticipation as Carmen seemed to ponder her next words.

Suddenly, Prissy appeared in the doorway with Carmen's leather wallet between her teeth.

"You little shit!"

The moment shattered, Judith followed the action into the living room. Whatever Carmen had started to say was lost.

Carmen peered over Judith's shoulder as they watched out the window for the limo. They were so much closer now than they had been on Friday night, and the mysterious emotion of their initial hug had been unveiled. Carmen had wanted to share her revelation all weekend, but the timing had never seemed right. And now, her time was running out.

"I'm sorry you didn't get to see more of the city than my bedroom."

"Are you really?"

"No."

"Me neither. I can be a tourist anytime."

"You make me want to play hooky and come to New York."

"That sounds like a great idea. I could play hooky too. Then Todd would fire me and we could just lie around in bed all day. And I would—"

"You would call Sofia like I told you to, and get out of that sweatshop."

"And into another one."

"Yes, but Sofia would give you time off anytime I asked her to."

"The others would treat me like a pariah."

"But you wouldn't care because you'd have your legs wrapped around my head." She buried her face into Judith's neck, averting her eyes from the sight of the limo pulling up in front of the building. "I'm supposed to have a meeting in Philadelphia on Thursday. What if I try to change that to Friday and come up on the train when I get finished?"

"And stay the weekend? I'd love it." She tried to wriggle free but Carmen held her firmly in place. "Shouldn't I go down to meet the car?"

"He'll call up when he's ready. Would you like me to get a hotel room?"

"Why? Afraid of a few steps?"

"I can do steps. But I remember you said your place was perfect for one."

"I think we can manage for a weekend. But I have to see Victor on Sunday."

"That's okay. I'll get a midday flight back here."

Judith spun in her arms. "Or you can come with me if you want."

"We'll see. I haven't decided for sure if I'm even going to let you leave." Now facing each other, Carmen couldn't resist a kiss. As their lips moved together, their arms tightened in a desperate hug. "I think you should just stay."

"I wish I could."

"Judith, I—" The ringing phone cut her off. "That's your ride."

She picked up the phone and confirmed with the driver.

Judith put on her coat and grabbed the handle of her suitcase. "Is it Friday yet?"

"Wait. Before you go, I need to tell you something." Carmen

swallowed hard and steeled herself. Judith probably wasn't going to believe what she had to say. "You're going to think I'm nuts. I know we still don't know each other all that well, but that's not the way these kinds of things happen for me. I'm sort of weird that way."

"What are you talking about, Carmen?"

She took a deep breath. "I'm in love with you."

From the look on her face, Judith was stunned. Whether that was good or bad was an open question until she finally burst into a grin. "If that makes you nuts, we're both in trouble."

"You feel it too?"

Judith nodded. "I was too scared to call it love, though. But that's sure what it feels like."

"Whatever it is, let's take care of it." She folded Judith into an embrace. "This is going to be the hardest part, saying good-bye."

"We'll just have to look ahead to next time. I'll come back as soon as I can."

"Come on. We have time for one more kiss in the elevator. Let's do it right."

Chapter 15

Cathy filled Carmen's doorway, waving a note in the air. "I guess I don't have to ask what kind of weekend you had."

Carmen grinned with satisfaction. "Can we get that meeting with Hinkle changed? Otherwise, there's a pretty good chance I won't be in the office on Friday."

"There's nothing wrong with you taking a day off."

"Except that everyone else here is working their ass off to meet that deadline."

"That's not your project. You can always take your laptop and do some work if it makes you feel better." She came in and plopped onto the sofa, clearly eager to hear details of the weekend. "How was the boat tour?"

"We didn't exactly get out much . . . what with the nasty weather and all."

"How ever did you fill your time?"

"How do you think?" Carmen answered with a smirk. Then she related the story of Judith's plane delays, and their few forays out of the apartment to walk Prissy and pick up coffee. "Before she left, I told her I was in love with her."

If Cathy was the least bit surprised, she didn't show it. "In love as in relationship? Or diversion?"

It wasn't love like she had with Kim, with whom she had spent five tenuous years, wondering which of them would leave first. And it certainly wasn't like Robin, who was fun and sexy, but never more than an amusement. "No, more like . . . as in Brooke."

That drew the look of surprise she expected, and then some. Cathy sighed heavily and glared at her sternly. "Do you hear yourself? You've known Brooke thirty years and Judith . . . what? Thirty days?"

"I know. I don't mean like I love Brooke now. But this feels like it did thirty years ago, and I knew I'd feel that way . . ." She almost said all her life, but that sounded crazy, even to her. She shook her head and slumped in her leather chair. "It's hard to explain."

"You don't have to explain anything to me, Carmen . . . as long as you're not looking for more things to compare just because Judith and Brooke happen to look alike."

"I'm past that. It jumps back every now and then, but it's not an issue." She opened her desk drawer. "Why don't I keep a bottle of scotch in here?"

"Because you don't want anyone else to keep a bottle of scotch in here."

"Oh, yeah." She got up and came around her desk, taking a seat in a chair across from her friend. "Do you remember when you first knew you were in love with Hank?"

"Not the exact moment, but I do remember why I fell in love with him. It was after I got so sick with the flu and he came to the dorm every night and held my head while I threw up in the trashcan. I figured a guy who would do that was too special to let get away."

"And you were right. You knew it in here, didn't you?" She tapped her fist on her chest.

"I suppose so. Did you have a moment like that with Judith?"

"Sort of. It was like that with Brooke too. I realized how I felt all of a sudden and it turned into a filter for everything else." Carmen got up and shut the door. The whole office would be talking about her by this afternoon anyway, but she wanted at least the illusion of mystique. "Am I making any sense?"

"Barely. But that never stopped you before."

She paced around the couch as she gathered her thoughts. "I remember when I first knew I was in love with Brooke. It was a weekend and we were alone in the dorm because you guys had gone home or something. I went into her room to see if she wanted dinner and I found her crying." Carmen had kept this story to herself out of loyalty to Brooke, but it was old news now. "You guys know all about Brooke being molested when she was little, right?"

Cathy nodded.

"And she made a big deal about how she wasn't going to have sex with anyone unless she really loved him. Remember that?"

"Until that basketball player."

"Right . . . Dumfrey or Dumb Shit, whatever his name was. And then he dropped her a week later."

"I remember."

"She was devastated. She said it was the only time she had ever felt sure enough to share that part of herself, and this guy just basically threw it back in her face. I wanted to go kick his ass."

"Like you wanted to kick Anthony's?"

"Exactly. That's when I knew things were different between Brooke and me, but I didn't have a handle on the lesbian thing, so I wasn't ready to face what it was. I just remember holding her that night while she cried, and all I could think of was how much I wanted to protect her, to make her laugh again and forget the awful things that had happened."

"And that's exactly what you've done with her ever since."

Carmen returned to her chair. "It was like being hit in the head with a hammer."

"And now you want to protect Judith?"

"No, Judith doesn't need to be protected." Still, it felt like it had with Brooke. "But I got this feeling about her last weekend. She's just such a . . . nice person. Nice doesn't even describe it." Judith was so much more than that. "She feels for other people, no matter who they are."

"She's compassionate."

"That's it. There isn't a selfish bone in her body. Anyone who does things for other people like that deserves to have them done for her."

"And just like that, you're in love?"

"That's all it took. And when I opened that door on Friday night and saw her there, it hit me again like a hammer. I want to make sure good things happen to her."

"I'm happy for you, Carmen."

But she didn't sound happy. She sounded dubious. "What?"

"What do you mean what? I said I was happy."

"I know your happy voice, and that wasn't it."

Cathy chuckled. "That was my 'now that you've found a lesbian, why couldn't she live in Chicago' voice."

Carmen sighed. "There is that. But it's too soon to worry about it."

"You're right. You should be worrying about how you're going to introduce her to your best friend."

She stood up and headed back to her desk. "Thanks so much for coming in here and letting the air out of my balloons. I didn't need to feel good today. I have too much work to do."

"Somebody has to keep your feet on the ground. And you'll

need to be more efficient if you're going to be running back and forth to New York."

"Right. You can go away now. And don't come back unless it's with a latte—a double . . . no, a triple."

Carmen smiled and let out a satisfied breath as Cathy left her office. It was good to be able to share what she was feeling with someone, especially a friend who could reel her in when she started getting ahead of herself. It was fine to be in love with Judith, but way too early to start planning their future.

And Cathy was right that she needed to talk to Brooke. Her head was already working on coming up with a painless way to do that.

Judith wiped her feet on the bristled doormat on the porch of the group home and pressed the buzzer to announce herself. She had been eager to see Victor, but that changed to apprehension after talking to the staff at the group home. When she called this morning to say she was coming by, they were struggling to convince Victor to go to work. He had been frantic since lunchtime on Sunday, unhappy she hadn't come to pick him up.

"Come on in, Judith."

"Hi, Russ. How is he?"

"He's better. I don't understand why he got so upset yesterday. Stacey said he didn't eat all day, and he refused to go to work this morning."

Judith felt awful. It wasn't unusual for Victor to get a little agitated when his routine was disrupted, but it rarely lasted more than a few hours. "Did you call our mom?"

"Stacey did. She got Victor to come to the phone and listen, but it didn't do any good. He kept going to the door and looking out."

"Poor guy." She wished now she had caught a morning plane back from Chicago. She would do that next time. Carmen would understand. No matter how much fun they had in the extra hours, it wasn't worth the anxiety it caused her brother.

She signed in and started down the hall to Victor's room. The moment he saw her in the doorway, his face lit up and he blushed.

"Hi, Vic. Did you miss me?"

Stacey joined them, scooting past her in the doorway and carrying a small stack of Victor's laundry. "He sure did. But I bet he's okay now. Aren't you, handsome?"

"You want to go get some ice cream?"

"Sure he does. He likes ice cream." Stacey pulled his jacket from the closet and handed it to him. "Put this on."

When they stepped out into the cool air, Judith hooked her arm through her brother's. "I'm sorry I didn't come yesterday. I was in Chicago with that pretty lady I told you about." If there was one good thing about Victor's emotional immaturity, it was that he never held a grudge. The instant his needs were met, he was appeased. "You're not going to believe this, but I'm already in love with her."

They crossed the street and walked up to the ice cream store. Judith led the way inside and ordered a cone for each of them. Grabbing several napkins, she guided him to a small table near the wall.

"We need to get Mom over here to see you, Vic. She'd like your room. And you could show her your pictures and where you keep things. Would you like that?"

What Victor liked was vanilla ice cream. His cone was already half gone, while Judith had eaten only a few licks of hers.

"One of these days, I'm going to bring my girlfriend to see you. You'll color something for her, won't you?"

She grinned as he looked at her, his chin covered with melting ice cream. It was one of those moments she almost expected him to answer.

"She's going to like you."

Victor finished his cone and Judith handed him the rest of hers. Nothing made her feel better than to see him happy.

Carmen pressed the button on her phone to beep Cathy at her desk. "Can you help me in here?"

Moments later, her assistant darkened her door.

"I've got the Franklin files, but I need the Southwest data," Carmen said.

"That report isn't due until the end of next week."

"I'll be in Tokyo at the end of next week. I want to work on it on Friday." She had decided to keep the Philadelphia meeting on Thursday and work from Judith's apartment the next day.

"You have a conference call with Berger and Gould on Friday at eleven. That's noon for you."

"I know, but it's not going to take all day. I want to get ahead as much as I can."

"Aren't you spending the day with Judith?"

"She has to work. I thought if I took the Southwest data, I could get that report written at her place."

Cathy nodded. "Okay, I'll see if Kristy has it. You want it on your laptop?"

"Yeah, but I need printouts too . . . the crosstabs."

"You're going to carry all that?"

Cathy was right. The last thing she wanted was to lug those notebooks on the plane and then on the train. "Can you overnight them?"

"To Judith?"

"Yeah." Carmen retrieved Judith's business card from her desk. "I'll let her know they're coming."

The intercom beeped. "Carmen?"

"Yes?"

"Art Conover's on line two."

Carmen rolled her eyes and flipped her middle finger at the

phone.

"Should I take a message?"

"No, I'll talk to him." She sat down at her desk and looked back at Cathy. "I'll come find you when I'm done."

She burned a few seconds before answering, hoping Art would grow impatient and hang up. Finally, she pressed the button on her speakerphone. "Art?"

"Carmen. Good to talk to you. How are things in Chicago? You folks getting any spring weather?"

"Eh, springtime's overrated. What's up?"

"I just wanted to follow up on what we talked about in New York . . . see if you'd had a change of heart about joining forces."

"I can honestly say I haven't thought about it at all, Art. We're just not providing the same service."

"That might be true now, but it's going to change soon."

"Fuck you." Carmen mouthed the words silently, snarling at the phone.

"My board met this week and we've decided to make the investment in our expansion of the travel sector, including the implementation of the customer surveys. That means we're going to go after your clients, Carmen. It may take us a couple of years to get there, but we will. And our operation won't include all the seminars and consultations, which means we can offer the same data for less money."

"Art, you know we can run circles around you on customer service and usability. Why do you terrorize me like this?" Despite her bravado, Carmen had a sudden sinking feeling in her gut. It was true her product was better now, but Art would be a serious threat if CDS redesigned its methodology to yield the same data.

"Because I want to give you one last chance to come on board. Your people are smart. They can save us two years of prep, and that's worth a lot of money to us."

"We like who we are."

"But you won't like who you're going to be. If we come out in two years with a data service for less money, your company's value is going to drop like a rock. You won't be able to compete with us."

"Art!" She jabbed at the phone with both middle fingers. "We're not selling out to you."

"Your people will end up working for Conover Data Services for half the money they make now. I'm telling you, we can make a very sweet deal, and I can have a team of auditors there tomorrow to go over your books."

"I can't talk about this anymore. You've got something in your ear that keeps you from hearing me."

"Just think on it some more, Carmen. Think seriously."

"I used to think you were such a nice guy."

"I'm still a nice guy. I'm trying to make us both rich."

Carmen groaned. "Good-bye, Art."

"Good-bye, Carmen."

She disconnected the line and let out an exasperated scream. Within seconds, Cathy and Lenore were in the doorway.

"Get in here and shut the door!" she barked. "Art Conover has just graduated from pest to threat." She related the details of his call.

"How much truth is there in what he's saying?" Lenore asked.

Carmen sighed heavily. "If he delivers all the data we do without the client service? He'll eat our lunch—and our breakfast and dinner, as well. Analysts will make a cottage industry out of providing data consultations for anyone who wants it, and we'll be out in the cold."

"But we're the experts. We've been showing our clients the way for years. Why would they dump us for Art?"

"Because if they had a choice, most of them would buy just the reports, and not the seminars and consultations. The little guys would save thirty thousand a year, and the big guys would save three times that."

"Still," Lenore argued, "Art isn't as smart as we are. Why would they trust his data?"

"Because he plans to pretty much duplicate what we're doing. We're smart, but who's going to want to pay that much more for it?"

"How can he afford to deliver it for so much less?"

"He plans to replicate this across all of his consumer industries—real estate, electronics, automobiles, everything. He'll be printing money."

Cathy shrugged. "So what are we going to do?"

"I'm thinking of putting out a hit on Art Conover. You got any relatives in the business?"

"Not that I know of, but I can ask around."

Lenore's serious expression hadn't changed since she came into the room. "What do you want to do about it, Carmen?"

"I don't know. We'll brainstorm on the way to Philadelphia. Are you all packed?"

"I'm ready."

Carmen stood, her signal that this impromptu meeting was over. "I have one more thing to finish before I leave."

"Two," Cathy said. "Brooke called and wanted you to call her back."

No, Carmen definitely didn't want to deal with Brooke right now. "Tell her I'm . . . shit." It wasn't fair to ask Cathy to cover for her. This whole business about ducking Brooke had started when she met Judith. It was silly on her part, and it wasn't fair to Brooke. "Would you mind calling her back and telling her I'll call her from the airport?"

"Not a problem. What else do you have to do?"

"I have to finish this checklist for Richard. I want to meet with him in the conference room on Monday afternoon on the stuff I have to take to Tokyo."

"Do you want to dictate it to me from the car?"

"What would I ever do without you?"

⁂

Judith pressed the phone to her ear to muffle the sound of the passing truck. "Mom, I told you. It was hard on him, and I think one of us has to see him every Sunday, no matter what . . . No, I'm not going to be out of town every weekend, but sometimes I have something else I need to do. I can always see him during the week, but you could see him on Sundays if I'm not there."

She always dreaded this conversation, but the problem wasn't going away. Her mother had to get over herself and go see Victor at Wyckoff.

"You don't have to spend any time there. They can have him ready to walk out the door." She crossed the street and turned toward her agency. "We can go together. I'll come by on Sunday at noon and we can both ride down and get him."

As usual, her mother staunchly refused.

"Mom, all I'm asking is for you to consider picking him up at the center. I don't think having you spend five minutes at Wyckoff is too much to ask for Victor's sake." That's the argument she wanted to leave with her mother. "I'm at my office now. I have to go. See you Sunday."

She glanced at the clock on her way to her desk, then locked eyes with Todd as she walked past his office. She usually took a full thirty minutes for lunch, but made it back today in only twenty-two. Todd had given her grief about not coming on Saturday, but she didn't care. She would have her forty hours in by the end of the day tomorrow, and she was spending Saturday with Carmen.

Her boss suddenly appeared in the entrance to her cubicle. "I've been thinking about what you said a couple of weeks ago . . . about paying the lower commissions on existing clients. I've changed my mind."

"What?"

"You can have the higher commission on all of your clients.

But you're going to have to enter all of them into the new system so when they call in, it goes to you."

"I can do that." She almost let out a laugh. Apparently, he interpreted her staunch refusal to work on Saturdays as an indication that she wasn't going to go quietly along with his plans. No problem with that. She was the senior agent in the shop, after all, and she brought in more revenue than anyone else. He needed to keep her happy.

As he returned to his office, her phone rang.

"Rainbow Getaways. Judith O'Shea."

She was startled to hear Cathy Rosen's voice. She never even got a word in as Cathy rattled off instructions.

"Yes, I can pick it up. It's on Seventh Avenue, about three blocks from where I live." Cathy had sent a package for Carmen. No problem. She had time to collect it, drop it off at her apartment and still meet Carmen's train at seven.

"Noon tomorrow . . . and she already knows about this call?" A reminder for a conference call. "I can set an alarm for her, or if you want me to call her just before—"

Apparently, Carmen's forgetfulness when it came to turning on her cell phone was a chronic problem. "I'll make sure it's charged and turned on when I leave for work. And I can leave her a note about the time . . . no, believe me. She won't be able to miss it."

As Cathy spoke, Judith wrote down all the information about Carmen's return flight, and took two phone messages to pass on. Then she gave Cathy her home phone number, her cell number and her e-mail address, just in case she needed anything else.

The last bit was nice, Cathy thanking her for helping to keep Carmen organized. It was a big job, she said. "I'll help you however I can. What would she ever do without you?"

For some reason, that set off a fit of laughter on the other end of the phone. Then Cathy collected herself and said good-bye.

Chapter 16

Carmen blinked a few times, taking in the unfamiliar surroundings in the dim light. She was comfortable on the futon, much more than she had expected. Who knew these things gave such good back support? Or that sleeping with Judith would be so restful? Between the new environs and sharing a bed, she hadn't anticipated such a good night's sleep.

Of course, being totally worn out probably had something to do with that.

By the green digital display next to the bed, she had seven minutes before the alarm went off. Judith was facing her, asleep on her side. She was the very picture of morning, with her hair mussed and her face puffy and white. Smitten didn't even begin to describe what Carmen was feeling.

She couldn't believe how excited she had been to see Judith last night. They had rushed back here and fallen right into bed.

Their lovemaking had been adventurous and fulfilling, even sending them to the floor in laughter when Carmen had gotten tangled in the sheets. Judith was the first lover ever that seemed to share her attitude about the bedroom—that it wasn't just about orgasms and passionate ecstasy. It was about fun.

"My whole apartment smells like sex," Judith mumbled, not opening her eyes.

"It damn well ought to."

They both began to giggle as Judith snuggled close. "Did you sleep well?"

"I did. But whether I can still walk or not is a whole different question."

"Good thing you don't walk on your breasts, huh?"

"No kidding. Sitting may be hard enough."

"You can soak in my tub."

Carmen poked her in the ribs. "You don't have a tub."

"Oh, yeah. You can soak in my sink."

"Perfect. One cheek at a time. I'll be all better before you know it."

"At least you don't have to get dressed and go out."

"There is that. Will you bring me a latte before you go to work? I'd be ever so grateful."

"And I was thinking how nice it would be for you to do that while I was in the shower."

"I'm afraid I'd get lost. I'd be wandering around in New York . . . naked . . . with coffee."

"And a banana nut muffin." Judith stretched across her to turn off the alarm. Her nipple was within millimeters of Carmen's mouth. "Don't even think about it."

"But the muffin thing got my mouth all watery."

"I'll go get us coffee. You lie here and think about ways to thank me . . . much, much later . . . when I've recovered."

"Mmmmm." Carmen pulled the covers up to her chin. "I like being spoiled."

Judith kissed her on the nose. "You deserve it. Now go back to sleep for a little while."

Carmen rolled toward the window and snuggled deeper into the bed. She could hear Judith getting dressed, and eventually, going out.

She couldn't imagine how a place so foreign could feel so familiar. Between rounds of explorations last night, they had talked about this room, what Judith did here most nights, how she spent her time. The neatness, organization and efficiency bore Judith's stamp, and that's what made it familiar.

With every day they spent together, Judith seemed as much a best friend as a lover. Carmen was embarrassed to even think that because they had known each other barely a month. But Judith not only encouraged her to be herself, she demanded it. After being strong and responsible for those around her for so long, Carmen rarely felt free to relax and let someone else do for her. Cathy was the only friend truly inside that sanctum. Until now.

On the surface, she had always considered Brooke her best friend. But beneath the layers of friendship was a barrier that separated what they were from what they could never be. The deepest parts of her lay beneath that barrier, out of Brooke's reach.

Judith could get all the way inside. She had shown herself to be a kind person, a person she could trust to take care of . . .

The keys jingling in the door startled her awake.

"This is your wake-up call."

"I was hoping for a magical kiss that would turn me into a beautiful princess, and then let me sleep all day."

Judith presented her with coffee and a muffin, and a sweet kiss on the lips. "Looks like you got your first wish."

Carmen groaned and sat up in bed. "I'm actually looking forward to working here today. I rarely take a day at home, but when I do, I get so much done."

"You're welcome to come here and work anytime you want. I'll even guarantee breakfast in bed."

"I like dinner in bed too, and snacks."

Judith sat on the edge of the futon and devoured her muffin. "I have a whole stack of menus in the kitchen. They all deliver. You can call out for lunch if you want, or you can have last night's leftovers."

"That's fine with me."

"But you have to eat something. And don't forget you have a conference call with the San Diego people at noon. Where's your phone?"

"It's in my purse." She pointed to her handbag on the chair.

"And your charger?"

She had to think about that one. "My briefcase?"

Judith rummaged in the leather attaché and produced the charger, then dug the phone from her purse. "I'm going to plug this in next to the table in the kitchen. Cathy said for me to tell you not to turn it off."

"Yeah, yeah." It was funny that Judith seemed to be taking over as her assistant in Cathy's absence.

"All your printouts are in the FedEx box. You can use my printer if you need to, but it's slower than the Six Local. Paper's in the bottom drawer of my hutch." As she talked, she pulled off her clothes and went into the bathroom. "If you wait until about nine to take your shower, you'll have plenty of hot water."

"What if I come in there with you right now?"

"It'll be like your butt cheek in the sink."

" . . . two nights in Barcelona, returning to Madrid on the fifteenth. All that for twenty-two-eighty a person."

Judith typed in her client's personal information on the screen as Todd appeared in the entry to her cubicle. He motioned for her to come see him, and she nodded her understanding.

"You want me to book it? I'll need credit card info from all four of you . . . That's okay. I can put a hold on it, but I leave at five thirty, so try to call me back by five."

Judith printed the specs and placed the form in a folder. She wondered how Carmen was doing at home and was tempted to call her. Then she remembered her boss.

"Did you need something?"

"Come on in and shut the door."

That was a first. Todd usually made a public display of his interactions with the agents, whether for praise or criticism. Judith complied and took a seat opposite his desk.

"I just wanted you to know that I've been getting some complaints from the others about you not working Saturdays. You know how this business is. People need us to be here on the weekends when they have free time."

In the last five weeks, Judith had missed three Saturdays completely, plus the one when Carmen came to New York and she worked for only a couple of hours. Of course people were upset, but she wasn't going to miss being with Carmen for their sake. "It fits my schedule better to get my hours in during the week, Todd. It's not like I'm sitting around burning the clock. I'm productive during my time."

"I know, but it isn't just a question of you. When Pauline and Raja see you skipping out on weekends, they want to skip out too. I can't let everyone just decide not to work on Saturdays."

"Fine, don't do it for everyone. Do it for me and tell them it's because I'm your senior agent. Tell them I've paid my dues and I deserve a more flexible schedule. When they've been here seventeen years, you can give them a few perks too."

"I wish it was that easy."

"Why isn't it?"

"Because I can't have two sets of rules. Nothing sinks employee morale like a double standard."

Judith fought hard not to roll her eyes at his MBA recitation. "It isn't a double standard if they see it as an earned reward."

They sat silently, Todd seemingly digesting the arguments and Judith lining up more.

"Can you at least come in for a couple of hours this weekend?"

"No." She was loathe to share her personal details at work, but she would do it to drive home her resolve. "I'm seeing someone who happens to live in Chicago. The only time we have free is weekends."

"We all have things we'd rather be doing."

She stood up. "Then I'll find another job, Todd. My relationship is worth more than working here."

"Wait! Don't . . . shit."

"It's up to you to make it work. I'll come in on Saturdays whenever I can, like next weekend." Carmen would be in Tokyo. "But I'm not going to let this job take precedence. I've been here too long to be a minion."

He ran his hand through his hair and started to speak. Clearly exasperated, he swallowed his words and waved her out.

Judith found herself shaking as she walked back to her desk. It felt good to be standing up for herself, but she didn't like hearing that she was letting down her coworkers. Still, it wasn't going to change her determination to set her own schedule. Between her mom and Victor, she and Carmen had precious little time as it was.

Judith emptied the contents of her basket on the conveyor. They had agreed to eat in tonight, preferring total privacy for their last night together. The next two weeks would be long, but Judith was already booked for Chicago for the weekend after next.

Carmen rested her chin on Judith's shoulder and whispered

in her ear. "Tell them to hurry."

"This is New York. Everything is done as fast as is humanly possible."

"But I want to get home and spend some more quality time with your pussy."

She felt the blood rush to her face as she suppressed a smile. "I can't believe you just said that in the middle of the Chelsea Market."

"Judith's pussy." Carmen softly hissed the words.

"Oh, God."

"Judith's sweet, tasty pussy and her pointy nipples."

"Behave yourself."

"Only if you promise me I can have your sweet, tasty pussy for dessert."

"You can have anything you want if you'll just be quiet."

Carmen obliged for all of fifteen seconds, but her chin never left Judith's shoulder. "I get Judith's pussy for dessert," she sang softly.

Judith did her best to ignore the taunting as she pushed her items toward the checker. When he called out the amount, Carmen reached around quickly and dropped three twenties on the counter.

"I should get this. You're my guest this weekend."

Carmen collected the change and scooped up two of the plastic bags. "I'll buy dinner. You can save your money to buy me presents."

She grabbed the last bag and followed Carmen out onto the sidewalk. "I have to buy you presents?"

"How else will I know you care?"

Judith snorted. "I guess just telling you wouldn't work."

"Words can be so insincere. Nothing says 'I adore you' like presents." She held out her hand for the third bag. "Let's try a little experiment. Hand me that bag too."

She hooked it on Carmen's outstretched fingers.

"Now reach into my pocket and take out the little box."

Judith did, her eyes growing wide.

"Open it."

Her mouth dropped as she peeled back the top to find a jade pendant on a gold chain.

"Now don't you feel adored? Doesn't it just toast the cockles of your heart to know I was thinking about you during lunch on Thursday in Philadelphia?"

"You are so sweet!"

"And here's the best part. Now that you know how sweet I am and how much I adore you, don't you want to take me home and fuck me till my eyes cross?"

Judith gripped her forearm with both hands and squeezed. "Yes! Yes, I want to do that."

"And I bet you thought I knew nothing about relationships."

Judith laughed and shook her head. "People are so wrong about you, Carmen." The look of shock that comment produced was priceless.

"What people?"

"You know . . . the usual people." She reached again for one of the grocery bags.

"Someone's been telling my secrets?"

"Don't worry. I don't believe some of it."

"Only some of it?"

"Well, the part about you having a dirty mouth is true."

"And to think I gave them all that money not to talk."

"You can't trust anyone these days." They reached the front of Judith's building and started up the stairs.

"Not even you?"

"You can trust me, Carmen. Unless, of course, you can't."

"I have to find my camera. This is surreal," Judith said.

"What? You think the great Carmen Delallo doesn't know

how to do dishes?"

"I just never imagined you'd be doing mine."

"And now my mystique is shattered."

"Maybe, but your stock went through the roof."

Carmen laughed. She couldn't believe it herself, but she actually liked this domestic turn, as long as it was cozy and very, very rare. "The analysts predict I'll outperform all others in the sector."

Judith's arms went around her waist from behind. "How about in the galaxy?"

"Do I have competition in the galaxy?"

"Not that I know of."

"Good thing." She spun in Judith's arms and wiped her wet hands on her back. "Did I tell you I'm in love with you?"

"I don't think so. I would have remembered something like that."

"Mind like a steel sieve."

"What was your name again?" Judith asked.

"Bruno." She wriggled free and crossed the small kitchen to pull the shade. Then she proceeded into the living room to do the same.

"Are you expecting an air raid?"

"I thought we should have a little privacy for our contest." She casually began to loosen the buttons on her shirt. "Last one naked gets coffee in the morning."

She threw off her shirt and fumbled with the clasp on her bra. Judith was wearing a pullover and sent it flying across the room, along with her sports bra.

Carmen gave up on the clasp and tugged the bra over her head. She had already noticed Judith's lace-up shoes. That would buy her at least two seconds. She kicked off her clogs and unzipped her pants, sending them to the floor with her panties.

Judith had somehow managed to kick off her shoes without undoing the laces and also pushed her jeans and panties to the floor. But she caught her socks on the way down and was trying to step out of everything at once.

Carmen was hopping on one foot trying to get her last sock—

"Ta-da!"

"Damn it!"

"Double shot, skim milk, no sugar," Judith said. She stepped close enough for their pubic hair to mingle. "Good thing we didn't bother with making the bed, huh?"

Carmen fell backward onto the futon and pulled Judith on top. "You make me want to do this all day."

"We have."

"I know, but it has to last for two weeks this time." That seemed like an eternity and she hadn't even left yet. "I wish you were coming with me."

"To Tokyo?"

"Wouldn't that be fun? We could take a couple of extra days to sightsee."

"I can't believe you're going all that way for just three days."

"Me neither. But that's how long the meetings will last. I don't want to wander around by myself."

"Still, it must be fun to go to such an interesting place. You should take at least some time to get out and see things."

"I think they're giving me a little tour. I should have arranged that for them when they were in New York."

"Are those the people I talked to at your reception?"

"Yeah."

"They were nice. Will they be coming to Chicago?"

"Not until May."

"I can get you some DVDs that highlight the sights. You can set them up on that boat tour, but they can plan ahead on what else they want to do."

"That's a great idea."

"You should do that for all your clients. Make them want to visit Chicago so you won't have to go see them."

"You're smart." It was funny to be lying naked and stroking each other while they brainstormed marketing strategies. "Do you have any other skills?"

"None whatsoever."

"I'll probably have to disagree with that." She leaned into Judith and ran her tongue around the rim of her mouth. "I find some of your skills to be exemplary."

"What can I give you tonight that will last you for two weeks?"

"Nothing lasts that long. I'll want you again tomorrow."

Judith dipped her head and licked a nipple. "Then what do you want to miss most? That's what I'll give you tonight."

With her finger, Carmen tipped Judith's head so she could look her in the eye. "I love it when you go inside me . . . and then you work my clit with that lovely mouth. That's got to be the most exquisite sensation I've ever felt."

"I love doing that."

"So do I. What do you say we have another contest?"

"Such as?"

"Who can hold out the longest without a climax?"

"That would be me."

"Care to wager?"

"Wager what?"

"The first one to come gets tied up and made to watch the other one have a climax all by herself."

"Hoo boy!"

"Are you game?"

"Sure. I just have to think of what I'm going to use to tie you up."

"We'll see about that." Carmen pushed her onto her side and quickly shifted to position her head between Judith's thighs. "Somebody's excited already. Is that from thinking about me putting on a show for you?"

"No, it's from imagining you tied up."

Carmen swiped a finger through the wetness and tasted it. Then she ran her tongue the length of Judith's sex, slipping her tongue inside and swirling it around.

Judith must have been overwhelmed, Carmen thought, because it took her several moments to remember this was a contest, and she had a duty to perform. When she did, she wasted no time burying her face between Carmen's legs, teasing her opening with her fingers.

In tandem, they kissed and caressed, sliding fingers inside as if in harmony.

Carmen began to feel a pulsing warmth with every pass of Judith's tongue over her sensitive clit. Nice . . . she might be wrong . . . maybe it was about orgasms and passionate ecstasy after all. If that tongue crossed her clit one more time, she was going to burst.

"That's it. Give it to me," Judith murmured.

In retrospect, Judith probably meant she wanted Carmen to release. Instead, her command earned her three fingers deep in her vagina and a relentless assault on her clit. They climaxed within seconds of each other.

But Judith came first.

That was Carmen's story and she was sticking to it.

"Thank you very much." Judith hung up the phone and finished her notes in Carmen's day planner.

"Did you get it?" Carmen came out of the bathroom, one towel draped loosely around her and another binding her wet hair.

"The Waldorf at twelve thirty." If Carmen came closer, Judith wouldn't be able to resist giving that wrap a tug.

"I better call Sofia."

"And I got you switched to the four twenty flight. Bulkhead seat."

"Perfect." Carmen picked up her cell phone and called her friend to confirm their lunch date. "Who knew it would be so handy to have a travel agent for a girlfriend?"

"With all the things you have to do, I think Cathy should have been your girlfriend."

"I told her that not long ago. I dread going to Tokyo by myself."

"Why don't you take one of your assistants?"

"They're all trained researchers. That would be like asking one of them to get me coffee or pick up my laundry."

"But they're your assistants. Doesn't that include helping you organize your materials and get you where you're supposed to be?"

"I suppose." She unwrapped her hair and brushed it with the towel. "The truth is, I'm embarrassed about being such a space cadet. Cathy has to come in my office and cut tags off my clothes."

"No one's expected to do everything. You have the whole industry hanging on your every word, and you can work a room like no one I've ever seen."

"Are those my greatest skills?"

Judith got up and followed Carmen as far as the bathroom doorway. "Not by a long shot."

Carmen stopped her ablutions and looked up, locking eyes with her in the mirror. "I love you, you know."

The words seemed to steal all the air in the room, and Judith floundered for something to say.

"I know we still don't know each other all that well, but it feels right," Carmen went on.

"You're not taking it back, because I love you too."

Carmen turned and held out her arms. Judith fell into the embrace, a hug so strong she couldn't doubt its meaning.

"This could be a serious thing, Judith," Carmen whispered, pressing a kiss on her temple. "But it's going to be hard to be so far apart."

"I know." The warning tore at her heart, but it was true. "I just can't think about that now."

"Okay, we don't have to."

"I want to be with you as much as I can."

"Then I'd say we want the same thing."

Chapter 17

As the doors closed at the First Avenue station, a thin woman limped gingerly to the front of the car. A dirty elastic bandage was wrapped around her knee.

"Ladies and gentlemen, I am ashamed that I have to ask for your help. Last week, I was hit by a car that kept right on going . . ."

Judith looked away to hide her smirk. She recognized the woman from last Monday on the F train, when she had appeared with her arm in a sling made from this same elastic wrap. That story had been more compelling—a man dislocated her shoulder when he snatched her purse that contained the money she had saved for her baby son's operation. She almost said so when the woman walked by with a plastic cup, but instead dropped a folded dollar inside. People needed what they needed.

As she feared it would, the week had dragged by at a snail's pace. With Carmen headed to Tokyo this weekend, she had worked longer hours, banking a few extra so she could leave early for the airport next Friday. Todd was in a better mood about it all, especially after she showed up this morning to work her obligatory Saturday.

Carmen was in the air now, one hour into a fourteen hour flight. Her plane would arrive this time tomorrow in Tokyo, giving her half a day and all night to rest up for three days of meetings that started Monday. Though they could speak by phone every day—as she got ready for work and Carmen got ready for bed—she hated being half a world away.

A crackly voice announced Bedford Avenue and she got off, heading upstairs to the sun. It was a beautiful day, but that didn't make what she had to do any easier.

For better or worse, she was on her way to her mother's to have the talk she had been putting off for fifteen years. She would tell her about Carmen, about what they meant to each other and why she couldn't be available every weekend anymore. It would be difficult for both of them. But what she needed from her mother wasn't for her. It was for Victor.

Ironically, it was Carmen who made her see she had to do this. Their thoughtful phone conversations over the past week were a testament to how important their relationship had become. Carmen had sympathized with her mother, whose only perspective was that her daughter was choosing time with friends over loyalty to family. Her mother needed to understand that the choice was more profound, that Judith needed to be with Carmen because they were in love and headed down a serious path.

She skipped up the steps to her mother's door and rang the bell. After almost a minute, she rang it again. Finally, the door opened.

"Sorry, hon. I was finishing the dishes."

"It's okay." She handed her mother a brown paper bag filled with Polish pastries. "Faworki."

"Where did you get faworki?"

"I saw them last weekend when I was at the Chelsea Market."

"You got these last weekend?"

Judith shook her head and chuckled. The eternal pessimist, her mother expected hail behind every silver lining. "I went back and got them last night."

"Let's eat them."

"They're for you. I had one for breakfast."

They went to the back of the house to the kitchen, where her mother poured a cup of coffee from a decanter that had probably been sitting there since six this morning. "You want a cup?"

"No, thanks." She had to get this conversation going before the goodwill from the faworki wore off. "I need to talk to you about something . . . something important."

They sat down at the small kitchen table.

"Is Victor all right?" Again, expecting the worst.

"He's fine, Mom. I still plan to pick him up tomorrow, but I'm hoping you'll go with me."

"It's silly for both of us to go. Victor doesn't need that."

"He needs you to come when I'm not here, though. You saw what happened to him last time."

"I know." She could see on her face that her mother wanted to blame her for being away, but held back. "But I need for you to go get him and take him back. You don't know how awful I feel when I go to those places and see how he lives. All those bad smells, everybody screaming. It's like they're not even human." Halina sniffed and wiped her eyes. "And it's my fault he's there."

Her mother usually waited until later in the discussion to play that particular guilt card, which meant she probably had come up with new arguments since the last attempt to get her to visit the group home. "Some of the people at Wyckoff are more handicapped than Victor, but a lot are like him, Mom. He really likes it there. The staff is nice and they take good care of him. The only time he ever causes trouble is when we break his routine."

"That's why you have to be there, Judith. He needs you."

"He needs us." She scooted her chair closer and laid her hand on top of her mother's. "I've met somebody . . . somebody who lives in Chicago."

Immediately, Halina started shaking her head. "No, you can't leave us. You know what will happen to Victor if you leave him."

"I'm not . . . I don't . . ." What was the truth? "I haven't even thought about moving away. We haven't been seeing each other that long. But the only time we can see each other is on the weekends, and it makes me feel guilty not to be here for Victor. That's why I need your help."

She hadn't expected her mother to be happy for her, and she wasn't surprised. Not since Kevin had she even mentioned dating anyone.

"So the friend you mentioned was a man. You told me it was a woman."

Wonderful segue. "Well, no. The person I went to see was a woman . . . like I said, it was a woman I met at the convention." Before her mother could try to fill in the blanks, she drew a deep breath and finished. "She's the one I'm in love with."

"That's just ridiculous."

"Mom . . ." Her mouth suddenly dry, she got up and ran herself a glass of water from the tap. With her back turned, she continued. "I never said anything about dating women because it never mattered before. There wasn't anyone I cared about this much."

"Judith, don't stand there and tell me you care about some woman"—she said the word with contempt—"more than you do about your only brother."

"I think I already know how you feel about this sort of thing. It's going to take some time to get used to, but—"

"I'm not going to get used to it. It's not natural."

"It is for me, Mom. It's the only thing that is." She took her seat again at the table, but this time, slumped back in her chair.

"You were married to Kevin."

"I know. That seemed right to me at the time, but it wasn't."

"How do you know? If you had stayed with him, you wouldn't be so confused."

The obvious retort, which Judith suppressed, was if she had stayed with him, she would have moved to Boston. "I'm not confused, Mom. This is who I really am."

Halina just shook her head, not making eye contact at all. "It's not who I raised you to be."

"No, but sometimes I feel that you raised me to be Victor's caretaker." She could see that her words stung, but the issue of Victor—and not her sexuality—was what she needed to confront with her mother. "I love Victor. You know I do. And I've been there for him my whole life. That isn't going to change because I'm in love with a woman."

"It will if you're never here."

"I will be here, Mom. But I need you to step up when I can't be. Whether you agree or not with my choice, I deserve to be happy with somebody I love. It's not fair for you to ask me to give that up for Victor."

A cold silence followed, which Judith took as her cue to leave. That was a lot to dump on her mother, and they both needed time to think about it.

"I want you to come with me tomorrow to pick him up. I'll call and ask them to have him ready to go so we won't even have to go inside."

Halina's expression of angst hadn't changed. Nor did her resolve not to speak.

"And by the way, Mom . . . her name's Carmen. Carmen Delallo. It would have been nice if you'd asked."

Bed . . . hotel . . . Japan. Bits and pieces of information filled in the blanks in Carmen's head as she jerked herself awake. Phone . . . Tuesday . . .

"Hello."

After a beep, Cathy's voice broke through, followed by an echo of her words.

"What? Hold on." She sat up and turned on the light. Six thirty, which meant it was six thirty p.m. back in Chicago. She slapped the speakerphone button and ran both hands through her hair. "Good morning."

"To you. Lenore's here with me, but we're about to go home."

"What are you guys doing there so late?"

"Something happened we thought you should know about."

"This doesn't sound good."

"It's not," Cathy said. "I'm going to let Lenore tell you about it."

Her bladder was screaming. She would have gone to the bathroom had it been just Cathy. But her vice president warranted a show of decorum.

"Carmen?"

"Hi, Lenore. What's up?"

"I got a call on my cell phone today from Art Conover."

"That asshole. Let me guess. He wanted you to persuade me to sell him the company."

"No . . . actually, he wanted me to come work for him. And he offered me a lot of money."

Carmen felt the muscles in her chest and arms tighten. Losing Lenore to Art Conover would be a body blow. "And what did you tell him?"

"I told him my cell phone was for my private use, and to please tell whoever gave him the number not to do it again."

She blew out a breath of relief. Whatever she had done to earn the loyalty of her staff, she was glad she had. "I appreciate that, Lenore. And I appreciate you." And she was infinitely thankful she had made her vice president before this ever came up.

"I know, Carmen. I'm happy where I am. But there's more, I'm afraid."

"More?"

"I'm not sure, but I think he talked to Raul too."

Raul leaving would gut them, especially in the middle of the transition project. "What do you mean you're not sure?"

"I'm really not. I was with him in the break room when his cell phone rang. He didn't take the call, but I heard him ask Richard who had that area code. It was the same one as when Art called me."

"Dallas?"

"Yeah."

"I guessed I shouldn't be surprised." She heard mumbling on the other end of the line.

"Cathy says to remind you about the no compete clause. Raul signed one, didn't he?"

Right, the no compete. "Yes, everyone did. Cathy has them in the personnel files." No one in her company could just leave and go to work for Art. They all had signed agreements not to work for an industry competitor for a period of two years after leaving TDG.

"So we're safe, right?"

"Yeah, except two years from now it may not matter. We need to head this off, or we're all going to be looking for work."

"That's more or less what Art told me. You want me to talk to Raul? Remind him about the clause?"

"Not just Raul. Call a full staff meeting for tomorrow and tell them you heard from Art."

"You want everyone to know about this?"

"He may be talking to everybody—Richard, Kristy, all the assistants. Tell them they might get a call, and if they do, they should mention the no compete clause in their contracts. If he's going to play hardball, he's going to have to play it with me, not my staff."

"Good enough. How are things going in Tokyo?"

"I have two contracts to write today, and one more tomorrow. Then my plane leaves at three."

"And you'll be back in the office on Thursday?"

"Physically. No telling where my head will be."

"Cathy says bye."

"Bye to both of you. Thanks for staying late to call."

She hung up and went straight to the bathroom. The idea of hiring a hit man to take out Art Conover was growing on her.

She sure picked a hell of a time to travel halfway around the world. Art Conover was poaching her staff, and Brooke was clamoring for attention. And all Carmen seemed to want was more time with Judith.

She turned on the shower and went back into the bedroom to lay out her clothes for the day. She needed to finish these contracts and get back home. Judith would arrive on Friday night, and they weren't going to worry about anything but each other for two whole days.

She drew a small bottle of prescription pills from her purse. She hadn't taken one of these in over three years, not since her niece died. Back then, the stress of Susanna's declining health and eventual death had twisted her chest into a permanent knot.

Screw Art Conover, she thought angrily as she stepped into the steamy spray. If he thought she was just going to hand over her life's work, he had another think coming. She was the industry leader because she knew the business better than anyone else, she worked harder and she surrounded herself with the best people. That's what her clients expected, not some off-the-rack book of numbers.

And what was up with Brooke? For the first time in her life, Carmen found herself actually wanting to say no to Brooke.

Cathy had teased her about it at first, but hit it right on the nose when she pointed out that it probably had everything to do with feeling guilty that she hadn't told her about Judith.

"By the way, did I happen to mention my new girlfriend looks just like you? No, not just a little bit. A lot, actually." Carmen cranked up the hot water in the shower. "But it's not like I'm pretending to make love to you or anything. It's all just a coincidence. Well, yes. I was in love with you, but not like that . . . because you weren't like that. If you had been like that, I could have loved you like that . . . but you weren't . . . so I didn't."

She had no idea how Brooke was going to take the news, and no clue about how to break it to her without her feelings becoming transparent. Maybe it was time to finally come clean, to tell her how she had felt all these years. That was ironic, telling her now that it didn't matter anymore. Why hadn't she done it when she got involved with Kim? Life would have been so much simpler.

"Because you would have left Kim in a New York minute if Brooke had even waggled her finger in your direction."

She just had to hope their friendship was strong enough that Brooke could handle the awkwardness of knowing she had been the object of lust for thirty years. Maybe now she would understand why Carmen had practically run out of the room every time she had started to change clothes, or why she had always preferred sleeping on the couch to sharing a bed.

"But I don't need you anymore, you see. I've replaced you with a look-alike, my own personal Brooke Healey doll."

She finished rinsing and turned off the spray. Her words disgusted her. That wasn't how she felt about Judith. It was why she had noticed her initially, but it wasn't why she fell in love.

She wrapped in the hotel's oversized robe and stepped out, going straight to the bedroom to find her phone.

"Amie? It's Carmen. Is your mom there?"

She rubbed the towel through her hair and tossed it back into the bathroom. She could hear conversation in the background. It was stupid not to have told Amie this was costing her about three dollars a minute.

"Hi, stranger . . . Yeah, I'm sorry I've been so busy. Let's try for dinner next week." Brooke had other ideas, pumping her for when she got back in town. "No, I've got some fires to put out at work when I get back. How about Monday night?" She wrapped one arm around her midsection, shivering against the cool air. "Of course I miss you. I can't wait to see you."

They finalized arrangements to meet at their favorite restaurant and said good-bye. Then she dialed again and waited. In moments, Judith's voice came on the line.

"Someone in Tokyo is thinking about you." The feeling of relief was instant. "I love you . . . No, I only have a minute, but I wanted to hear your voice before I headed out. You have no idea how much I needed it . . . It's mostly stuff going on at work. I'll tell you about it tonight, but you just made it all better."

They traded sweet words and she hung up. It was as if she could actually feel the tightness in her chest begin to dissipate. She reached for the bottle of pills again, squeezed it and dropped it back into her purse. Yes, she was feeling better already.

Chapter 18

Judith moaned as the last waves of her orgasm receded. "That was a nice surprise."

"You didn't expect to come?" Carmen eased herself upward, allowing the dildo to slip out of her.

"I didn't know what to expect. I thought since I was wearing it, you would be the one . . ."

"When I wear it, you can expect to be face down across the coffee table." Carmen loosened the strap of the harness and tugged, prompting Judith to lift her hips so it could be removed. "But it's always going to be about your pleasure."

Judith had no doubt about the veracity of Carmen's simple declaration. Even before they moved into this realm, her body had known Carmen would be a perfect lover. "You don't have to make it about me all the time."

"What if I want to?"

"And what if I want to make it about you?" She wrapped her arms around Carmen's neck and pulled her down.

"I've always thrived on competition." Carmen latched her lips onto Judith's earlobe for a gentle nibble. "I love it that you like to share these wonderful things with me."

"I draw the line at animal costumes."

"Damn. And I have this great duck outfit."

Judith chuckled and tightened her grip. "You're so good for me."

"Because of the animals?"

"Because I know you love me. I can feel it."

"That's probably just my hipbone."

"You aren't capable of being serious, are you?"

"I'm serious about you."

Their playful mood shifted dramatically as a tremor seemed to pass between them. Carmen followed her words with a deep, soulful kiss.

"Tell me what that means."

"You don't know?"

"I want to hear it from you."

Carmen didn't answer right away, but Judith knew from the rare pensive look this wouldn't be a lighthearted response. "It means I think about having you in my life all the time. I want you to be a part of it all—my family, my friends, my work. And I know how hard it is for you to imagine a life like that, but it doesn't stop me from wanting it."

For Judith, it wasn't hard at all to dream about a life with Carmen. The hard part was her obligation to Victor.

Carmen went on. "I want to show you off to all the important people in my life, even though every one of them is going to think I'm insane."

"Because I look like Brooke?"

"And because they're all going to think the same thing you did—that you're a substitute for something I couldn't have."

"I don't think that anymore."

"I know you don't. We couldn't do this if you did."

"Why does that worry you?"

"I just want people to know this is about you and me."

"That may not be something they'll accept right away. But if we love each other, it's going to show eventually."

"I know." Carmen laid her head on Judith's shoulder. "I'm worried about what Brooke will think."

"Have you thought about when you're going to tell her?"

"I'm having dinner with her Monday night. I plan to do it then. Don't you wish you could be a fly on the wall?"

"No, I don't want to be anywhere near. You two have to work that out on your own."

"I don't suppose there's any chance you . . ."

"What?"

"My brother Paul is a plastic surgeon. He could give you a big nose and a pointy chin and a—"

"You are insane." She should have known Carmen couldn't stay serious. At least she hoped she wasn't serious.

It was easy to see why Carmen liked it here, Judith thought. The neighborhood was old and distinguished, and who could beat having a park and Lake Michigan practically in your front yard? Not to mention the Starbucks around the corner. Though it was only her second visit, she was starting to feel at home, enough to make the coffee run by herself while Carmen talked to her mother.

She balanced one cup on top of the other and reached for the door. It swung open as the doorman got there just in time.

"Thank you."

"You're welcome," he said. He continued to hold the door for another woman she had noticed getting out of her car at the curb.

She stepped onto the elevator and shuffled the cups again, balancing the drinks so she could punch the button for Carmen's floor. The other woman jumped on and pressed a number, and sensing Judith's predicament, asked, "What floor?"

Before she answered, she looked up. The woman before her was Brooke Nance, and she looked every bit as shocked as Judith was. "Uh . . . seven."

They couldn't stop staring at each other, but neither spoke. The pictures Carmen had shared didn't do justice to the brilliant blue in Brooke's eyes. Those had to be contact lenses. No one had eyes that color. And Brooke's blond hair was longer now, long enough to pull back from her face. She was even prettier in person, and that was saying something.

The door opened on seven and Judith immediately stepped off without a word, turning left down the hallway in the direction of the stairs. This was going to freak Carmen out, and she didn't want to make it worse. If Brooke said anything—and of course she would—Carmen would figure out she had run.

She exited the stairwell at the outside of the building and followed the sidewalk back around to the front, where she crossed the street to the park. From a bench, she could watch the main door of the building, and wait to return when the coast was clear.

" . . . No, Mom. I do want everyone to meet her, but she has to leave early in the morning." Carmen had finally broken the news to her family that she had a new girlfriend, and that her girlfriend bore more than a passing resemblance to her best friend. Now their curiosity was piqued and they couldn't wait to meet Judith. "Sundays are hard for her because she needs to get back to New York . . . I told you, her brother lives in a group home and she picks him up every Sunday to go to dinner at her mom's."

A shuffling sound at the door told her Judith was back with their coffee.

"I need to go, Mom . . . Fine. Seven o'clock. We'll see you then."

She disconnected and let out a sigh. Now to break it to Judith that she had just committed them to dinner tonight in Evanston.

She grabbed for the handle to open the door. "You'll never guess what I've just gotten us—" Her stomach dropped as she realized the face at the door belonged not to Judith, but to Brooke. "What—" She caught herself before blurting out something that would have certainly sounded rude. "I didn't know you were coming by."

"I had to drop off something at work. You're never going to believe what I just saw on the elevator!"

Carmen had a sinking feeling she was going to believe it very much.

"There was a woman who looked so much like me we couldn't stop staring at each other. She was a little taller, and her coloring was darker, but we had practically the same face. We could have been sisters."

"Where . . . did she go?"

"She got off on seven. She must not live here or I know you would have noticed her before. It was amazing."

So Judith got off on a different floor. When she recognized Brooke and realized where she was headed, she ducked out to let Carmen deal with it. Smart girl . . . or a chickenshit.

"I think I know who you're talking about."

"No, you haven't seen the woman I'm talking about, or you would have said something before." Brooke walked in and dropped her purse on a side table in the foyer. From there, she continued into the living room to sit on the couch.

At a loss for how to dissuade her from sticking around, Carmen followed her. Like it or not, the time had come to tell her about Judith. She walked over to the glass doors of the balcony and peered out. Judith was sitting on a park bench across the street, a cup of coffee in each hand.

Where to start? She pushed her hands in the pockets of her jeans and turned around to face Brooke. "I have to tell you something."

"Is something wrong?"

"No, no. I was planning to tell you tomorrow night at dinner, but since you're here . . ."

"What is it?"

"You remember back in college when I told everybody I was a lesbian? I started by saying how it took me a long time to be sure about it, and I hoped they wouldn't think I'd been dishonest with them all along."

Brooke looked at her dubiously, clearly curious about where this was going. "I never thought you were dishonest."

"I know you didn't. And I would have told you about this sooner, but I wasn't sure where it was going."

"Quit beating around the bush, Carmen. If you're going to tell me something, just do it."

Beating around the bush was exactly what she was doing, trying to couch her words in something Brooke might find sympathetic and acceptable. "I was going to tell you all about Judith, the woman I met in New York." Still beating around the bush. "That was her in the elevator."

Brooke squinted with confusion and shook her head. "No, that woman got off on seven."

"It was her. I guess she did that because she recognized you."

Her eyes grew wide as realization dawned. "Your new girlfriend looks just like me?"

Carmen nodded and came over to sit on the couch. "This is going to sound crazy, and for all I know, it is. I met her at that conference we all went to, the one where I asked you to come hang out with us."

"Wait a minute." Brooke sat up and held up her hand, clearly agitated. "You're not making any sense at all."

"Brooke . . ." Carmen took a deep breath and steadied herself.

"She's a travel agent from New York. She was at the conference. Cathy noticed her because . . . well, I guess it's obvious why. She pointed her out to me and I had a chance to talk to her. I really liked her and we hit it off."

Carmen held her tongue while Brooke put it all together. She expected confusion, awkwardness, maybe even teasing. What she hadn't counted on was hurt.

"Now I get it. I wondered why everybody laughed when I said I wish I'd been there with you guys, and Priscilla said it was like I was."

Carmen was heartbroken to see the tears that had begun to pool in Brooke's eyes. "If anything, they were laughing at me, not you . . . because they knew I hadn't told you yet."

"In other words, it was a private joke. I'm used to that from all the others, but not from you."

"Brooke, I—"

"They think I don't know how they talk about me, how they look down on me because I don't have a big, fancy career . . . or because I didn't marry the perfect man."

"That isn't true. They love you, just like I do."

"I've always counted on you to stand up for me. You have no idea how much it hurts to know you kept this from me and everybody made it their little joke."

She suddenly stood up and started for the door, but Carmen caught her arm. "Brooke, please. You're so wrong." She wanted to wipe the tears away but she didn't dare. "Please sit back down. I'll tell you everything."

"You mean there's more?" Her question dripped with sarcasm, but she wiped her own tears and sank back onto the couch.

"The truth is, I noticed Judith because I thought she was beautiful . . . like I've always thought you were beautiful." She was relieved to see Brooke's face soften with her admission. "Of all my friends, you've always been the special one. There have been times when . . ." Her heart was pounding in her throat.

"There's no easy way to say this."

"You were in love with me."

So much for her secret. Brooke had known about it all along. "Off and on." Mostly on.

"Why didn't you ever say anything?"

"Like what? Leave your husband and do something that goes totally against your nature?"

Brooke pressed her fist against her mouth as she seemed to weigh whether or not to say what she was thinking. "Who knows, Carmen? If you'd asked me at the right time, I might have said yes."

The words came down like a sledgehammer inside her, and her first thought was to ask herself when that right time might have been.

"It's not like I could have fucked things up any worse."

Brooke had always needed a port in a storm, but Carmen knew deep down she would never have been more than that. "That wouldn't have been enough for me. I wouldn't have settled for anything less than you being outrageously happy." She held up a hand to stop Brooke from cutting her off. "If we had gone down that road and it hadn't worked out, it would have killed me. And it might have screwed up our friendship. That's a risk I would never take."

"Oh, Carmen." Brooke scooted along the couch to wrap her arms around her waist and lay her head in her lap. "Next to my girls, you being my friend is the best thing in my life."

Carmen returned the embrace, such as it was. "That's how I've always felt about you too."

Brooke sat up again and faced her. "So where does that leave Judith?"

Judith . . . who was probably still sitting on the park bench. "I'm in love with her."

"And you're sure it's her you're in love with?"

"There isn't a doubt in my mind."

"Obviously, she knows about me."

"I've told her the truth—that you and the girls are like family to me, and I expect things to be that way forever."

"So what's going to happen? Is she going to move here?"

She told Brooke about Victor, and how Judith felt obligated to take care of her brother. "When has anything having to do with my love life been easy?"

"Never, but you've got me beat. At least you haven't had a whole life of misery."

Words like those always melted Carmen's heart, but Brooke had no idea of the lonesome sadness of unrequited love.

"You would have been the perfect husband, Carmen."

"I know. I used to think the same thing." She chuckled at the irony. "I need to let Judith know that everything's okay. It is, isn't it?"

Brooke nodded, but didn't look up.

"Would you like to meet her?"

A quick shake of the head told Carmen that things weren't as okay as she hoped. "Not today. I'm feeling a little bit . . . jealous." She finally looked up and waved her hand at Carmen's confusion. "It's not rational. Don't try to make any sense out of it . . . I just feel like she's stealing the only person who always puts me first."

"You know I'll always be there if you need me. And I'll always need you."

"So this Judith thing is serious."

"I think it is."

Brooke stood and looped her purse over her shoulder. "At least promise me you won't ever leave Chicago."

"I can't"—a part of her brain said she should stop right there—"imagine leaving my home."

" . . . and this is where I spent my formative years," Carmen said, swinging open the door of a small bedroom. "I had the smallest room in the house, but at least I didn't have to share."

Judith stepped inside to look around. A twin bed was situated beneath a window, and a bureau and dresser crowded the opposite wall. "I wish I'd had a camera when we walked in the front door. Your mother's face was priceless."

"I told you she'd freak out."

"But your dad acted like he didn't even notice anything unusual."

"Probably because he didn't. Before he retired, he was the best surgeon there was—totally focused. But outside the operating room, he couldn't find his car in the parking lot."

"That sounds a lot like someone else I know."

Carmen glared at her before breaking into a grin. "I remember the things that really matter . . . most of the time."

"Especially when Cathy reminds you." Judith walked over to the window and looked out. "Did you ever climb out this window onto the roof?"

"Just once. I sneaked out with Mark one night, but Dad heard us walking around out there. The next day, he made us go out again and clean the gutters."

"That sounds fair." Judith loved the image of a teenage Carmen filled with mischief. It almost rivaled the adult version. "I love how this house feels, Carmen. I bet it was fun growing up here."

"It was a crazy place most of the time."

"I can't imagine living with so many people."

"I couldn't even take a shower without somebody coming into the bathroom. Did you know that all guys flush the toilet while they're still peeing?"

Judith laughed, instantly thinking of Kevin. "Yes, I think I did know that."

Carmen tugged her into an embrace. "Did you also know that I love you?" She followed her question with a tender kiss, then shot a sideways glance toward the bed. "I used to lie there in that bed at night, touching myself and dreaming about you."

"You did not."

"I did." She looked intently into Judith's eyes, her expression serious. "I never imagined your face, but you touched me with the love I always wanted to feel."

Judith was moved by the rare show of solemnity and candor, and buried her face into Carmen's neck. "I love you so much."

"Carmen?" Elaine Delallo was calling up from the bottom of the stairs. "Dinner's ready. You and Brooke—I mean . . ."

"It's Judith, Mom."

"I'm so sorry."

As they started down the steps, Judith was amused by the mortified look on the woman's face. "It's all right, Mrs. Delallo. Carmen does it too."

"I do not."

In a gloomy scene Judith thought was becoming too familiar, she and Carmen stood at the window watching for the airport limo.

"I'll try to come to New York on Friday. It's my turn."

"There's no rule that says we have to take turns. I'm not the one who has to go to San Diego next week."

"I know, but I hate for you to have to turn around and make this trip again."

There was more to Carmen's reluctance than that, but Judith couldn't put her finger on it. "Do you not want me to come?"

"That's not it."

Judith shook her head. "Then what is it? I feel like you've been holding me at arm's length ever since we got home last night."

"I have not. Why would you even say something like that?"

"Because this thing with Brooke is eating at you, whether you admit it to yourself or not."

"What thing with Brooke are you talking about? I told her about you—that I loved you."

"Yes, and . . ."

"And what?"

The growing agitation in Carmen's voice was unsettling. "Why were you so upset on the way home last night?"

"Why do you think? My mother called you Brooke twice."

"And I made a joke both times. That's all I can do. You don't have to make it such a big deal."

Carmen sighed and stared out the window.

"And I'm also worried because you didn't want to make love last night. It was like there was a wall between us."

"A wall?" Carmen's pained look took her by surprise. "I went to sleep with both arms around you and my head on your shoulder. When did I ever do that before?"

It was true that she usually slept on her stomach facing away, even after intense lovemaking. Last night had been different in more ways than one.

"Judith, I felt closer to you last night than I ever have, so I don't know anything about this wall you're talking about."

"Carmen . . ." They both looked up as the limo pulled to the curb in front of the building. "I'm sorry. I didn't mean to—"

"This isn't all about sex for me. I hope it isn't for you."

"Of course it isn't. But last night was different, and you should have talked to me about how you were feeling."

"Brooke made me think about things." Carmen took both of her hands. "But they were good things, like how much I love you and why."

Judith sighed, frustrated with herself for misreading Carmen's sweet gesture last night. "Can I just backspace and erase the last five minutes? I'm sorry I said that."

"What if I just forgive you instead?"

The phone rang to announce the car. Prissy began to bark when Judith grasped her suitcase and rolled it toward the door.

"Let me come to New York on Friday," Carmen said when she hung up the phone. "I promise to make love to you all weekend."

"With me, not to me. Then we have a deal."

"You drive a hard bargain."

"I want what I want."

"And you shall have it."

Chapter 19

"It's one of these along here on the right," Carmen said, peering through the the window of her taxi. All of the brownstones on Fifteenth Street ran together, especially at night. "Here is fine."

She climbed out on the curb as the cabbie scrambled to get her bag. A quick call would bring Judith—

"There you are."

After her hectic week, Judith's warm smile was a sight for sore eyes. "I'm so glad to see you."

"Me too you," Judith answered, giving her a quick kiss and a long, fierce hug. Then she picked up Carmen's bag and led the way up the steps to the top floor and into the small apartment.

"I'm so glad this week's over." Carmen wanted only to collapse on the futon and relax.

"I knew you were going to San Diego, but why did you have

to go to Denver? I couldn't understand what you were saying."

"I was so tired when I talked to you." She kicked off her shoes and threw her feet up on the coffee table as she leaned back. "The scumbag who's trying to steal my company had a meeting in Denver with one of my oldest clients, Pete Cowen. Pete called Cathy about it and she put him through to me in San Diego. I flew up there on my way back to Chicago to see what Conover was pitching, and talked with Pete about what it would take to beat him back."

"Will you be able to do it?"

Carmen rolled her head around her shoulders to loosen the muscles, prompting Judith to scoot in behind her and start a shoulder massage. "I don't know. The syndicated study throws off a couple of million dollars a year after expenses. That covers payroll and benefits for most of the staff, with a nice tidy profit for yours truly. If he lowballs us, he could eat up half of it in five years, all of it in six or seven."

"So how do you compete with him?"

That was the same question she had been asking herself for the past three weeks. "One option is just to sell him the syndicated division. That's what he wants. It would be better than watching it disappear over time, especially if I have to stomach the idea of him having all my clients." A sharp pain gripped the center of her chest, and she pressed a fist against it. The sensations had been coming more frequently, and she mentally located the pills in her purse in case of an emergency.

"What's wrong?"

"Nothing, I just . . . I've been sitting on the plane and the muscles in my chest are cramped." Judith would probably freak out if she suddenly jumped up and put a pill under her tongue. "Our only other choice is to cut the service way back and try to salvage the bare bones. At least we'd be able to keep the custom work that way."

"That's the part you like, isn't it?"

"Yeah, but it's also the part with the lowest profit margin, and the first thing to go when companies start tweaking their budgets." Carmen leaned back into Judith and tried to relax. "I won't be able to support a whole staff on just the custom side."

"Is that what worries you most, not being able to support your staff?"

"They've worked as hard as I have."

"No one works as hard as you do, Carmen. At least you can relax this weekend."

"I wish. I lost a day on the San Diego report and it's due on Tuesday. I was hoping you'd let me work on it tomorrow."

Judith stopped her massage and hugged her from behind. "Are you sure that's more important than you getting some rest?"

"I know I'll feel better when it's not hanging over my head."

"Okay, then you should get some rest tonight. Why don't you get ready for bed?"

It was only ten thirty—nine thirty in Chicago—but that seemed like a great idea. "Bed sounds good. I believe I promised to make love with you all weekend."

"And I believe you showed me last weekend that making love can be a lot of things, including just holding you while you sleep."

Carmen felt a swell of love inside. Judith was the most unselfish lover she had ever had. "I'm so glad I'm here."

"Me too."

Carmen unzipped her suitcase and pulled out her toiletries. Once inside the bathroom, she popped two antacids, hoping they would calm the burning in her chest. If this pain and tightness continued, she would probably have to go back through all the tests again and get back on the regular medication. She had worked hard to avoid that, but stress was her trigger, and she had it coming from all directions—Art Conover, the report that was due, Brooke's cool attitude toward her after learning about

Judith . . . and having the one person she seemed to need most live a thousand miles away.

Judith waited at the crosswalk with a half dozen others, oblivious to their faces or purpose, mindful only of getting back to her apartment with coffee and breakfast. It was a beautiful spring day in New York, the kind of day one never wanted to waste working indoors, but Carmen needed to get her report done in order to relax. Judith understood that. She was the same way about getting errands done on Friday night or Saturday morning so she could have the rest of her weekend to take it easy and be with her family.

Carmen had gotten up early, stacking her printouts on the small kitchen table as she fired up her laptop. The workspace wasn't big enough to spread things out, but she was gamely making the best of it, balancing some of her papers on the lid of the trashcan. In her Chicago apartment, she had an enormous desk and workspace, an ideal atmosphere for getting things done. That she was now crammed into the corner of a tiny kitchen to crank out what she said was a fifty-thousand-dollar report was absurd.

Judith knew Carmen loved her, but she wasn't going to kid herself about the reality of their differences. People like Carmen—successful businesswomen used to the finer things—didn't simply adapt to spending their free time in two hundred square feet on the top floor of a walk-up. It made so much more sense for Judith to be the one doing the traveling back and forth, especially since Carmen traveled so much already and she had a dog at home that needed her attention. But Carmen insisted it wasn't fair unless they took turns. She might change her mind after a few more weekends like this one.

As she turned the corner on her street, her cell phone rang from her purse, and she hurried to the next stoop so she could set down her tray. The number in the display had a Chicago area code.

"Hello." It was Cathy Rosen. "No, I guess she forgot. She was so tired when she got here last night." Carmen hadn't turned on her cell phone today.

Judith took a seat on the third step of the brownstone as she listened to Cathy's instructions. Carmen was booked tomorrow on the five o'clock return from LaGuardia . . . a package came late yesterday from Pete Cowen in Denver, probably Art Conover's sales packet . . . one of the research associates had a question about the San Diego report. "She's working on the report for San Diego today. I wish I could help her . . . Sure, I could do that." Carmen had a habit of transposing digits, Cathy said. Someone needed to go behind her and check the numbers in her report and charts.

"I feel so bad that she has to work today, Cathy . . . Yeah, but she's really tense about it. Last night when she got here, she said the muscles in her chest were cramping, and—no, she didn't take anything, at least not that I know of."

She sat in stunned silence as Cathy grilled her for more details, then explained why she was so concerned.

Carmen marked the page of numbers with a blue sticky note from her briefcase so she could find the figures she wanted later. The blue ones marked statistics for outbound travel for those living in or around San Diego. The yellow ones marked local attractions for day-trippers. And the pink ones marked visitors to the area from other parts of the country. It was easier to conceptualize her report in terms of color coding the sections. As soon as she wrote the basic framework, the meat of the text would fall into place.

She had done this hundreds of times, but she prided herself on never letting it become rote. Her clients wanted new and clever interpretations, things they could use to attract new business and outsell the competition. Ordinary wouldn't do.

She jumped to open the door when she heard Judith jiggle the lock with her key.

"Coffee, coffee, coffee. Just what I need."

"I got fruit and yogurt too."

"That's not as good as coffeecake, but it'll do. What took you so long?"

"I got a call from Cathy. Your cell phone's turned off again."

Carmen went into the other room and fished it out of her purse. "Just the ringer. I don't have any messages."

"I do."

She sipped her latte as Judith relayed the messages about the plane, the package from Denver, and the question from Richard. "I guess I should call him first since I'm working on the report now. Did she say anything else?"

She was surprised by Judith's stern look as she turned. And there was something almost confrontational about the way she folded her arms and leaned against the sink. "As a matter of fact . . ."

Carmen cocked her head, waiting for whatever Judith needed to get off her chest.

"I told her about how tired you were when you got here last night, and I mentioned that bit about when you were holding your chest."

Great, she thought. So not only did Cathy know she was having trouble again, she had probably told Judith all about it. No doubt, both of them would make this a bigger deal than it was. "And I bet Cathy told you things she had no business telling you."

"Is your health something you think isn't my business?"

"No, but I should be the one to decide what to tell you and when." She fought the impulse to grip her chest as the familiar ache returned. Thinking or talking about it always seemed to make it worse. "It isn't all that big a deal. I didn't want you to think it was worse than it was."

"No, you didn't want me to be like Cathy and ride you about what you eat and whether or not you get out and exercise."

That was part of it too, Carmen admitted to herself. "Look, that's not the sort of thing I tell people that I'm just getting to know." She took a step toward Judith and grasped both of her hands. "But now that I know you better, I'll tell you all about it."

"You should have done that already, especially if it's bothering you now."

"I don't want you to treat me like I'm fragile or something."

"Tell me how you're feeling right now."

"Right now . . . it hurts a little bit. This always happens when I feel stressed about something, like needing to get this report done."

"Sit down."

She grabbed the kitchen chair and started to turn it around.

"Not there. Let's go in the other room."

Carmen led the way into the main room and sat on the futon, still in its unmade condition. "It's not usually this bad, but this mess with Art Conover has been bothering me for a couple of weeks. That's the kind of thing that makes it act up."

"What is it that's acting up?"

"My cholesterol runs a little high. And then when my blood pressure goes up, my chest starts to feel tight."

"Do you take medicine?"

"I used to. But after a couple of years, we agreed to try to control it with diet and exercise. I always carry a bottle of pills in my purse—some nitroglycerin tablets—in case I have an emergency. I haven't taken one since Susanna got so sick." The time before that was shortly after Brooke married Geoffrey and moved out with the girls, but Judith didn't need to know that.

"Carmen . . ." Judith wore a pained look, but it was obviously concern, not anger or disappointment that she hadn't been told about this. "You know how Cathy watches over you? I'm going to be ten times worse than that."

"I figured you would. Between the two of you, I'm guessing all of my fun is gone forever." She had hoped for a smile, but it didn't happen.

"You know what?" Judith intertwined their fingers, never once looking up to meet her eye. "Forever sounds pretty good to me, but I want it to be a very long time."

Yes, forever did sound good. She squeezed Judith's hand and leaned over to place a tender kiss on her temple. Now probably wasn't a good time to tell her that this New York-Chicago thing was second only to Art Conover on her list of problems she had to solve if she really wanted to deal with her stress.

Carmen sat nervously on the couch beside Victor, wondering if, at any moment, one of them would jump up and dash out of the room. It wasn't that she minded sitting with him, but she worried he might become spooked at being left alone with a relative stranger.

He was sweet, this toddler inside a man's body. He certainly loved his sister. That was obvious from the way his face lit up every time she was near. No wonder Judith felt such a strong sense of responsibility for his well-being.

Halina appeared in the kitchen doorway. "Carmen, would you like coffee?"

"No, thank you. I'm stuffed. Lunch was delicious." She had eaten the meatloaf graciously, though ground beef in any form usually gave her indigestion.

"I would have fixed something more suitable for company, but Judith didn't tell me you were coming until just before you got here."

"It was wonderful, Mrs. Kowalczyk." She had practiced pronouncing the surname on the subway with Judith as they rode to

Brooklyn. It was too soon to tell what sort of impression she was making on Judith's mother. At least Victor seemed to like her.

Judith returned from the bathroom and sat on the couch between Carmen and Victor. "I think my mother likes you," she whispered as Halina disappeared into the kitchen.

"How can you tell?"

"When you helped Victor hang up his jacket . . . she really liked that. Most people don't interact with him very much, but you did."

"It wasn't anything. He just looked like he needed a little help."

"I know, but it was the way you did it. You helped him do it, instead of doing it for him."

"That's what you do."

Halina returned with a cup of coffee. "Carmen, do you have brothers and sisters?"

"There are six of us. My brothers aren't as handsome as Victor, though." She leaned forward to peek at Judith's brother, who was blushing from the compliment. Now that Carmen knew how to earn Halina Kowalczyk's approval, she wasn't ashamed to pour it on.

Judith pulled the front door closed on her mother's house and stepped onto the sidewalk to wait with Carmen for her limo. "This would be a nice day for them to be late."

"But if I miss my plane, I'd have to stay a whole extra day. What would we do?"

"Believe me, I can think of plenty." Judith was bubbling over with excitement over how well the afternoon had gone. The last-minute decision from Carmen to join them for Sunday dinner had paid off for everyone. Her mother had been a gracious hostess, and Victor had liked Carmen right away, even coloring a picture for her after lunch. "What are you going to do with that picture?"

"I'm going to put it on my refrigerator just like you do."

"You're sweet."

"So is Victor. I can see why you're attached to him."

"He's pretty special."

"Your mom was nice to me. I was expecting something more along the lines of Cruella De Vil."

"So was I. But then, you always seem to bring out the best in people."

"I think that describes you more than me, but I'll thank you for the compliment."

Judith wished she could put her arms around Carmen and hold her until she had to leave. But it didn't seem right to leave a trail of gossip among the older women in her mother's neighborhood. "Do you promise you're going to take it easy this week?"

"As much as I can. Sure you won't change your mind about next weekend?"

Judith had decided they should spend next weekend apart so Carmen could enjoy peace and quiet in her own apartment with her poor, neglected Prissy. Carmen had argued that she could relax better if Judith was with her.

"You need your time, Carmen, whether you admit it or not. Things in your life need to settle down."

"See, that's a perfect example of what I was talking about yesterday. You're making a decision for me. I don't want to be coddled over this." Her voice had a sharp edge, but she softened it immediately. "I can think of dozens of ways I'd rather be coddled."

A dark green Town Car turned the corner and slowed.

"And I promise I will do all of them weekend after next. Maybe I can get Todd to spring me an extra day."

"You need to call Sofia. She'll let you off whenever I tell her."

Judith didn't want to spend their last moments together

debating the merits of a job change. "Call me when you get home. Do you have the dog treats?"

"Yeah, but I'll probably let her think they're from me."

"That's okay. You need to make up with her after being gone so much."

The limo driver silently plucked Carmen's bag from the sidewalk and stowed it in the trunk. Then he opened the back door and waited.

Judith decided she didn't care who was watching, and buried herself in Carmen's arms. "I love you."

"Can't have enough of that." Carmen kissed her full on the lips. "I love you too."

"Thanks for coming this weekend . . . and especially for coming to Brooklyn."

"It's always a pleasure . . . to come." With a wink, she got into the backseat and was gone.

Judith smiled to herself at Carmen's last remark. From the fervor of their lovemaking this morning, neither of them seemed to think Carmen was fragile. Her neighbors probably didn't think so either.

She went back inside to find her mother, already in her jacket, and helping Victor with his. It was almost time to take Victor back to the group home, but the walk was her mother's favorite part of the visit. "We have enough time for a quick walk, Mom. I told them I'd bring Victor back by four."

"I thought I might go back with you to drop him off."

The offer shocked her, but she wasn't going to look this gift horse in the mouth. "That would be great."

She hung back as they walked outside, pleased to see her mother take her brother's arm.

"Your friend is very nice."

"She said the same thing about you."

"Your brother liked her."

"Is that right, Victor? Did you like Carmen?" His smile was

only a small one, but that was because she hadn't used the key word. "Did you think she was pretty?"

He grinned broadly at that.

"Look at you teasing your brother."

"He likes to hear about pretty girls."

They descended into the subway, where Judith watched with pride as Victor pushed his card through the slot and tripped the turnstile.

"I didn't know he could do that by himself," Halina said.

"He's very smart," she said, slapping her brother lightly on the back.

A train came within moments of their reaching the platform and Victor led the way through the open door, taking the first empty seat he reached. Judith gestured for her mother to take the other available seat, and she stood facing them.

"It's usually easier if he gets to sit down. Otherwise, he sometimes forgets to hold on." She chose her words carefully, afraid to sound as if she was giving a lesson. The fact that her mother had decided to come along didn't mean she was willing to do this on her own, but Judith saw it as at least a small sign that she was considering the possibility. "When there aren't any seats, I usually hold his arm like I do when we walk."

At the first stop, the man sitting next to her mother got off and Judith quickly took his seat.

"Will you be going to Chicago next weekend?" her mother asked.

"No. Carmen wanted me to come, but she needs a break. Things are tough for her at work right now, and I told her she should take a few days on her own to relax." She tried not to sound nervous as she talked about her relationship, but the difficulty both of them had making eye contact underscored the sensitive nature of the topic. "This is Bergen," she said, standing up and motioning for Victor to do the same.

Victor was familiar with the station and led the way from the train up the stairs to the exit. Halina was clearly impressed.

"Watch the light, Victor," Judith said when they reached the corner at Wyckoff. "I always tell him that just to be sure."

They waited, then crossed the street and turned toward the home. Judith noticed her mother slowing down, likely in anticipation of reaching the place she dreaded most.

"Someone's getting excited about being back home," Judith said, nodding her head in the direction of her brother, who was smiling and watching the door. "He's always like this, Mom. This is his home."

Her mother said nothing, but watched intently as Victor walked up the steps and pressed the buzzer. A voice crackled and Judith announced them. Moments later, Stacey opened the door.

"You brought my boyfriend back!"

Victor grinned and blushed, then started to enter.

"Wait, Victor." Judith caught his arm. "Go give Mom a hug."

He complied in his own way, standing close enough for his mother to embrace him. Then he did the same with Judith.

"Stacey, this is our mother, Halina Kowalczyk."

Halina simply smiled her greeting, but Stacey responded in her typical animated style. "Uh-oh, we'd better behave ourselves. Mamas watch out for their babies."

Victor went inside and Stacey waved good-bye. Judith hooked her arm in her mother's as they turned back toward the subway.

"It's true what she said, Judith. Mamas watch out for their babies."

"Wyckoff is the best. Victor's really happy—"

"I wasn't thinking about your brother. I was thinking about you."

"You watch out for me?"

"Of course I do."

Judith loosened her grip so they could walk down the stairs and go through the turnstile. Her mother then continued along the subway platform until she reached a spot well beyond the other waiting passengers.

"Judith, I never meant for you to feel like Victor was more important than you. It's just that he needs more."

Judith searched her memory for what she had said to prompt this declaration, then remembered her comment about feeling as if her only purpose to her mother was what she did for her brother. "I know, Mom. I was just frustrated when I said that because I didn't think you were listening to what I wanted."

"I was." She leaned against the tile wall and folded her arms across her chest. "I know I've depended on you too much. If I'd done more myself, you and Kevin might still be married."

"I doubt that." Invoking Kevin's name probably meant her mother had been thinking a lot about the lesbian issue. "It never felt right with Kevin, Mom. It's hard to explain, but I think I would have figured out what was wrong eventually and we wouldn't have stayed together anyway."

"Maybe, maybe not. But it's probably my fault that you ended up feeling like you belong with a woman and not a man."

Yes, this was about being a lesbian. "It isn't anyone's fault. Look, will you try to do something for me? Try not to feel like there's something wrong with me, okay? Because I don't."

"But how can you be happy this way? Even if it was all right with me, it wouldn't be with everyone else. It's not normal."

"I don't care about what other people think, Mom. I know it's going to take some getting used to, and I don't expect any miracles overnight. But this isn't a choice I'm making. It's just who I am. And you have to believe me when I tell you that I'm happy."

The train pulled into the station and they climbed aboard an empty car.

"Your brother does seem to be happy at Wyckoff."

That seemed to mark the end of the lesbian discussion, but Judith was fine with that. They were light years ahead of where they had been just two weeks ago.

Chapter 20

"I want to know everything," Cathy demanded, storming through the door into Carmen's office.

"Well, I've got the San Diego report ready for—" By the look on her friend's face, this wasn't the time for joking around. "Everything's okay. We had a nice, relaxing weekend."

"Have you taken your blood pressure this morning?"

"It's down a little bit."

"To what?"

So much for that ploy, Carmen thought. Cathy was relentless and knew all of her avoidance tricks. "One-forty over ninety."

"You call that down? I'm calling your doctor right now."

"I'm okay, really. It was way up last week with everything going on, but it's getting better. I haven't eaten a single bad thing since last Friday, and I got that report done so it isn't hanging over me anymore."

"Carmen, you can't screw around with this. You need to go back on the medicine when your blood pressure starts to spike."

"I know, and you're right about me screwing around. But I've got a grip on it now. Judith and I talked about it—thank you very much for that, by the way."

"So Judith doesn't think you need to see a doctor?"

"I promised her I'd make an appointment, so there. And thanks to you, she's now part of the food police."

"Good for her. But I bet you didn't tell her how close you came to checking out, did you?"

"She doesn't need to hear those horror stories. Besides, that was a long, long time ago, before I even knew what to watch out for."

"In other words, if you have a heart attack now, you'll know what's happening."

"It wasn't a heart attack."

"It was close."

"But there wasn't any damage. That's what matters. And I'll call Dr. Marshall today."

Cathy stood up. "Let's call her right now and get you on the schedule."

"Fine." It was good to get this done. Judith would be happy to hear it, and it might even convince her to change her mind about coming to Chicago this weekend. She busied herself with the finishing touches on the San Diego report while Cathy made the arrangements from the phone next to the couch.

"Thursday at nine o'clock. And she wants you fasting."

"My blood pressure should like that."

"So what are you going to do about Art Conover?"

The name alone was enough to send her stomach roiling. "I had a conference call with Lenore and Kristy when I got home last night. They've been working on a business model for a quarterly study, which will save us two-thirds of the field costs."

"Won't we lose all the big clients doing monthly ad buys?"

"Maybe not. They might sign up for Art's service, but if they want custom work, they're going to have to subscribe to ours too."

"And a quarterly service gets our price under Art's."

"Right. So he might pick up a few clients, but we'll still own the sector."

"How much revenue do we drop?"

"A shitload. But we make up forty percent when we launch the time-share stream. That will keep us in the game. I can't imagine Art's going for that sector too."

"And there's no other way to stop this?"

Carmen shrugged. "We can fight him off for a while, but eventually, all of our clients will probably shop at Art-Mart."

Cathy looked at her dubiously. "How come you're taking this so well?"

"It's not like I can fight it. We'll have to look for other expansion opportunities. Asia's a good bet, and Australia ought to be right behind." She got up and walked around her desk to sit in the wingback chair. "Can I talk to you about something else?"

"Since when do you have to ask a question like that?"

"I mostly just need to vent. I'm not really looking for advice . . ."

"Noted. So is this going to be about Brooke or Judith?"

"Both."

"Have you talked to Brooke yet?"

"She hasn't returned any of my calls. All I got was that message last week canceling dinner."

"Does that have anything to do with why your chest is hurting?"

"Maybe some." Carmen absently rubbed a palm across her sternum. "She's never pulled away from me like this before."

"You want me to talk to her?"

"No." She felt certain none of their friends could fix this, especially since Brooke admitted she didn't really trust anyone but Carmen. "I'm sure we'll talk whenever she's ready. There's no real point in trying before then."

"Except that it's bothering you. And I don't mind telling her that. One of these days, she needs to realize she's not the center of the—"

"I don't want you to talk to her, Cathy. I need to do it on my own. She's already embarrassed about everything, and so am I."

"Which brings us to Judith."

"Judith." She leaned forward and ran both hands through her hair. "I'm so crazy in love with that woman I can't stand myself."

Cathy laughed. "That's great. I wouldn't mind seeing more of the two of you together."

"The together part . . . that's not so easy." Carmen couldn't bring herself to share the laugh. After seeing Judith with her family yesterday, it was clear she could never leave New York. "This going back and forth is hard."

"Will Judith consider moving here?"

"I can't ask her to do that. Did I tell you I met her brother yesterday? And her mother too."

"So what? She met your mother and father too. She knows you're close to your family."

"Yeah, but I can leave my family and they'll be okay. That's not true for Judith."

"But Judith doesn't have a dozen employees in New York."

Carmen sighed and leaned back. Her chest was starting to tighten up, but letting Cathy know that right now was out of the question. "That's pretty much why I've been thinking about her so much . . . because I can't figure out how we're going to fix this distance thing."

"Is it bothering you?"

"Having her here might make all the rest of it manageable." What she feared most—but wouldn't say—was that not having Judith with her might be more stress than her body could stand.

Judith scrolled down the screen, checking the results of her search. The cheapest flight to Chicago was over four hundred dollars, and the only return flight that would get her home in time to pick up Victor left at six a.m. on Sunday. That pretty much buried any notions of surprising Carmen tomorrow night, though she knew if she put the bug in Carmen's ear she would find an electronic ticket in her inbox within minutes.

It was just as well, she thought. All of the arguments about Carmen needing some time to relax alone with Prissy were still valid. But four days into their first week apart, she was already missing her so badly she was ready to cave.

It was a miserable feeling, but she never wanted their time apart to be easy. If either of them began to take it in stride, it would mark the beginning of the end. So she had to be miserable in order to be happy. It seemed as though her whole damn life was filled with that sort of convoluted logic.

Her cell phone chirped faintly in her purse. A quick check revealed an unfamiliar Chicago number. Carmen usually called around lunchtime when she knew they could talk.

"Hello." It was Lenore Yates. She knew all about Carmen's vice president, but they had never met. It was curious that she would call—"She did what?"

Immediately she stood up and looked across the top of her cubicle to Todd's office.

"Where are they taking her?"

Her hands shaking, she grabbed her mouse and shut down her computer. Then she opened her top drawer and raked everything on her desk into it.

"And Cathy's with her?"

She slung her purse over her shoulder.

"Please tell Cathy I'm on the way. And tell Carmen I'll be there as soon as I can."

"They're taking care of me, Mom," Carmen said, holding out her free hand for a squeeze. Her other was attached to an IV that kept her hydrated. The leads from her chest fed a steady blip on a digital display, along with the cuff that inflated automatically to monitor her blood pressure. "Dr. Marshall thinks we can fix this with some beta blockers."

"Your brother Chris thinks you ought to consider bypass," her father said. "I'm inclined to agree."

"That's because you're both surgeons and you like to cut." She stuck her tongue out, which prompted her father to smirk. "It's not blocked, so Dr. Marshall wants to—"

"It's not blocked yet."

"Joe, you know better than to interfere with what her doctor is telling her. This is between them."

Carmen was glad for her mother's support.

"Besides, I bet her new friend Judith will make her take better care of herself. She's coming tonight, right?"

"Yeah, Cathy went to pick her up at O'Hare. She should be getting here any minute."

"And you think they'll let you out of here tomorrow?" her father asked.

"That's what Dr. Marshall said. She just wants—"

"Can anybody come to this party?"

For an instant, Carmen thought it was Judith in the doorway, but she quickly realized her mistake. She had given up on Brooke coming, since Cathy had left her a message over six hours ago.

She watched as her parents greeted her friend with the usual hugs and smiles. If anything was amiss with Brooke, she was hiding it well.

"How are you, honey?" She bent to give Carmen a light hug.

"It looks scarier than it is, just a little stress attack. I'm glad you came."

"That teenager of mine only remembered an hour ago to give me an urgent message."

So that's why she hadn't come sooner. It wasn't that she didn't care.

"I've been on the phone with Cathy ever since I heard. She said you had a catheterization and they found a bad spot."

"Just a little one. It's going to be okay. Dad wants them to cut me open and tear it all out, but you know how he is."

Her parents gathered their things to leave and said good-bye.

"I'll call you tomorrow from home," Carmen called as they walked out. "Don't worry about anything."

Brooke came to sit beside her on the bed, looking as if she might cry at any moment.

Carmen took her hand. "See what I have to do for a little attention from you?"

"Don't you dare joke about this. You scared the shit out of me."

"I'm sorry."

"I would never have forgiven myself if anything happened to you." Her tears were coming now in a steady stream. "I wasn't mad or anything, Carmen. I promise. I just needed to step back and think about things."

"It's fine. I know I threw you for a loop with all that. I can't blame you for feeling weird about it, especially after you ran into Judith in the elevator."

Brooke wiped her eyes with her sleeve. "I was probably more mixed up worrying about why it made me so jealous. I never got that way before when you had girlfriends."

"But none of them looked like you."

"Maybe." She drew a deep breath and exhaled loudly. "I've been thinking about leaving Geoffrey. Surprise, surprise."

"I know you haven't seemed very happy lately."

"I've had this silly fantasy that Amie and I would move in with you again. She goes off to college in the fall, so in my perfect little world, things would work out. We'd have fun all the time and you'd never let me do something stupid, like get married again."

After all the times she selfishly dreamed of Brooke leaving Geoffrey, she was strangely ambivalent it had come to this. It saddened her to realize this would be the first time in thirty years she wouldn't be there to break Brooke's fall, but it was also the first time she could honestly say she wasn't in love with her. "Whatever you need to do, you know you can count on me to help."

"I know. You're the only one in my whole life I've ever been able to count on. But the strangest thing happened after we talked last week. When I realized leaving wouldn't be so easy, I started wondering if it was worth doing."

"And?"

"And maybe I'll hold off. I don't think we're a good pair right now, but we used to be. We haven't given each other much of a chance lately, and I think we need to do that. At least I need to do that."

"All I care about is you being happy."

Brooke flashed her killer smile. "And all I care about is you being healthy."

"I will be. I've just had a lot of headaches at work and I let them get to me."

"That's what Cathy said . . . something about somebody trying to take all of your business."

"That's right. I thought we had it all worked out, but this morning we got a call from our biggest time-share client, the one in Philadelphia whose ass we all kiss on a regular basis." She felt the tightening return to her chest as she related Bill Hinkle's call telling them he couldn't commit to their new service for more than a year or two. Art Conover had come to him with ideas for a new service.

"You need to calm down, Carmen."

"I know."

"You need to quit worrying about all this work shit and concentrate on the happy things, like your new girlfriend."

Brooke didn't understand that a company head couldn't just step back and let the chips fall. "I had no idea how hard this long-distance thing would be."

"Is that worrying you too?"

"Some." Quite a bit. A great deal. "She'll be here in a few minutes, by the way."

"I know. Cathy was at the airport when I talked to her. I'll get out of here before she gets here."

"You don't have to." Despite her words, Carmen didn't want another awkward meeting between her lover and best friend. There would be another time, preferably one that didn't include heart monitors.

"Yes, I do. If she's got this as bad as you do, she's going to want you all to herself."

"I'm glad you came. I've been worried about us and I feel a lot better now."

"Don't ever worry about us, sweetie. I love you, and nothing will ever change that."

Judith gave up on getting her bearings in the city as Cathy spun through the surface streets on their way to the hospital.

"I'll drop your bag off at Carmen's. It's not far from here. You can just get a cab. Now are you sure you want to deal with Prissy? I can always take her home with me."

"No, you don't need to do that. She'll be good company . . . unless you think it's too much for Carmen to have her there when she gets home."

"It should be fine if you can handle taking her out. Carmen's supposed to take it easy for a couple of days, but other than that, she'll be fine."

"This was just a scare then."

"A big one, especially for Lenore. She didn't know what was

going on. Carmen just collapsed all of a sudden and passed out."

"I'm just glad it happened when she was with people who knew what to do."

"No kidding. If she had been by herself, she probably wouldn't have done anything at all. And she wouldn't have told anybody either."

Cathy pulled into the circle at the hospital's entrance and stopped.

"Thank you for everything, Cathy."

"I'm glad you were able to get here so fast. It'll make a big difference to her to see you."

"I hope so."

"You have the key?"

She slapped her pocket as she got out. "Right here."

"Call me if you need anything."

As Cathy pulled away, Judith walked anxiously through the double doors, bypassing the information kiosk when she spotted the visitor elevators. She knew the room number already, and wanted to get there as soon as she could. What she hadn't planned was coming face to face with Brooke Nance when the elevator door opened on the fifth floor.

For a moment, they simply stared, both too shocked to speak. Then Brooke broke into a broad smile and extended her hand. "Hi, Judith. I'm Brooke."

"I know." This wasn't at all the reception she had expected, given what Carmen had said about Brooke avoiding her. "I'm . . . I'm sorry about before."

"It's okay. I probably would have done the same thing, except I doubt I would have been able to think that fast."

Judith welcomed the gracious overture, but this wasn't the time for making new friends. "Is Carmen okay? Have you seen her?"

"She's fine, and she's going to be very happy to see you." She turned and faced down the hall. "Next to last door on your left."

"Thank you. I—I want to talk to you later, but . . ."

"We will. Go."

Judith gave what she hoped looked like a genuine smile and started down the hall.

"Judith?"

She turned back.

"One more thing." Brooke walked closer and lowered her voice. "This isn't any of my business, but I'm going to say it anyway because Carmen is very dear to me, and I care about what happens to her."

Judith expected a friendly warning to treat Carmen well or else.

"She's worrying about a lot of things right now, including how hard it is on her for you to be in New York."

"It's hard on both of us."

"Well, if you really care about her, you need to do something about it." Brooke gave her an earnest look, one that drove home the gravity of what she was saying—that the stress of being in different cities was causing Carmen physical pain. "And don't tell her I told you that or she'll kick my ass."

Judith sighed and looked away as a massive wave of guilt enveloped her. If any of this was her fault, she would have to fix it, no matter what it took.

Carmen felt a flood of relief the moment Judith walked through the door. In that instant, she recognized the strain this had put on everyone who cared about her, and the extraordinary effort Judith had exerted on short notice to be at her side. She also saw a look of panic.

"It's not as bad as it looks. These are all just monitors."

Judith hurried over and took her face between her hands, kissing her solidly on the forehead. "You scared me half to death."

"I'm okay, really. This was just one of those freaky things."

"I want to hear everything, and you'd better not leave anything out."

"I was just—"

"Not yet, though. Right now I just want you to be quiet and let me tell you how much I love you." Judith's hands caressed her, wandering up and down her arms and across the top of her chest, careful to avoid the IV and electronic leads.

"I love you too. I'm so glad you came."

"I thought I'd never get here."

"I bet your boss had a fit."

"I didn't stick around long enough to hear it. Getting here was all that mattered."

"Your timing was perfect. Everyone else just left."

"Yeah, I just saw Brooke in the hall. We actually said hi this time. She was glad you were feeling better."

Carmen shook her head at the weirdness. "One of these days, maybe we'll all sit down together and talk like civilized people."

"I'm sure we will." Her warm hand brushed Carmen's hair off her forehead and she perched on the side of the bed. "Now tell me what happened."

Relishing the physical closeness, Carmen related the tale of her sudden chest pain, blackout and collapse, all capped off by a dramatic trip to the hospital in the back of an ambulance. "I almost told them to do the bypass surgery so I wouldn't have to face everybody in the building when I walk in next week."

"What do you mean bypass surgery? Do you have a problem or don't you?"

"I have a trouble spot. It's a narrowed artery, but it isn't blocked. Dr. Marshall suggested a stent, but first, she'll put me on medication to dilate the blood vessels, and something else to get my cholesterol and blood pressure down. We're hoping that takes care of it."

"And if it doesn't?"

"Then we consider bypass."

"How will we know? Do we have to wait for you to collapse again?"

She could sense Judith's anxiety. It was the same as her father's and brother's, both of whom wanted her to fix it once and for all. "No, I promise to have frequent checkups and follow all of the doctor's orders—exercise, diet, everything. I'd like to stay away from the knife if I can."

"But you'll do it if you need to?"

She nodded once. The people around her needed assurances that she wouldn't be reckless or stubborn. "This was all just a ploy to get you to come to Chicago."

"That was the first thing I thought when Lenore called me."

"And since I knew you were coming, I asked my doctor if I had any sexual restrictions and she said no."

"You did not!"

Carmen was relieved to finally see a smile. "In fact, she said I could have sex right here in this bed if I wanted to."

Judith sighed and shook her head. "Do you ever not think about sex?"

"It's the only thing that doesn't make my chest hurt."

"In that case"—Judith kissed her again, this time on the mouth—"you should think about it all the time."

Chapter 21

Judith paced the guest room, trying to sound more encouraging than exasperated. "It'll be easy, Mom. All you have to do is call ahead of time and tell them to have Victor ready to go. Then just ring the doorbell when you get there and they'll bring him out."

Her mother was adamant she couldn't manage the simple handover on her own. She wanted Judith to come home early in the morning as she had done before.

"No. I need to be here. Carmen's family is coming tomorrow after church, and I need to take care of things."

Next, her mother tried the guilt trip, reminding her how the change in routine would upset Victor.

"That won't happen if you go get him and take him home . . . I can't do it, Mom. I won't. Carmen needs me here."

So much for her mother's grand show of going back to

Wyckoff with her last week. If she wouldn't do it on her own, what difference did it make?

"Then that's how it has to be. I'll just have to deal with it when I get back." She wanted to turn the tables and lay on the guilt, but that wouldn't help anything. Her mother wasn't being stubborn. She was genuinely afraid, not only of seeing how Victor lived, but of the possibility he would act out in a way she couldn't handle on her own.

Judith hung up the phone, but made no move to go back to the living room. She needed to lighten her mood so Carmen wouldn't worry. That was what really mattered.

Carmen was feeling fine, no residual effects beyond a little soreness in her groin where they had inserted the catheter. The parade of friends and coworkers had marched through yesterday after they had returned from the hospital, and tomorrow, they would host Carmen's parents and siblings. Today was to be their day, time out from everyone just to watch TV and relax. She would worry about Victor later.

She gathered herself and walked out to the kitchen. "Do you want something to drink?"

"Can I have a scotch?"

Yes, Carmen was definitely getting back to normal. "It isn't even noon."

"What time can I have one?"

"Alcohol's on your forbidden list until your blood pressure comes down. How about a glass of orange juice instead?"

Carmen groaned. "Just kill me."

Judith set two glasses of juice on the coffee table. Prissy raised her head momentarily, but settled again in Carmen's lap once she determined neither glass was for her.

Carmen patted the couch and she sat down, leaning underneath an outstretched arm. The firm embrace told her Carmen had gotten the gist of the phone conversation and was offering her quiet support. It was a frustrating situation, but Carmen didn't need to be worrying about Victor or anything else.

Carmen grabbed the remote and muted the TV. "I take it your mother was less than helpful?"

Judith sighed and shook her head. "I thought she would come through, but she won't go there by herself."

"Because she hates the group home?"

"That's part of it, but I don't think it's the main reason. I think she's afraid of being alone with Victor, like he might go off on her or something."

"He looked pretty mild-mannered to me."

"He usually is. She's just worried something will upset him and she won't be able to calm him down."

"What happens then?"

"He can get out of control pretty fast. The last time, he had to go to the hospital. He fought with everybody and they had to put him in restraints."

"What set him off?"

"Just . . . his routine got disrupted." She hoped Carmen wouldn't press for more.

"Because you were gone?"

"I was on a tour for three weekends in a row. It was a few years ago."

"Are you worried it's going to set him off if you're not there tomorrow? I don't mind if you want to go home in the morning."

"I mind, Carmen." She grew irritated, not at Carmen, but at her mother for not helping, and even at Victor for not being able to control himself. "I deserve to have my own life."

"Of course you do. And you should do whatever you think is best. But if that's being with Victor, I'll support that."

"You shouldn't have to. What just happened to you was a big deal. You have a right to a girlfriend who can be here with you." She was going to cry any minute if they didn't change the subject. "Besides, you need me here to keep you from living on scotch and potato chips."

"I need you here for more than that. You give my dog something to do." Carmen wiggled her feet, which were propped beside Judith's on the coffee table. Both women had holes in the toes of their slippers.

"I can't believe she did that." Judith had found her slipper under the guest bed this morning.

"I warned you not to leave your shoes there, but did you listen?"

Judith stroked the sleeping hound, which caused Prissy to stir and roll halfway onto her back. "It's good for you to spend time with her. She keeps you calm."

"She definitely likes it when I'm home. I feel guilty for leaving her so much, so I understand a little about what you're going through with Victor." She hurriedly added, "Not that I'm comparing Prissy to your brother. I mean, she's a dog and he's a person."

"It's okay. I know what you meant." Yes, Prissy was a dog, but her turmoil was symbolic of the disruption in Carmen's life that paralleled that in her own.

Carmen settled under the blanket and waited for Judith to finish in the bathroom and join her in bed. Under other circumstances, all this special attention would be the sort of thing she would celebrate. But it had been a quiet day, almost too quiet, especially after this morning when Judith had talked to her mother. It was clear she was worried about how Victor was going to react to her absence this weekend.

Just what they needed—more stress in their lives. In her own current state, she wasn't much help to Judith. Even if she got this mess with Art Conover settled, she couldn't keep shuffling her work schedule to end up in New York two weekends a month. And Judith couldn't sacrifice her brother's well-being—not to mention her job—to go back and forth to Chicago. At best, they might be able to manage being together for a few days a month without pushing themselves too much. But that introduced a potentially bigger problem—how to deal with the frustration of being apart.

"Do you need anything?" Judith asked, her finger hovering above the light switch.

"Just you." Her eyes not yet adjusted to the darkness, she didn't see Judith drop her robe in the chair. But the cool, bare skin against hers was every bit as thrilling as the vision of her nude form. "Just you like this."

"I love you." Judith moved closer, her whole body aligned with Carmen's. "How are you feeling?"

Carmen hoped that was an invitation. "Never better." She wrapped her arms around Judith's waist and pulled her on top.

Their relationship would have been manageable if Judith had been just a pleasant distraction in New York, someone to enjoy a few times a year without strings. Falling in love had changed everything, stoking a need that could only be met by having her close, a need that fed itself with every word or touch they shared.

And it was falling all to hell this weekend, even if Judith didn't know it. How would she stand it if she returned to New York to find her brother in the hospital, out of control? Or what if something even more horrible happened because Victor's routine was disrupted?

"Relax. I want to do this for you," Judith whispered. "I don't usually get to have you like this."

Carmen loosened her grip and took a deep breath, focusing on the feather-like touch of Judith's fingers along her collarbone. Warm lips tickled her neck and she felt her whole body respond with a gentle upward thrust. "That's because I must be crazy."

Judith covered her breast with one hand and kneaded it softly, never letting her lips break contact as they drifted lower to capture a nipple. Carmen willed herself to lie perfectly still and let

Judith have her. Why did she always fight for the top when this was so deliciously exquisite?

The hand left her other breast and traveled slowly across her stomach to her pubic hair. Anticipating the touch, she bent one knee to open her legs. "I can't wait to feel you inside me."

Judith obliged, sliding in and out gently with first one, then two fingers. Then she spread the slickness around her clit and started a slow, tantalizing massage, all the while nibbling and sucking her nipple.

"If I promise not to come, will you do that all night?" She knew she couldn't keep that vow. Her body was already rocking with desire, her clit seeking solid contact with the fingers that teased her.

A sudden wave of sadness swept over her. There wasn't any light at the end of their tunnel without a great sacrifice. She would never let Judith abandon her brother, and Judith would never ask her to leave her business and family in Chicago. The longer they pushed this, the more likely it would lead to anxiety and heartache.

As Carmen drew closer to her climax, Judith released the nipple and kissed her on the mouth once again. Then she held her place to look into her eyes. "Don't you ever forget that I love you, Carmen."

The sorrow in her words was unmistakable. Carmen wanted to speak, to tell Judith hers was the best love she'd ever had. But her climax took her away.

"Judith, we all appreciate you getting here so quickly and taking care of Carmen this weekend."

"I'm glad I could." Judith genuinely liked Carmen's mother. It wasn't hard to guess that Carmen would age just as beautifully as Elaine Delallo, her black hair turning silver and her skin taking on a deep olive glow. "It's been a nice restful weekend for both of us."

"Has she been out of the apartment at all?"

"We took Prissy for a walk this morning and stopped in at Starbucks."

"I heard her groaning to her sisters about having to drink decaf." They looked over at the couch, where Carmen was sitting between twins Angie and Lizabeth. "But she can groan all she wants. We stocked her refrigerator with salad and fruit. There's a fish filet all seasoned and ready for the oven."

"What time do you leave?"

"She ordered a car for five. My flight's at seven."

"It's too bad you have to go. She's going to miss you."

Judith wanted to stay. It was already too late to do anything about Victor, but she needed to get back to her job or Todd would probably blow a fuse and fire her.

Elaine joined her three daughters on the couch and Judith followed to gather the used plates and cups. Back in the kitchen, she could hear the men talking in the dining room. Carmen's father and her brothers Chris and Mark, whom she hadn't met before today, were discussing her condition. Mark wasn't a doctor like the others, but that didn't stop him from having a strong opinion.

"She doesn't want surgery and I don't blame her. All you cutters ever want to do is cut."

"But you know her better than any of us, Mark." She recognized Chris's voice. "And you know she probably won't do what it takes to get her stress under control. She'd be better off getting the bypass now so this doesn't happen again."

"She thinks she can manage it. She did it before."

"It's worse now, son." Carmen's father. "The arteries are compromised. She admitted in the hospital the other night that she hadn't been keeping up with her exercise and she wasn't eating right. She's just asking for trouble."

"And with all that mess at her company . . ." Chris added.

"If you want to know the truth," Joe said, lowering his voice, "I think her biggest problem is her new girlfriend. Don't get me wrong. I like Judith. But this running back and forth on the weekends to see each other isn't good for her."

"Yeah, Carmen told me a couple of weeks ago that she didn't know how they were going to keep this up. Judith has a mentally retarded brother in New York, so she can't just pick up and move."

Judith shuddered as Mark's words sank in. This was the brother who was closest to Carmen, the one in whom she confided. And apparently, the one to whom she had voiced her doubts about their future.

"She could be killing herself over this," Chris said. "I was happy to hear she'd met somebody, but it's just not worth it if you ask me."

The room was quiet for several seconds before Mark solemnly asked, "Who's going to tell Carmen that?"

Judith started the dishwasher and gave the kitchen counters one last swipe with the sponge. "Okay, that's the last of the chores. You're on your own now, kiddo."

Carmen leaned in the doorway, wishing there were some way out of the box they had built for themselves. It was obvious by the awkward conversation since everyone left that something ominous was in the air. Judith clearly couldn't deal with the guilt about Victor anymore. Carmen knew she shouldn't fight it, and she hoped Judith wouldn't drag things out for her sake. The sooner they ended things, the sooner Judith would settle her guilt.

She refused to accept that falling in love had been a mistake. It was going to hurt like hell, but she was better for knowing someone like Judith, and for seeing what was possible.

Judith stepped into the foyer and fussed with her suitcase,

checking its zippers and name tag. Carmen was equally nervous, but buried her hands into her pockets to hide it.

"You want to talk about it?"

Judith looked as if she might cry. "It's always so hard to leave. And Victor's going to be a wreck by the time I get home."

"I know it's . . ." Carmen felt a lump form in her throat. It was more than just Judith leaving. It was the likelihood she was never coming back. There was no better time than now to settle this. She had to show Judith a door and see if she walked through it. "It's selfish for me to keep taking you away from him when it's obvious how much he needs you. I don't know if that's a problem we can solve."

Judith's tears broke loose. "What else can I do?"

She had her answer. Judith could have argued but she hadn't. Carmen pulled her into her arms for what she knew would be the last time. "It's okay."

"And I'm so worried about you."

"I'm fine. But I can't keep doing this either. It's probably better this way." Judith was sobbing, and it was all Carmen could do to hold it in.

They held each other tightly, soaking up the last of their love, until the phone rang to announce Judith's car.

"It was a lovely ride, Judith O'Shea."

Chapter 22

Judith angrily ripped the form in half, hoping the woman on the other end of the phone could hear it. Some people seemed to think travel agents were their personal slaves. "Why don't you talk it over some more with Trisha and call me when you've decided something definite? There's no sense in wasting everybody's time making reservations if you're just going to cancel them."

She hung up the phone and clicked on her Web browser, checking her e-mail for the hundredth time that morning. Why had she just left Carmen's without making some sort of pact to keep in touch? Surely what they had was worth trying to maintain at least a friendship.

The fact that their romance was over hadn't really sunk in until the plane ride home last night. The more she thought about it, the more it seemed as though Carmen had practically shoved her out the door. Granted, she knew she had given the impression it was all about Victor, but only because Carmen's family and friends seemed to think she was the cause of Carmen's stress problems. When Carmen hadn't resisted at all, it seemed as though she was eager to end things.

And Judith had cried all night.

"Judith? Can I see you in here?"

She didn't have the patience to deal with Todd today, especially after his display last Thursday when she told him she had to leave for an emergency. He was sympathetic to her situation, he had said, but he wasn't under any obligation to treat everyone's boyfriend or girlfriend like a spouse unless they filed domestic partner papers with the agency. She had been ready that day to tell him to shove it, but now she was glad she had held her tongue. Whether she liked it or not, she needed this sucky job.

She drew a deep breath and walked into Todd's office. "Something I can do for you?"

"I was just thinking you might want to take an early lunch and cool off. You need to deal with whatever's up your butt and stop taking it out on our customers."

"Great, so when I really need time off, you give me a hard time. Now you're telling me I need to get out and take a break."

"All I'm saying is I've been listening to you talk on the phone this morning. If that's how you're going to treat our clients, we're better off with you somewhere else. It's up to you whether that's going to be permanent or not."

She bit the inside of her cheek to keep from lashing out. "Fine. I'll be back at one."

"I mean it, Judith. Either fix whatever's bugging you or don't bother coming back."

She returned to her desk and grabbed her purse. As soon as she reached the sidewalk, she pulled out her cell phone and dialed the main number for The Delallo Group. "Cathy Rosen, please."

After a few moments, Cathy came on the line.

"Cathy, it's Judith. Did Carmen make it to work today?" She covered her other ear as a garbage truck rumbled past. "Could you say that again?"

Carmen was in her office with the door closed, Cathy said. She seemed to be bothered by something, and wasn't in the mood to talk. Cathy had no idea what that was about, but she was concerned.

"I don't know if this is it, but we, uh . . . we decided yesterday that this long-distance thing wasn't working out." She was surprised by the sharpness in Cathy's voice. "No, for either of us . . . Yes, part of it was my brother." Evidently, Cathy knew all about Victor. "But he wasn't the only reason . . . I don't think this going back and forth is good for Carmen. She needs somebody who can be with her all the time. I can't do that."

She turned the corner down a side street to get away from the traffic, straining to hear Cathy's diatribe about giving up just because things weren't easy. "I know my timing left a lot to be desired, but I didn't want to make things any worse than they already were . . . Look, she didn't exactly throw herself in front of the car when I left. If anything, I'd say she was relieved about it."

Cathy's reaction was odd. It wasn't as if she was showing some great loyalty to Carmen by taking her side. Instead, she seemed angry at both of them, saying they didn't deserve to be happy.

"Cathy, I know this may sound stupid, but I broke up with Carmen because I love her, and because I'm not going to be the one that pushes her too hard and causes her to break. She needs somebody who can be there for her, and I wish that could be me. But it can't." Her voice was shaking with frustration. "I just need to know she's okay."

The sound of a siren drowned out most of Cathy's response, but Judith distinctly caught the word "idiots" before the line went dead.

~

"That's right, by Wednesday, or you can forget it. We're done here." Carmen let the phone drop into its cradle, not caring what kind of noise it made in the ear of the person on the other end of the line.

A sharp knock sounded on her door. Before she could answer, Cathy barged in. "I just talked to Judith. She had some rather strange things to say."

"I hope you told her I was fine." Cathy waited near the couch, obviously in the mood for a heart-to-heart talk about her love life, which didn't interest Carmen at all. She busied herself with the stack of papers in her inbox. "I'd appreciate it if this didn't turn into some big drama. It didn't work out and we're both dealing with it."

"Fine." But she made no move to leave the office.

"Would you get out a memo to the whole staff that the office will be closed tomorrow? Everyone is to stay home. Paid holiday."

"A paid holiday on a Tuesday? What the hell is going on?"

"Just do the memo, Cathy."

"Yes, ma'am," Cathy snapped, spinning on a heel before marching out and slamming the door.

Carmen took a deep breath and checked herself. It was bad enough that outside circumstances affected her stress level. Being an asshole to her friends made it worse.

Judith widened her stance and gripped the pole tightly, bracing herself for when the train started again. There was no telling what she would find once she got to Wyckoff. Russ said Victor hadn't gone to work today, but he didn't know any more than that. She would have to get the details from Stacey once she got to the group home. At least Victor hadn't run away.

Her stop was next and she squeezed between two young men to get closer to the exit, holding her breath to ward off someone's body odor. As soon as the doors opened, she leapt off, starting immediately up the stairs to the outside. She turned on State Street and slowed her gait.

She loved her brother dearly. But for the first time in her life, she actually had considered turning her back on his needs in order to make a life with Carmen. No sooner had that possibility entered her head than she was faced with its consequences—fear that his life would come apart and his small windows of joy would turn to tortured confusion. How would she have lived with herself if choosing Carmen had meant putting out the only light in Victor's life?

None of this was Victor's fault, and she wasn't going to entertain resentment for what it meant to be there for him. What mattered now was spending time with him to get him back on an even keel and recommitting to his needs.

She climbed the steps to the stoop, rang the buzzer and announced herself. Stacey opened the door.

"Hi, Judith. Come on in. Victor's back in his room."

"How is he?"

"He's better now. I don't know what it was he ate. Did your mother figure it out?"

Judith wasn't following at all what Stacey was saying. "What are you talking about? He didn't go to work today, right?"

"Right. He threw up a couple of times last night so we kept him in today. I called your mother to tell her and she was going to look around and see what he might have gotten into at home yesterday."

"Victor went home yesterday?"

"Your mother didn't tell you? She called in the morning and asked us to have him ready. We did, and she picked him up and brought him back."

"She came all by herself." Judith was astounded.

"I was surprised, if you want to know the truth."

So her mother had come through for her after all, and for Victor as well. But could she do it again? "I guess I need to talk to her and see how it went."

"I'd say it went fine. She looked a little scared at first, but when she brought him back, she was smiling . . . seemed pretty proud of herself."

"And Victor was okay? He didn't mind going with her?"

"Not that I could tell."

They walked into Victor's room, where he sat coloring at his desk. His face brightened immediately with recognition, and Judith almost cried with joy.

Carmen balanced the large box of doughnuts in one hand as she struggled with the key to the office. When the lock clicked, she pushed the door open and held it with her hip while she worked the key out. Her first stop was the receptionist's desk, where she programmed the outgoing phone message that simply announced the business was closed. Then she walked down the hall to the conference room, dropping her gym bag on the floor outside of her office.

The sweet pastries smelled tempting, but they weren't for her. They were for the audit team coming in at seven thirty a.m., and she didn't care if the sugar gave them a collective migraine. She dropped the box on the conference table and continued into the kitchen, where she started two pots of coffee, one regular and one decaffeinated.

From her bookkeeper's office, she emptied two file drawers into boxes and carted them into the conference room. They could access everything else over the wireless network.

She had a pretty good idea what the bean counters would find today. She had pored over the numbers last night, along with Lenore's business plan for the syndicated side of the company.

The math was straightforward—six and a half million was the magic number, either what Conover paid her today or what she would earn before that revenue stream went down the tubes.

Walking back toward reception, she gave the gym bag a kick into her office. When those guys cut out for lunch, she would go down to the fitness center on the third floor and log her time on the treadmill. It wouldn't do to skip her workout on only her second day back in the routine.

Carmen was determined to get a handle on her life, not just her health, but the other big pieces too. Selling out to Art Conover, no matter how distasteful, would settle the uncertainty of her company, and free her to focus on the custom work she enjoyed. There also was the matter of her home life, which she wasn't going to spend darting back and forth across the country for snippets of time with someone she loved. From the very beginning, that had disaster written all over it. What she needed in her life was—

The elevator deposited three men and two women, all dressed in dark business suits and carrying laptops. Carmen almost laughed aloud at the cliché. They would systematically undervalue her business, but she was prepared to bump it up with demands she knew Art wouldn't be able to resist.

"Come in. I'm Carmen Delallo."

They rattled off their names and followed her to the conference room, where they methodically spread out and opened their laptops, dividing the contents of the file boxes. She hurriedly located extension cords and power strips, and left them on their own.

Before settling in her office, she checked the front door and found it locked. She was free to work undisturbed.

But when she walked into her office, all thoughts of work evaporated. Cathy sat on her couch, dressed in jeans and a casual sweater, her face buried in a magazine. Without looking up, she handed Carmen a cardboard cup.

"It's a decaffeinated soy latte."

"Sounds nasty . . . I mean tasty." Carmen accepted it and tried a sip. She was pleasantly surprised. "Is that vanilla?"

"It is." Cathy dropped the magazine on the couch beside her. "I take it they're auditors?"

"From Conover Data Services."

"What sort of timeline are you looking at?"

"For reaching a deal? Tomorrow afternoon."

"And after that?"

"Handover of the syndicated division in three months. I provide consultation for a year after that."

"You'd actually be working for Art?"

"Hell, no. The company keeps its name till I walk out the door." She walked over to the window and stared out at the western horizon. She hoped the rest of her staff was out enjoying this gorgeous day. "Art's ramping up for a major expansion. He wants the whole research staff in Dallas."

"And if they don't want to go?"

"Six months severance."

"That could be sweet."

"I'm going to encourage everyone to consider a move to Dallas. Salaries go a lot further there than here, and CDS is a growing company. It's a good time to get on board."

"Does this mean I finally get to retire?"

Carmen sighed drearily. "If that's what you want."

"I'm sure as hell not going to Dallas."

"But I'm not going out to pasture. This gives me a chance to get back to what I love, which is working directly with clients to solve their problems and answer their questions."

"Isn't that how you started? You're turning the clock back twenty years."

"Yeah, but with one big difference. I'm not so hungry now. I don't have to compete for every dollar out there, and I don't have to sell myself. I can pick and choose which jobs to do . . . I'll sit back and be the grand dame of travel research. And I'm going to ask Lenore to be my partner."

"Maybe you should just retire early. You won't have anyone to manage your projects and keep you on schedule."

"I have an idea about who could handle a job like that. She could handle all of our travel arrangements too."

Cathy arched both eyebrows and smiled, obviously delighted. "Now there's an idea. What happens to all this office space?"

"The lease is up in November. Art can pay the rent after the handover."

"And where will your new office be?"

"Wherever I am."

"In Chicago?"

"I haven't decided."

Pressing the phone to her ear, Judith rose from her chair slightly to locate her boss. He was in his office with the door closed.

"I have everything now, Jules. I can send the packet to you by courier this afternoon, or I can drop it in the mail . . . Okay, but someone has to be there to sign." She folded the documents and stuffed them inside the sleeve. "You guys are going to have a great time. I want to see a picture of Phoebe in the helicopter." She chuckled amiably and hung up.

It was too bad Todd couldn't hear her falling all over herself to be nice to people. Then he could take the credit for her so-called attitude adjustment and feel like a great manager, or whatever other delusions he wanted to entertain. She was back in the hunt for a better job, and a lot less picky than she had been before last week.

She checked her e-mail again to see if Carmen had responded to the note she had sent last night asking when they could talk. The sooner they settled things, the better, especially since she now had a mountain of doubts about Carmen's feelings after the way she was shuffled out of Chicago so fast on Sunday. Carmen's easy agreement had been a shock. Maybe she felt she was being abandoned in her time of need. Or that Judith was choosing Victor again, just as she always had.

But today was a new day. With her mother finally able to fill in the gaps, Judith had newfound freedom. She had awakened this morning with the thought she could even move to a new job in Chicago. Carmen could handle it if she came back to New York on her own a couple of times a month to see Victor and her mother. Those barriers to things working out didn't have to exist anymore if they could just smooth over what had happened on Sunday.

It was unsettling that Carmen wasn't answering her e-mail. She had always been very quick about that in the past. Surely, she wasn't traveling again already after just getting out of the hospital. Unfortunately for Judith, the alternative was that she was being ignored.

Too bad. She was determined to get through, whatever it took. She checked her watch and grabbed her purse. It was a bit early for lunch, but she wasn't about to try to have a phone conversation with Carmen from her desk. She dropped the travel packet in the courier box and scooted out before Todd even knew she was gone.

Two blocks from the office, she ran into Agnes, who was rummaging through a pile of garbage bags at the curb.

"Hello, Agnes."

The old woman smiled a toothless grin, but said nothing.

Judith opened her purse and gave her a five dollar bill. She had no idea how Agnes used money, but the woman accepted it eagerly.

"Look, I might be changing jobs soon, so I won't be around as much anymore." If Agnes understood her, she gave no sign. "You take care of yourself, okay?"

Judith smiled and started to walk away, but the old woman caught her arm. No words passed between them, but Agnes's heartening look was unmistakable.

"Yeah, I'll try to do the same."

Judith felt buoyed by the encounter, her mind made up that she could take her life in her hands and mold it into what she wanted. Whatever shape it took, she wanted Carmen at the center.

She reached Washington Square and settled on a park bench, well away from the street noise. Taking a few deep breaths for courage, she dialed the number for The Delallo Group. After only one ring, the line cut to voice mail, where a generic voice said the office was closed.

On a Tuesday?

Her mind raced for a possible explanation. Carmen hadn't said anything about closing the office in the middle of a work week. Even if she was out of town, they wouldn't shut down the whole business.

She quickly dialed Carmen's cell phone, only to have it go straight to voice mail also. It was probably turned off, or lying in a drawer, its battery dead. And there was no answer at Carmen's home.

She had Cathy's home number from the time she had called a couple of weeks ago, and she dialed it nervously with hands that had begun to shake. After twelve rings, she hung up, her anxiety mounting.

She stood up and started to pace, trying to imagine any reasonable explanation for the office to be closed and everyone in The Delallo Group to be out of reach. No matter how many ideas she came up with, none seemed more plausible than the worst-case scenario—an emergency, like the one involving Carmen last week, but more serious. Maybe she had a heart attack for real this time.

Panic took over as her mind's eye conjured images of the

whole staff at the hospital, frantically awaiting word on their boss.

Carmen cut the chicken breast into small pieces and placed it in Prissy's dish. "What am I going to do with you when you get so rotten you stink?"

The dachshund twitched her tail and pranced on the kitchen floor in anticipation of her special treat. It was hard to deny how excited she was to have her mistress at home.

"I know. I'm going to enroll you in obedience classes where they make you sit perfectly still until I give you permission to move."

She lowered the bowl and sat cross-legged beside it as Prissy dug in. "Who loves you, sausage dog?"

In only the last couple of days, she had started to feel as if she was getting control of her life again. Here she was relaxing at home, and back into her exercise and diet regimen. The world was lifted from her shoulders when she made the decision to sell out to Art Conover, especially since getting quite a bit of money for the business she had built was far better than watching it circle the drain.

There was one last piece to put into place. She stretched upward and plucked the phone from its stand. With one hand gently stroking Prissy's back as she ate, Carmen dialed the familiar number with her thumb.

"Hey, sweetie." On the other end of the line was a voice she would never tire of hearing. "I was hoping we could have lunch this week . . . Because I blew you off in the hospital the other night when Judith was coming in."

Prissy finished her treat and crawled into Carmen's lap.

"I'm fine. I feel great and I'm doing everything the doctor said . . . Yes, the auditors came today. I should know something by tomorrow, but I can't imagine it isn't going to go through."

Brooke was showing an uncharacteristic interest in her business dealings, especially when Carmen told her she was considering a sale.

"No, she went back on Sunday night. What about you? How are things at home?" Brooke gave her an upbeat answer without going into detail, pressing Carmen instead for more information on Judith.

"My news isn't so good. We sort of reached an impasse, but I'm going to try to talk to her again and see if we can work things out . . . No, I think we still love each other. But you should have seen the look on her face, Brooke. I felt awful . . . Because of her brother. If she isn't there to see him every Sunday, he gets wild. Then she feels guilty about it. I think it got to be too much for her last weekend."

Brooke surprised her with a defense of Judith, suggesting Judith's real reason for backing away was that she felt responsible for Carmen's stress.

"I don't know where she would have gotten that idea. The only time I ever felt relaxed was when I was with her. It didn't matter if it was here or New York."

Carmen listened with growing dismay as Brooke described her brief conversation with Judith at the hospital.

"No wonder she took off. She thought this was her fault." Carmen stood and began to pace the kitchen. "She probably thought I wanted her to because I—shit, I have to go . . . No, I'm not mad, but I have to call her."

Judith slung her duffle bag over her shoulder and scooted to the taxi door, straining to see signs of life in Carmen's apartment. In the twilight, it was difficult to tell if the lights were on.

She thumbed through her wallet and pulled out several bills. "Here's an extra twenty. I want you to wait for me. If no one is home, I'll be right back down and I'll need you to take me somewhere else."

The driver nodded toward a metered space in the street. "I'll wait there."

"Thanks. If I'm not back in ten minutes, that's a tip. Okay?"

She got out with her bag and headed for the lobby, where the doorman met her with a smile.

"Miss O'Shea."

"Hi, Luis." It was a good sign that he was smiling, she thought. If something terrible had happened, he would have shown more concern . . . if he knew about it, that is. She wanted to ask if Carmen was home, but if he didn't know, he might ask her to wait while he called up to the apartment. Instead, she forged ahead to the elevator as though she was expected.

"Please be home," she mumbled several times before the elevator reached the fifteenth floor.

When the doors parted, she charged out and down the hall, her heart racing at a frantic pace. The instant she knocked on Carmen's door, Prissy began to bark. She waited anxiously for what seemed like an eternity. She was about to knock again when the door suddenly opened.

"Judith?" Carmen's face broke into a broad smile.

"Oh, my God!" Judith rushed forward into her arms, burying her face into Carmen's neck, where she smothered it with kisses. "I was so scared."

"Scared? What were you scared about?" Carmen put her hand on the back of Judith's head and held it in place against her neck. "Keep doing that. I like it."

Prissy stood on her hind legs, scratching first Carmen, then Judith in a vain plea for attention.

"I've called you all day and couldn't get an answer anywhere. I thought something happened."

"Something did happen, but it wasn't anything scary. Please say hello to my dog before she tears our legs to shreds."

Judith didn't want to let go, but she complied with Carmen's request.

"I was about to call you," Carmen said. "I was talking to Brooke and she said the most ridiculous thing. She said you broke up with me because you thought you were causing my stress."

"It wasn't good for you to be running back and forth so much. I heard them say so in the kitchen, and they're doctors."

"Heard who?"

"Your dad and Chris. They said you might have a heart attack."

Carmen grabbed her and pulled her again into an embrace. "That's not going to happen. I let things get out of control, but I've got a handle on them."

"I can move to Chicago. Todd fired me today when I told him I had to go, so I need a new job anyway. Mom's helping with Victor." Her words were coming in a tangled rush. "I just need to go back a couple of times a month."

"Or I can move to New York."

"I'll send my résumé to all the big agencies here and—" She stopped short. "What did you say?"

"I have a lot to tell you. But the most important thing is this." Carmen hugged her tightly, brushed her lips along Judith's temple before whispering in her ear. "Don't leave your shoes there."

Publications from
BELLA BOOKS, INC.
The best in contemporary lesbian fiction

P.O. Box 10543, Tallahassee, FL 32302
Phone: 800-729-4992
www.bellabooks.com

ASPEN'S EMBERS by Diane Tremain Braund. Will Aspen choose the woman she loves . . . or the forest she hopes to preserve . . . 978-1-59493-102-4 $14.95

THE COTTAGE by Gerri Hill. The Cottage is the heartbreaking story of two women who meet by chance . . . or did they? A love so destined it couldn't be denied . . . stolen moments to be cherished forever. 978-1-59493-096-6 $13.95

FANTASY: Untrue Stories of Lesbian Passion edited by Barbara Johnson and Therese Szymanski. Lie back and let Bella's bad girls take you on an erotic journey through the greatest bedtime stories never told. 978-1-59493-101-7 $15.95

SISTERS' FLIGHT by Jeanne G'Fellers. *SISTERS FLIGHT* is the highly anticipated sequel to NO SISTER OF MINE and *SISTER LOST SISTER FOUND.*
978-1-59493-116-1 $13.95

BRAGGIN RIGHTS by Kenna White. Taylor Fleming is a thirty-six year old Texas rancher who covets her independence. She finds her cowgirl independence tested by neighboring rancher Jen Holland. 978-1-59493-095-9 $13.95

BRILLIANT by Ann Roberts. Respected sociology professor, Diane Cole finds her views on love challenged by her own heart, as she fights the attraction she feels for a woman half her age. 978-1-59493-115-4 $13.95

THE EDUCATION OF ELLIE by Jackie Calhoun. When Ellie sees her childhood friend for the first time in thirty years she is tempted to resume their long lost friendship. But with the years come a lot of baggage and the two women struggle with who they are now while fighting the painful memories of their first parting. Will they be able to move past their history to start again? 978-1-59493-092-8 $13.95

DATE NIGHT CLUB by Saxon Bennett. *Date Night Club* is a dark romantic comedy about the pitfalls of dating in your thirties . . . 978-1-59493-094-2 $13.95

PLEASE FORGIVE ME by Megan Carter. Laurel Becker is on the verge of losing the two most important things in her life—her current lover, Elaine Alexander, and the Lavender Page bookstore. Will Elaine and Laurel manage to work through their misunderstandings and rebuild their life together? 978-1-59493-091-1 $13.95